Little Teashop of Horrors

Jane Lovering

Choc
Lit

Where heroes are like chocolate – irresistible!

Published 2018 by Choc Lit Limited
Penrose House, Crawley Drive, Camberley, Surrey GU15 2AB, UK
www.choc-lit.com

A CIP catalogue record for this book is available
from the British Library

ISBN 978-1-78189-420-0

Printed and bound by Clays Ltd

This book is dedicated to the memory of my big old dog Dylan (2002–2016), without whose weight on my feet, life is not quite the same

Acknowledgements

Firstly, a huge, huge 'thank you' to Charlie Heap and all the staff at Duncombe Park's National Birds of Prey centre, who put up with me asking stupid questions and walking around making 'awwww' noises at the burrowing owls. Seriously, those birds are cute! If you are ever passing Helmsley in North Yorkshire, do pop by and watch a flying display. I can promise you won't get your nose eaten off. Well, *practically* promise.

Secondly, another huge 'thank you' to all the staff at Nunnington Hall (which, if you happen to be passing Helmsley and need something to do to celebrate keeping your nose, is not that far away and belongs to the National Trust). I loosely based Monkpark on Nunnington – although none of the shenanigans that takes place at Monkpark are based on anything in real life – and visited more times than was strictly necessary, on account of the very good cafe.

Thirdly, another, and only slightly smaller, 'thank you' to everyone in my corner of North Yorkshire, my workmates, my family and even complete strangers, who have so far failed to have me certified mad for walking around muttering to myself. I would like several cases of 'wearing my pants on my head' to be taken into consideration …

Fourthly, more thanks are due to the Choc Lit Tasting Panel, who read the books before they are accepted for publication, and therefore go above and beyond the call of duty. Special thanks to Stephanie H, Catherine L, Jenny M, Lizzy D, Elaine R, Gill L, Linda Sy, Jean L, Jenny W, Joanne O, Cindy T and Toos H for liking *Little Teashop of Horrors* enough for it to see the light of day!

Prologue

The falcon lifted off from the glove and rose effortlessly. She flew a lap of the field, swooping by the tall, scruffy-haired young man whose arm wore the gauntlet that had launched her. Up, up, higher, catching a thermal and climbing, until the walled garden was no more than a focus spot, the old house a grey L-shape set into the green bowl of the hills, like a rock at the bottom of a pool of water. So high now that, had she not been a bird and therefore ignorant of maps, the infrequent lines of roads and the blurring of agriculture into moorland would have looked like an Ordnance Survey sketch of the district. Then, tilting her wing to catch a breeze, she headed off towards the gleaming line of the horizon.

The watching audience gasped, one or two laughed, and then all eyes turned to the scruffy-haired man.

'Oh, bugger,' he said. Then, without acknowledging the onlookers, he set off at a run, out of the walled garden, eyes trained on the sky as his falcon became a diminishing black dot against the blue sky.

The small crowd, eyes straining to catch the last glimpse of the bird's flight, gave a collective groan, which may have been disappointment or, from some of the more reluctant visitors, a kind of vicarious thrill at the ability to so easily escape the claustrophobia of this remote place. Most turned away to go back into the house – after all, they still had to visit the Old Kitchen with its display of seventeenth century cooking implements, and they were determined to get their money's worth, the entrance fees to the Heritage Trust properties being what they were. Some, deciding that enough was enough where culture and history were concerned, headed for the small teashop that had been atmospherically converted from a coach house in the old stable yard. The disappearance of one of the display birds had been mildly exciting, but now what the day called for was a cup of tea and a slice of carrot cake.

Chapter One

The last customer of the day had drained the last of their tea, the last moistened finger had dabbed the remains of a scone into an eager mouth, and I'd squirted my last buttercream flower, when we heard the sound we'd been dreading. The heavy crunch of a large car, sweeping up the gravel drive to Monkpark Hall and drawing up at the main front doors. My heart thumped uncomfortably under my Edwardian outfit. *What if the new boss decides to change things? What if he decides on a shake-up of the estate? What if—*

'He's here.' Julia threw me a clean apron. 'Quick, get this on, Ames, you look like you've spent the afternoon face down in the European scone mountain.'

'And who died and made you Mary Berry?' I muttered, but rebellion was pointless with Julia. She could have ignored the Jacobites. 'Anyway, *is* there a scone mountain?' I discarded my butter-stained overall and threaded my arms through the new one. 'I mean, there's EU directives for scone storage, and a mountain would contravene hygiene regulations, you'd have Brian Blessed going up the North Face before you could say "clotted cream". And why should we have to change, just because some new guy is taking over the management of the big house? We're not going to be expected to line the steps as he comes in, are we? Like bloody *Downton Abbey*, all curtseying and rolling our eyes at the footmen. Which we don't have, and I am not rolling *anything* at Artichoke Sam, he is odd enough without encouragement.' I was talking to cover my nervousness, and Julia knew it. Or didn't know it, but didn't care why I was babbling.

'Shut up.' Brushing off my petty little mutiny, Julia

pulled off her mob cap, smoothed her hair down and retied her ponytail. 'This is no time to start getting all socialist. If new guy reports back to the Heritage Trust that we didn't sufficiently doff whatever we're supposed to doff, we could find ourselves out of a job and our lovely cafe being taken over by a couple of maiden aunts who believe in jam pot covers and white supremacy, so get that apron on and round to the front, double time.'

She disappeared into the back room, muttering about mascara, and I stuffed the loose bits of hair back under my cap. It was supremely unflattering and made me look as though I was about to dive into the sea circa 1880, but then I wasn't really worried about the way I looked, not like Julia was, anyway. She worried so much about her appearance that I was surprised she had a worry surplus, but clearly she was concerned with 'standards' today, in the face of the arrival of what was, technically, our new boss.

I checked my reflection in the cake cover. Yup. I still looked like the Human Cannonball in a daft hat, but, short of a fairy godmother with an encyclopaedic knowledge of Clinique products and a robust approach to corsetry, that wasn't going to change any time soon. A momentary wash of powerlessness swept over my linen-capped head. I *needed* this job, more than just about anyone else employed by Monkpark, I needed to stay. Yet I was the one nobody noticed – the one with the gritted teeth, carrying out the everyday tasks behind the scenes to keep the cafe running smoothly, cooking, serving, cleaning up – relied upon; as necessary as a Hoover, and given about as much attention. Although, I thought, adjusting my cap – although I didn't really know why because nobody would notice whether I doffed or didn't doff – my wheels were less likely to come off. I wasn't even going to think about whether I sucked more than the average Hoover.

I was steeling myself to go out and meet the newcomer, and scolding myself internally for wondering whether 'doff' was strictly a verb, when the doors at the far end of the tearoom opened and Josh shambled in, shedding feathers like a werebudgie mid-change.

'Any sign of Bane?' I asked.

'Mmm?' Josh looked around and finally saw me. He'd clearly been lost in his own, quite bird-specific world, as usual. 'Oh. Not yet. I've checked all round the estate, no sign. But she's got a tracker on, I'm going to go and get the equipment and find her ...' He trailed off, once more subsumed into a place where falcons making off into the wide blue yonder was far more important than the arrival of some bloke, picked up a leftover muffin from the counter, and continued his amble out through the door by the kitchen. His hair was half on end, he hadn't shaved for a while and his shirt was untucked at the back and flopped over the seat of his jeans like a gold-prospector's 'escape hatch', but that was typical Josh. Nothing mattered but the birds. I didn't think he'd ever actually looked me in the face since he'd arrived at the Hall in the winter, but I liked him. He didn't leer past me at Jules, like a lot of the men who worked here – which always made me want to stand right in front of them, waving – or talk to my, admittedly robust, chest. There was something gentle about him, something that made me think of the old china we had on the dresser in the cafe. Faded and fragile and a bit chipped around the edges.

I finally joined Julia in the gloriously oak-panelled Library. She was whispering conspiratorially with Wendy, who did admin and usually only worked mornings, and the motley collection of other people who worked at Monkpark Hall were milling around and making free with the Heritage Trust-provided glasses of celebratory wine that stood on side tables near the door. Clearly our new boss didn't know much about his potential workforce or he would have kept it to chilled mineral water. Monkpark stood alone amidst its acres with no civilisation for seven miles – and for 'no civilisation' read 'no pub'. The gardeners had already pinched a bottle and we were only moments away from having to fish them out of the verbena. James, who was in charge of the outside staff at the Hall, was turning a blind eye. In fact, he looked as though he might also have had more than one glass, and I was sure I could see a bulge in the pocket of his donkey jacket that might be a bottle 'for later'.

'Ahem.' A cleared throat from the stairs that led up to the gallery. 'Attention, please, everyone.'

'Prat,' muttered Julia from beside me, but with her mouth carefully tilted down into her wine glass, presumably in case our esteemed employer had 'lip reading' as one of his skills.

'Boss prat though, Jules.' I nodded towards the speaker being gradually revealed during his process down the polished oak of the staircase. He was very obviously someone whose previous exposure to the countryside had come from county shows and the odd point-to-point, judging from his clothing. Instead of warm, practical sweaters over rip-stop trousers he was wearing a beautifully cut hacking jacket, dark green moleskin chinos and the shiniest shoes I'd ever seen on someone not recently released from prison. His blond hair was immaculately cut into a short back and sides that my grandfather would have appreciated, and he wore wire-rimmed glasses, which emphasised fair-lashed eyes. He looked as if he'd walked off the cover of one of those magazines for people who like the idea of living in the country but can't cope with the lack of broadband, rubbish mobile signals and mice in the larder.

At Monkpark you were lucky if it was just mice in the larder. I'd once had to eject a full-grown deer that had been at the spuds.

'Plus, hot prat.' Julia was looking him over now too and I gave her a jab in the ribs. Julia's 'types' included everything from Richard Armitage down to the lean young work-experience boy who trimmed the hedges, so her fancying our new boss wasn't entirely unexpected, but it was going to make life awkward. Jules had a tendency to go off in full pursuit of any man that took her fancy like a whippet after a sausage. I was usually recruited to ride shotgun on these quests, providing advice, reassurance, tissues and, occasionally, sandwiches, if it looked like being a long job. It was a role I'd been born to. Next to Julia – oh, all right, even *without* Julia – I was the kind of girl that men's eyes just seemed to slide off. Nondescript. Chunky, serviceable body, brownish hair, blueish eyes ... if anyone had ever had to produce a 'Wanted' poster featuring me, they could have used 'ish' as my main descriptive factor.

'Mind on the job, Jules.'

'I'm sure you will all have been expecting me before now, but it turns out that the vagaries of North Yorkshire roads are beyond the reach of satnav.' Pause for laughter, some of which was a little raucous because of the free wine ... 'My name is Edmund Evershott and I'm here to take over management of Monkpark Hall on behalf of the Heritage Trust.'

New Boss began giving a speech about how he hoped this would usher in a new era in customer service and an increase in visitor numbers – the usual sort of talk you get when someone takes on an enterprise and wants to Make Their Mark. To be honest, I was too busy keeping an eye on Julia, who was using the speech-time to hitch her Edwardian skirt up to reveal her ankles, to really listen to his words, until he rounded off with 'and I hope we'll all work together very smoothly', which I only heard because I'd stopped looking at her and was looking at the slowly opening door under the staircase, which led into the Library from the hallway beyond. The door creaked wide, and Josh came through, the errant Bane, now hooded, on his fist. Josh walked into the crowd of wine drinkers, hesitated for a moment, then shrugged and walked on, causing New Boss's final words to stammer off into silence as he stared at the falconer and his bird wandering through the assembled throng towards the opposite door.

'Excuse me?' Edmund raised his voice, beautifully modulated, to carry across. 'Why are you walking through the Library?'

Josh didn't even slow down. He just raised his arm a little higher, to indicate the falcon perched on it and said, 'Short cut, mate,' then closed the door behind him without turning round. Everyone was so used to Josh and his vagaries that nobody reacted, because nobody else thought this was strange behaviour, apart from New Boss Edmund, who took off his glasses and stared at the door, then raised an eyebrow.

'Ooh, the eyebrow thing,' Julia whispered. 'Deeply sexy, that is.'

I gripped her elbow. 'It's only sexy when Mr Spock does it.'

I looked around the Library so as not to have to watch Jules doing her 'soft, interested smile, catch eye, bigger smile, head toss' routine. I'd been watching it in action since we were fourteen, when she'd made me start sitting behind her on the school bus so that the seat alongside was empty for her latest conquest. I hadn't minded as much as you might think, the school was a three quarters of an hour bus ride away, and I used to get a phenomenal amount of homework done on the journey, plus having it driven home to me on a daily basis how impossibly superficial XY chromosomes seemed to make you.

'Could Miss Amy Knowles and Miss Julia Neville stay behind please, everyone else, you are dismissed.' Edmund came down from his 'addressing the crowd' position on the staircase, slowly descending the polished oak treads as though he was going for maximum impact. There was a kind of smugness about him, as if he was used to having women follow him with their eyes, and their mouths going droopily slack. Jules was illustrating his point nicely, in fact.

People began milling around near the doors, everyone trying to head home without leaving any wine surplus so there were little knots of congestion in the doorways as glasses were emptied, sometimes repeatedly.

Julia's eyes had widened. 'Wow. Singled out already, Ames, we are *good*.'

But I'd already felt the conflict tightening in my chest, pulling me away. 'It's nearly six. You know I can't stay, the agreement is that I work until six and I never do overtime without prior arrangement ...' My voice was rising in panic. Even the thought of leaving Julia unattended in the vicinity of someone who signed our pay cheques wasn't enough to sever the tie that dragged at my heart, coupled me up between the cafe and home as though the weight of obligation and love hauled the two buildings together like a stone on a rubber sheet. 'We work in a teashop. There shouldn't *be* overtime. Once the scones are gone, it's lights out, goodnight Vienna.'

'*What?*'

'Just an expression that Gran ... never mind. And I had to walk up this morning 'cos the bike had a puncture, so I *have* to get off or I'll be late.'

Julia pulled the 'sensible one' trick, a move so rare that it was probably endangered. 'Look. It's not six yet. Give him a couple of minutes, he may only want to check us out – well, we can hope, can't we? Or maybe he wants our "insider perspective" into working at Monkpark, but either way, just hang around a bit, Ames.' Then, hitting home, 'We both need the job, we can't afford to go upsetting the new boss at this stage, can we?'

I closed my eyes for a second. Played the alternative scenarios in my head. 'Okay, you're right, I can't just disappear, but *please*, don't keep him talking.'

She was already heading across the polished wooden floor towards Edmund. Her heels clattered over the waxed and shiny boards, attracting his attention to our approach, while my sensible flats squealed and squeaked like distressed hamsters. 'Oh, don't worry so much,' she muttered over her shoulder. 'You are sooo boring sometimes, Ames.'

I bit my lip so as not to remind her that she knew *exactly* why I was 'boring', but she was already drawing up in front of Edmund, who'd replaced his glasses and was consulting an iPad, so she'd wasted the head tossing and the catwalk stride she'd used across the wooden floor. But, then again, in our Edwardian maid costumes, she'd looked less like Zooey Deschanel and more like a Dalek given a hearty shove. 'Ah. You would be …'

'Julia Neville.' She didn't bother to introduce me, but then I suppose someone who can't work things out from a process of deduction on a list of two isn't really management potential. 'How can we help you …' Toying with the idea of using his first name, but even Julia, with her blonde hair and long legs, couldn't be quite sure of a conquest. '… Mister Evershott?'

I fidgeted and looked down at my feet. The elastic of my cap was loosening, I could feel the whole thing beginning to ride up my head and preparing to sit on the top of my hair like a knotted hanky on the beach.

'You two run the cafe on behalf of the Heritage Trust?' He had pale blue eyes behind those thin-rimmed glasses, and a slightly chilly expression that made them look paler still, like bluebells in a frost. 'And the premises are part of Monkpark Hall …'

Julia launched into an explanation of how we'd set up the cafe in the old stable block when the Heritage Trust had restored the building six years ago, how we baked all our own produce on site, how she and I lived in the estate village … she stopped short of giving him her bra size and phone number, but I had the feeling it was only his slightly cool reaction to her spiel that prevented her.

'Hmm.' Edmund tilted back his chin and looked at us down his cheekbones like someone sighting down a rifle. 'Well, this is just a friendly warning then … I'm thinking of giving up the cafe and turning the stables into an education room.'

As he finished speaking I heard the dread sound of the clock on the top of the old coachhouse begin its pre-chime whirring noise, and the first strike of six o'clock rang its hollow tone out across the sheep-dotted Monkpark acres. 'I'm sorry, I have to go ...'

I was already turning, my rubber soles announcing my intentions to the room. 'But, Miss Knowles, we need to discuss—'

'I'm sorry, I *have* to.' I broke into a run and, as I did so, my Edwardian maid's cap gave up the last of its pretence of elasticity and pinged off my head, flying off to land somewhere behind me. I didn't bother to go back for it; instead I careered out of the main house doors and out along the gravelled driveway like a cheap Cinderella with time management issues, my shoes now crunching my departure as I fled towards home.

Chapter Two

It's a weird place, this. Not *weird* weird, I mean, buildings are all right, it's the people. Not all of them, some are okay, some are more than okay, but the rest? Just weird.

It's like they don't understand the birds. They seem to think we're just some kind of tourist attraction thing, as if the birds fly to order to look pretty, draw in the customers, they don't realise that these things are hunters, not decorations. That I'm here to try to show that, to try to stop people taking these birds and pretending like they're pets, keeping them all shut up in cages where they can't even stretch out their wings, let alone take off. I'm here to show that if you keep them right and train them right, then they'll fly for you …

Well. Usually. Bane now, she's a bit of a case, but she's coming round, she comes back more often than not, well … more often than she used to, anyway. And there's Skrillex, well, he'll never fly 'cos owls and cars don't mix and his wing'll never be right but he walks pretty and does the eye thing and people like him.

And I know they think I'm weird too. Maybe that's why I came here, because maybe weird attracts weird, but I know they'd never have found anyone else to live in this caravan, where the toilet is basically a bucket down the field and if you want a shower your best bet is to get your clothes off and hope for rain. But it's a roof, and there's a decent place for the birds, and the cafe's always got spare buns hanging around, so, yeah, could be worse. Just wish I knew why all people want to do is sit around and chat about stuff that means nothing; the weather, what's on TV, all things that we can't do anything about. Why does nobody talk about the things we can change?

About cruelty and loneliness and isolation and crap like that? It's like they don't want to mention anything that might want changing, just in case someone expects them to do something, but I reckon it's enough just to acknowledge that there *are* things out there beyond *Hollyoaks* and if it's going to rain at the weekend. But they all love to sit and chatter, all hunched up together like the rooks that sit in the high points of the trees.

Amy – she's different. She doesn't gossip with the girls who come in to clean, or the room guides that show the crowds around the old place. She keeps herself separate, she's like Bane. Like she doesn't need any of this stuff … So when I saw her running out of the house on the stroke of six just as I'd got the bike ready for a run into town, I didn't think twice.

'Jump on.'

'Josh, I haven't got a helmet.'

'Private land and I'm not going to crash. Jump on.'

She hesitated, but I could see that look in her eye, that look that said she was panicked enough not to worry about how legal it was. Then she was climbing up behind me, all cautious in that Edwardian maid's uniform that she and Julia wear in the cafe, I guess she was trying not to show her knickers to the world.

'Put your arms round my waist.'

'What?'

'Otherwise you'll tip off.'

She did it, but really slowly and all sort of loose, like she didn't really want to make contact with the jacket or me, but once I kicked the bike on and it did the slide on the gravel as the wheels tried for grip, she grabbed a lot tighter. I throttled back, compensating for the extra weight and the way she couldn't lean to counterbalance us and we crunched up the mile of drive that Monkpark is so proud of at no more than sixty. Over the cattle grid at the end, out onto the little country road linking us with the nearest town, then right and down the hill to the estate village. Geared down, braked and pulled up outside the cottage by the oak tree.

She gradually let go of the back of my jacket, sort of peeling off like she'd been sticking to me. Didn't think I'd been that scary, it was a slow old ride with the grit and the grid and then the hills, but I guess if you've not been on the back of a bike before it's a bit windy.

'You're home.'

'Thank you.' She sounded a bit breathless, and when I flipped the visor to look at her she'd got her hair all sticking backwards. She's got that kind of half straight hair, where it goes all curly at the ends and all sort of thick and crazy, but now it looked more like it was trying to be released into the wild. 'Seriously, thanks, Josh.'

I wanted to smile. Seriously, I wanted to give her a grin that said, 'Any time, just ask,' but she looked busy, like her mind was already on something else and I didn't want to intrude on whatever it was. I know, with the birds, when they're hunting they are so single-minded, so focussed that there's not really any point in trying to call them in, and she looked like that. So I flipped down the visor and just sort of nodded. Felt a bit of a dick, really, I mean, could have said *something*, but what was the point? So I just gunned the bike and headed off to the supermarket.

Chapter Three

Amy

I was lucky, Gran was just home from the day centre. I could tell from the way she was still walking around the room, tweaking everything into order even though nobody had been in all day and it was still as tidy as it had been when she left.

'Someone's been in, look at these curtains. Left these curtains hanging straight, now look at them! And someone's been fiddling with my spoons, comes to something when even your spoons aren't left alone. Place is a mess ...'

'It's all right, Gran, I'll sort it out in a minute.' I went through to the kitchen to put the kettle on, but she followed me. She always did, as though she was worried that if she let me out of her sight I'd be through the little window and heading for Scunthorpe as fast as my pedals would go. To be fair, she had a point.

'Let it boil properly this time. And two tea bags, one isn't enough.'

'Yes, Gran.'

'Did I see you on the back of that motorbike?'

I sighed. I'd been hoping against all knowledge of my grandmother that she hadn't seen my arrival. 'Josh gave me a lift back; my bike had a puncture this morning so I'd have had to walk back otherwise.'

'They're dangerous, those things. And this "Josh", who's he when he's at home? You're not going to start going out with some boy, are you? I mean, we know nothing about him, or his family, could be anyone. Could be one of these murdering incomers they're always on about, trying to get you to go off in the woods and you're never seen again.'

'You know who Josh is, he's been at the Hall for six months, he does the flying demonstrations with his birds of prey ... anyway, we've just got a new boss!' Distraction usually worked. Replace one menace with another. She couldn't cope with more than one train of thought at a time which was something to be grateful for, and she didn't mean any of it, not really, she couldn't help being this way.

'Mary left, has she?'

I poured the boiling water into the teapot, being careful to get it to *exactly* the point where the spout started, no more, no less. 'Gran, Mary left before I started. It was John running the place, remember? He's gone to Scotland to manage a house up there. Anyway, the new guy is called Edmund Evershott, and I've got a horrible feeling ...'

No Amy, don't. Don't even mention what he said about closing the cafe, she'll only start to worry ...

'... that Julia fancies him.' I managed to deflect myself.

Gran sniffed. 'That young lady is all fur coat and no knickers. She'll find herself in trouble one of these days, mark my words. Her mother was just the same as a girl, of course, eyes roaming around the entire male population of North Yorkshire, wasn't a man safe from young Annie in those days.'

I smiled and let her talk while I finished making the tea. Gran had been born and brought up here, not just here, but in this house; she'd worked on the estate back in the days when it had still been a family seat, before it had been handed over to the Heritage Trust in 1976. She'd met Grandad when he'd come in to advise on the gardens and my mother had followed her mother into working in the house. I was as much a product of Monkpark Hall as the orchard apples.

As always, we had tea, watched television until half past seven, and then Gran, with the air of one surprised by the sound of the clock striking said, as always, 'Well, been a busy day. Better get my beauty sleep.'

And then I, as I always did, got her a glass of milk, a cheese sandwich and the purple tablets for her heart. Watched her eat and drink, gave her the usual reassurances that the tablets were fresh out of the packet, no, nobody could have tampered with them, I'd taken them out of the blister pack myself, and kissed her goodnight. Listened to the sound of her moving about in her bedroom, which was like a cross between a cave and a Christmas bazaar, straightening the ornaments and pictures on the bedside table, the creak of the old metal bedstead as she climbed in, and let my breath out on the descending quiet.

All this business with the spoons, and her certainty that someone had been in the house while we were both out ... Was this the early sign of something going awry in a mind that had always been sharper than my best knives? What was I going to do if she got worse? It was the question that always circled at the back of my brain, which ate into any pleasure I ever took in anything. *What happens next? Is there a 'next' for me, or is this it?*

What actually happened next, it appeared, was 'nothing much'. Six weeks passed, summer arrived, and with it came the coach parties, the school trips and the carloads of visitors all arriving to tour Monkpark Hall, walk around the gardens, dabble their toes in the river which ran along the edge of the grounds, and hopefully to overindulge on our home-baked muffins, cupcakes and the fresh fruit juices that we made up to order. Edmund Evershott made no more reference to closing the cafe, just threw meaningful little glances around every time he came in. They were enough to make me keep polishing the chrome and titivating the displays, stopping just short of standing in the doorway and trying to force cakes on unwilling passers-by, and I wondered if he knew about my life and circumstances, the effect that his threat had on me, or whether he was just a major control freak trying to get extra hours of work out of Jules and I for no extra pay. Well, me, really. Jules hadn't given something for nothing since our school prom, and even thinking that made me feel like a bitch.

So, there we were, baking and serving and all Business as Usual.

'I'll have a ... strawberry and banana smoothie.'

I smiled and tried not to mutter 'please ...' behind my teeth as I bustled to get the fruit out of the fridge and into the blender, squeezing past Julia who was pouring boiling water into teapots. She looked up suddenly and did a wide-eyed stare, then jerked her head at me.

'The boss is in.'

I set the blender going and, undercover of getting a muffin out from the display case, I looked quickly across the tearoom. The far doors were thrown wide open to the sun and breeze, little tufted seed heads kept drifting in from the distant flower beds, and just outside I could see Josh bringing one of the birds down for the afternoon display in the walled garden. Behind the door stood Edmund, iPad in hand and a slight frown pulling his glasses towards the end of his nose.

'Right. This is worrying.' I trayed up the smoothie, added a straw and slid it along to the cash register.

'Why? Look how busy we are, Ames ... if he wants to change all this and get rid of the cafe, he'd better have a damn good reason.'

Bane flew from Josh's glove, spiralled up, and then came in, in a low dive through the watching audience, slicing the sunlight with sudden wings to the sound of applause. I could hear Josh, through his radio mike, explaining that Bane was a Lanner falcon, talking about birds of prey in general, while she hopped on the glove again. He seemed to look a little bit smarter today and I wondered if tidying Josh up was one of Edmund's projects – we'd already heard from staff about some of the 'improvement plans' being put into place, and it seemed that getting Josh out of his rumpled shirts and baggy shorts had been high on the agenda. Today he was wearing black jeans and a charcoal grey shirt, against which Bane's barred feathers looked like a sketch of light and shade.

'Can I put my PIN in now, or what?' Smoothie-woman asked me irritably, jerking my gaze back into the cafe. 'Only you really should be a little bit faster at this, you know. Are you new, or just simple?'

I smiled a little bit wider and recited 'customer service, the customer is always right, keep smiling' like a mantra, as I tapped her card through the machine, resisting the urge to splash strawberry juice over her cashmere top with everything I had.

'Hmm,' she blew down her nose at me as I handed back the card, my smile growing wider by the second, 'they really shouldn't let fat girls work in cafes. It gives such a bad impression of the place.'

'Have a nice day.' I passed her over the tray. 'And I hope Bane eats your nose off the second you step outside,' I finished, once she was well out of earshot. Sometimes I was convinced customers only said things like that to get a reaction, and then a possible free meal as reparation for staff telling them exactly how rude they'd been to their faces. But then, I'd always been good at keeping what I really felt hidden. Trained by Gran from an early age that losing my temper was a waste of time, I'd learned to sublimate any retaliatory urges so well that I'd only said, 'Oh, bum', when the bike had sustained its second puncture this month, even though it meant starting for work half an hour early, and having to rush back so I was home as Gran got in from the day centre, hot and sweaty and wishing the Edwardians had learned the value of ventilated costumes.

'Lips and teeth,' Julia muttered undercover of bringing a trayful of dirty crockery back, 'here comes Mister Gorgeous.' She'd affected a nonchalance that was belied by the way she swung her hips, noticeable even through her calf-length black dress with its high collar and fitted sleeves. In Julia's case, the way the aprons tied behind us enhanced her back view, while they made me look more like a badly organised parcel. 'Hello, can I help you?'

'Miss Knowles, Miss Neville.'

Maybe this is it. Maybe this is where he comes out and says what he's been building up to for the last month and a half. Feeling queasy, I tucked myself carefully behind Julia and tried to look busy; I didn't like anything I said or did to be noticed. I'd been born to be a backroom girl, why else would nature have given me this sturdily rotund frame? I let Julia be the 'face' of the business, while I was the brains of the outfit – the whole Edwardian theme had been my idea, to fit in with the era of the last remodelling of the house, and, despite dooming us to summers of chafing and itching, it worked well. Meanwhile Julia got paid to pout and smile whilst looking like one of those pert maids who seduced the master of the house, and I did the planning and accounts, looking like a funerary urn in an apron.

'An orange crush, please, if I may.'

Julia thrust bits of herself out so far that she nearly toppled into the Raspberry Crunch and drew the juice from the cooler. Black serge was not the most flattering of fabrics but she managed to make it look sexy and alluring, particularly when she wiped down the nozzle of the machine lovingly, as though imagining Edmund in swimwear whilst doing it. I set the ice to grind and muttered to her over our shoulders under the noise of the ice-crusher.

'You'd better ask him to pay.'

'Shouldn't we let him have it on the house?'

I looked at Edmund through the fuzzy mist that the ice machine threw up. His face was pale and narrow, giving him a sort of 'shuffled together' look, as though his features were furniture in an overcrowded room. 'We don't want to set a precedent. For all we know he's got an orange juice habit that could bankrupt us,' I whispered.

Julia gave me a sideways look. 'Really? Seriously, Ames? An orange juice habit? That's as racy as you can come up with, not snorting coke off naked women or designer drugs that make you dance all night then have crazy sex on the roof of a bus?'

'That is because ...' I hissed at her, putting the ice on for another crushing. '... we sell orange juice and we don't sell drugs.' Then, thinking of Julia's somewhat feral brothers, '*Please* tell me we don't sell drugs ...'

At which point, of course, the crusher cut out, leaving my words ringing into the air between our new boss and me. Edmund frowned.

'Three pounds fifty for the orange crush, Mister Evershott, please,' I said, a bit faintly, but keeping my eyes on his drink in case he might possibly have thought I was charging him for just standing around looking manly.

'Quite right too.' He handed me the correct change, carefully counted out from a zip-compartmentalised wallet. 'No favouritism here, ladies.' He looked around the cafe, gave a small sniff and a sigh which made my heart drum against my ribcage again. I couldn't see where his evident dissatisfaction was coming from. The cafe was full, the baking was all fresh and I hadn't thrown smoothies down the front of the very rude woman. Short of introducing waitress service – which we hadn't got the staff for – there weren't any improvements we could make.

Then Edmund beckoned to us, so we bent in closer. *Here it comes*, I thought, and the smell of the buttercream icing made me feel sick; my vision swam for a second. *Here is where he ends it all for me*. Edmund cleared his throat. 'By the way, I wonder ... could I recruit you two and your very fine catering skills for a little ... private party?'

At first I was flooded with relief. My liberty bodice sank a couple of inches as I relaxed, but then I saw Edmund's slightly furtive expression. *Great. This is where he turns out to be hosting orgies for the entire estate*, I thought, then, after a brief moment during which I mentally assessed the membership of the estate in question and their suitability for orgies of any kind, *two rounds of ham sandwiches and a couple of oatmeal cookies should do it, then. But at least he hasn't mentioned closing the cafe down.* My insides relaxed a little bit more. *Maybe he's forgotten about that.* 'I'll let Julia discuss that with you.'

Wow, that was business-like of you, I thought. *I could at least have said something about prices or asked him when it was going to be* ... but no, I chickened out and passed him straight to Jules, who, if the expression on her face and the wiggle on her Edwardian bum was anything to go by, was milking the situation for all it was worth. And now he was no doubt wondering just what the hell use I was to Monkpark. Probably assessing me as 'neither use nor ornament' as one of Gran's sayings would have it. I rang the money into the till so viciously that the receipt roll started disgorging itself and I had to take the whole thing to pieces, and then serve all the customers who'd built up while I was failing to be assertive at Edmund.

'I might have to do some late work sometime,' I said to my grandmother as she straightened the curtains that evening. 'Mister Evershott wants Julia and I to cater for some do he's having next week.'

'You can't cook.' She tweaked the hem again, although it already looked perfectly straight to me. 'Why is he asking you?'

'I don't know, Gran, perhaps he thinks I could stand around being decorative,' I snapped and then blinked slowly, trying to clear the words from my memory, as if my eyelids could work like Etch A Sketch erasers. 'I mean, we have to keep in his good books because ...' *Don't worry her, don't give her any reason to start one of her 'frets'.* '... because he's our new boss.'

Gran snorted. 'Place has never been the same since Lady Hawton gave it to those Trust people.' She followed me through to the kitchen. 'In my day people knew their place.

None of this "keeping in good books" rubbish, you did your job and you never stepped over the line, downstairs was downstairs and upstairs was upstairs and ... have you been having someone in here?'

Boiling water, up to where the spout starts ... 'What? No, of course I haven't, I've been at work all day.'

'There's too much water in that pot, tea'll be like widdle, and I'm sure someone's been in this tray, look at the spoons! You been having some man in here while I'm at my club?'

We kept the fiction between us, running like a story that no one else would ever understand. Gran went to a 'club' during the day, for company while I was at work; I couldn't cook but did 'little jobs' around the cafe because the lease of our house only applied while an occupant worked at Monkpark Hall. In her head, she ran the house and allowed me to live there only because I had nowhere else to go. Reality was too bitter for either of us to chew on.

'No, Gran, I haven't had anyone here.' I sighed and emptied the teapot down the sink. Once she'd got it in her head that the pot was overfilled, she'd never drink the tea. 'Besides, who would I have?'

Oh, I knew everyone who worked at the Hall, obviously. Most of us lived in the village, apart from the ones who drove in every day from town, and a lot of us had grown up together – there wasn't much alternative employment around here, and because of having to work at the Hall to live in the cottages that remained as yet ungentrified and unholiday-letted. Which meant that anyone of my age was known to be either married, gay or unsuitable through reasons of rampant sexism, racism or *very* odd attitudes to things. Like artichokes and, in one fairly extreme case, sheep.

Gran snorted again. 'Well, someone's been messing these spoons about.'

I looked over her shoulder. As far as I could tell, the spoons were lying exactly as they had this morning, neatly aligned and slotted into one another in the tray on the worktop, and I felt that cold grip of horror closing its fist again. *What happens next?*

'Look, I'll make another pot of tea, you go and sit down. I'll put *Pointless* on for you, shall I?' I recorded it every day, carefully setting it to play so that Gran could avoid watching the news. She had what I considered an irrational hatred of all news programmes, but then again, she also hated valences, John Cleese and any food with garlic in, so it wasn't worth arguing.

'You'll fill the teapot properly this time?'

'Yes, Gran.'

She smiled. It was a chilly sort of smile, a smile that's had all the empathy leached out of it from years of hard living and heartbreak, but it was the smiles that kept me going, like stepping stones in a river of angst. 'You're a good lass, Amy.' Her hand was as cold as her smile, but the thought was there, as she patted my arm. 'We muddle along all right between us, don't we?'

I gave her a quick passing hug. Any more and she would have brushed me off, accused me of 'being soft'. 'We do, Gran. We do.' And then I went to boil the kettle and fill the teapot and worry about Edmund's intentions until acid rose up my throat.

Chapter Four

Josh

Okay. No, I can do this.

I'd walked down from the van, once the birds were settled for the night; a long walk over the orchards, where the fruit was just starting to fatten up, down past the copse, making the rooks kick off. I like the sound of them reminding me that they're out there, 'Hey, mate, look, over here!', fussing and complaining, a football crowd of them hassling and taunting overhead. Some of them came most of the way with me, black clouding it and sounding like they'd got dry toast stuck in their throats.

Which is pretty much how I felt, really, giving myself a good talking to all the way down. Simple job mate, knock on the door, say what you've got to say and then get out. But that didn't help the way my hands had started sweating ... shit, better not touch anything, even the door knocker might be off-limits, maybe just tap on the door? Or ... or, stand outside the window and clear my throat?

In the event, I didn't have to do anything. When I got to the village, she was standing in the front garden.

'Oh, hi, Josh.'

She wasn't wearing that Edwardian stuff, and that's what undid me. I'd got this mental picture of her in that black dress all the way from her neck to just above her ankles, little white collar and that apron with the edges that make it look like it's been iced onto her. But here she was, wearing just jeans and a big old shirt and she'd got her hair all sort of pinned up on her head so I could see her ears and the way her neck sort of joined her shoulder in a smooth corner-thing that made me wonder what it felt like to touch it and my voice just went off with the rooks. 'Ptheh.'

'Are you okay?'

I coughed a bit to cover myself. Wished I'd bothered to change out of the black jeans that I thought were great, but had got a bit of bird-lime down one leg. Wished I'd had a haircut or at least worn a hat ... 'D'you want a lift in tomorrow?'

Wow. Yeah, well, that could have gone better. Could have been worse though too, let's be honest, words, in the right order and no swearing.

'Oh.' Doing that thing with her hair and her fingers that women do. Preening. Except the birds do it to keep their feathers in order, women seem to do it just because. 'Won't it be out of your way, though? The caravan is down at the bottom of Windmill Hill, you'd have to come all the way out here just to go back.'

Okay. Point one, she knows where the van is. Point two, she doesn't want me to go to any trouble. Is that good, or not?

''S fine. Couple of minutes on the bike, 's all.'

She leaned back up against the old oak tree like she was thinking. 'It would save having to leave before Gran gets on the bus,' talking almost to herself, hardly to me at all, which was good because I'd practically run out of words now. 'And that dress is really hot to walk in, although I suppose I could wear this and change up at the house. But then, I don't want to give Edmund any excuse ...' She looked at me now, not at the inside of her head. 'Thanks, Josh, if you really don't mind, it would be a great help. Dennis is fixing my tyre tomorrow, so it would only be the one day ...' And now, all the saints and ladies save me, she smiled. I'd seen her do it before, obviously, she has this kind of face which likes to smile, when she's not smiling she looks a bit pretend, but she's never smiled at me before, not like that, and suddenly I didn't know what I was supposed to be doing.

'Pick you up at half past then.' I had to turn away, had to leave, or she was going to notice that I'd come over all weird and my eyes were sort of sliding around her. Didn't want her to think I couldn't look her in the eye, or worse, that I was staring at her boobs. Like I was just one of those blokes that hang round in town, all shouting at the girls and talking about their tits as if they're independent things, not part of a real person. I'm so not like that, we're hardly even from the same planet, but she wasn't to know, she's hardly even met me, so, you know, better part of valour and all that.

Chapter Five

Amy

'Edmund says it would be a nice touch if we took him up some tea and cake mid-morning,' Julia announced as the opening rush petered out into the pre-lunchtime couples and the odd history buff.

'Does he.'

'Mmm.' Julia wiped down the surface with a quick spray and sluice. 'I know, Ames, but we really do want to keep our jobs, don't we? And did I see you arrive this morning on the back of Bird Boy's motorbike?'

I tidied cakes on the stand and started to fill the dishwasher. Gritted my teeth a bit. Julia's mum was a room cleaner and one of her brothers worked on the estate. *She* wouldn't lose her home if the cafe closed, although she would lose her chance at one of the tiny one-person flats in the converted apple store that she was always threatening to apply for. Her dad had left years ago and I sometimes wondered if her lack of a male role model accounted for her attitude to men.

'Yes, I know we have to be nice to *Edmund*, but when does it stop? I mean, today he's asking for tea and cake, tomorrow it might be a threesome on a piano or something.'

'Now you're just being silly.'

I stood up and put my hands on my hips. Looked around at our lovely little cafe, as Edwardian as we could make it, with starched table covers and some genuine old china on a dresser along one wall. 'Six years, Julia. And he could just take it all away from us, like that!' I tried to click my fingers but because they were damp there was more of a moist slidey noise. 'And if this goes, my house goes, unless I can find something else to do on the estate, and there's no vacancies except helping Sam out in the artichoke beds, and, let's face it, there's a lot I'll do to keep a roof over me and Gran, but working with Sam just might be a step too far.' Sam was noted for his wandering hands. It wasn't just his hands that wandered, either; according to Gran, some of those artichokes got about a bit. 'Besides, it's seasonal and I don't know how we'd go for the lease.'

'Okay, okay.' Julia bent down to adjust her skirt hem, which was tangling around a chair leg. How the original Edwardians had managed, I had no idea, and they didn't even have the benefit of supportive underwear and machine-washables. 'I wasn't suggesting we said yes to everything he wants us to do, just … some of it. And, let's face it, taking up some tea and a bun to the office, and doing some evening cooking stints for a bunch of townies isn't exactly crocodile wrestling, is it?'

'The moment the word "topless" leaves his lips, I'm out of here,' I said.

'Agreed. And don't worry, I'll be right behind you if he starts any of that sort of thing. Quite a long way behind, but I'll still be there. Now, shut up and tell me how you came to arrive with Orville.'

I made a face at her. 'His name is Joshua, as you well know. And he offered me a lift.'

Julia's immaculate eyebrows rose and her mouth went a bit pursed. She wasn't used to me getting assertive with her, that was what it was. I knew that I was the 'plain friend' to her prettiness, the dumpy one that made her look even taller and thinner in contrast. The straight man to her ditzy blonde. And just sometimes I got a little bit tired of the role.

'Oooooh, get you,' she said. 'Taking up with our very own Bird Man of Monkpark, are you?'

Julia had dismissed Josh as potential partner material as soon as she'd found out that he lived in the old caravan that the shepherd used to sleep in when the sheep were lambing out in the fields. Now they all came in and lambed in the big pens on the farm, so the caravan was pretty nearly derelict, not really Julia's idea of a shag pad. Julia was so upwardly mobile that she was practically rocket-fuelled.

'Don't be horrible. He's nice. Very quiet.'

Julia made 'brokkk brokkk bokkk' chicken noises in the back of her throat, but quietly because she was serving two juices and cupcakes to a couple of ladies. 'So, will you take up a tea tray, Ames?'

'Me?' I slammed the dishwasher door and waited until I heard it start to fill. 'Don't you want to baffle him with your charm and your way with a Cherry Bakewell?'

'I'm playing hard to get. He knows where I am if he wants me.' She did a pert little flounce and I was glad the cafe was nearly empty because it looked really odd from a girl in an Edwardian frock, a bit like the *Titanic* preparing to go down. 'Earl Grey tea and a Raspberry Crunch, okay?'

'All right, all right.' I started laying out the tray, throwing caution to the winds and giving him one of our best china teapots and the matching cup and saucer. Might as well go to town with that making a good impression thing. 'But this is under protest. And look, here's Wendy now for her morning coffee.'

I usually served Wendy when she came down from her office in the eaves. She'd have a cappuccino to take away and we'd spend a few minutes having a minor gossip in a whisper about the running of the estate.

'Yeah, I *think* I can manage to serve her, I mean, she's only had the same thing at the same time for the last four years.'

I gave Julia my best sarcasm-killing look

'Yeah, yeah. Go now, while we're quiet, there's a coach pulling in and, with a bit of luck, it'll be a road-crazed bunch of professional scone tasters.' She got down the mug that Wendy always had and held it to the steam nozzle.

I poured a jug of hot water and added it to the tray. 'It might be a coach load of American billionaires with dicky hearts and a cholesterol problem; you might be looking at the new

29

potential Mister Neville if you play your cards right.' I gave her a Cheshire cat grin, gave Wendy a little wave, and waltzed off through the kitchen and out across the yard that separated the old stables from the house proper, my china wobbling and chiming like a tiny set of bells as I went.

I opened the side door to get in. It was marked Private, kept me away from the crowds who might jeopardise my precious china, and took me up the old servants' back staircase to the top floor where the maids' rooms under the attic had been converted into an office suite and a small self-contained flat for the person who managed the house. Edmund Evershott had already got his name plaque on the door, with his title 'Monkpark Hall Administrator' underneath, all in shiny white plastic, which stood out among all the heavy oak doors and wood panelling like Dr Crippen in One Direction.

'Ah. Thank you so much, Miss ... Knowles.' He hardly looked up as I came in, busy tapping keys on his computer. I started carefully unpacking the tea things onto his desk, setting the Raspberry Crunch to one side because those things are *phenomenally* sticky. I did it all slowly and carefully, taking my time and taking trouble to make sure it all looked nice on the desk. Cup, saucer, teapot, milk jug, hot water – my eyes were fixed on the rose patterned bone china so as not to be accused by Edmund of trying to look at his computer screen – even if I sort of was. Not that I really *meant* to as such, but it was there and all covered in figures. If there's one thing my degree taught me, it's to pay attention to screens full of figures, even if you have to pay that attention out of the corner of your eye and upside down. My degree was business administration, not industrial espionage, but it was a close-run thing.

Edmund had a book on the corner of the desk, *1001 Summer Fun Activities for Children*, and I stared at it as I jostled the china to make room. He noticed me looking. 'Ah. Just trying to come up with a few ideas. Draw the younger crowd in, you know.'

'What about making paper boats and then racing them on the river?' I spoke without thinking. 'Or getting a load of sand in and making a pretend beach on the riverbank? We could sell picnic boxes for children in the cafe.'

Very slowly Edmund poured tea from the pot into the cup, focussing his attention on the pale golden stream of liquid. 'Those are interesting thoughts, Miss Knowles. Do go on.'

All right, I admit it, I'd spent way too many nights lying in bed thinking of what I'd do if I were in charge of Monkpark. Well, Gran monopolised the TV, and there's not a lot of other entertainment opportunities when you live in the middle of nowhere and are too old for whittling.

'Well, I've always thought the gardens would be a great place for Shakespeare performances, you know, like *A Midsummer Night's Dream*? And fireworks – we could have firework displays, not just on Bonfire Night, but other times. What about doing an *Alice in Wonderland* themed treasure hunt for the children, with like, set pieces in the grounds, Mad Hatter's tea party or croquet, things that the kids can take part in?' I ran out of breath and stopped, watching him carefully break the tiniest piece of Raspberry Crunch off and put it in his mouth.

He chewed thoughtfully for a moment. 'I'm not sure some of those ideas are practical, Miss Knowles, but thank you so much for sharing your thoughts with me.' He ran his fingers through his hair as if he was used to it being longer. His wrists were very slender and his fingers perfectly pink and white, which was disconcerting for me; most of the men I knew had 'grubby' fitted as standard. It threw me, momentarily, back to my university days.

Well, that's me told. Know your place, woman. I flicked another glance across at the computer. It looked as though Edmund was checking his bank statement. I wondered, for a moment, about asking if I could borrow the machine to check mine – our nearest town was Pickering, seven miles away, with a bank that only opened three days a week. An elusive broadband signal meant that it was pointless having a computer at home, so I borrowed Wendy's in the admin office once a month to do the shopping. Bank accounting tended to wait for the once-in-a-blue-moon trips to York, when I usually had to watch Jules try on a lifetime's worth of shoes.

Edmund looked between me and the computer quickly. 'Look, I'll bring the crockery down to you when I'm done, is that all right? You needn't wait for me to finish,' he said, a little tersely.

Oh Lord, did he think I'd been checking up on his bank balance? But then, his computer was tilted away from me; all I could see was the bank heading and some blurry lists of figures, it wasn't as though I could call him out on his expenditure in Burberry or anything. As if I *cared* about his expenditure in Burberry. Maybe he was just generally touchy. Hell, *I'd* be touchy if anyone queried my spending on clothes, although in my case it was more likely to be a question like, 'Why don't you buy some?' rather than anything condemnatory.

I couldn't think of any reply that didn't sound self-justifying, so I went out, caught my breath on the landing, and then headed back down the servants' stairs to the floor below, where I could hear tourists thumping about, moving between the Purple Room and the little art gallery set up in an old dressing room. As I reached the bottom I hesitated for a moment, wondering if I shouldn't pop back up and offer to come back and fetch the tea things later this afternoon, and, as I stood on the last step, one hand on the newel post ready to swing round and go down the main staircase now I was unencumbered with expensive china, a young boy of about ten or eleven who'd just come along the passage caught my eye and started to scream.

'There's a ghost! There's a ghost!'

Okay. Well, this was just shaping up to be a fabulous day, wasn't it?

The boy turned back the way he'd come, pale and breaking into a run, screaming all the way down the staircase. I heard him slip on the polished oak boards, and tumble down a couple of steps still screaming. From the noise he made, he wasn't badly hurt, but I could hear him carrying on to the assembled crowd that had presumably gathered on the landing, that he'd seen the ghost of a maid standing on the stairs, all dressed in an old-fashioned uniform, and the murmuring of people gathering their courage to come and look.

Right. Did I stay standing here and make that poor lad look really stupid when everyone came up and found it was only me? Or did I head down, freak everyone out until I, again, made him look stupid? Or ... I picked up my skirts and dashed back up the servants' stairs, past the 'No Entry' sign that blocked the public from access to the offices, and stopped, panting a bit because these costumes were really hard to run in, especially upstairs. I could hear Wendy tapping away on the computer in her office, her door half-closed, so I stood on the little landing, put my head down and gasped for a moment, listening to the general commotion on the floor below, the sound of voices muttering travelling up between the gaps in the old oak boards. I could hear the 'ghost spotter' reiterating what he'd seen, over and over, 'Honest, it was there, just standing really still like a photograph, with this like blank face expression and it didn't have any eyes, just these, like, big dark holes boring into me and everything!'

I remembered being his age. Only too clearly actually, that had been when my mother, sick of single motherhood – of the restrictions of the village where everyone knew everyone's business and indiscretions four generations back – and of 'this petty little life', had left to head to London. To find a job, somewhere to live, and then she'd send for me, apparently. I didn't really blame her, she'd been not much more than a teenager when she had, as my grandmother put it, 'got caught' by some passing stranger, and had brought me up as more of a sister than a mother. My grandmother had done most of the heavy lifting business of motherhood ever since, and, if truth be told, up till then too.

My mother had never sent for me and our contact had been limited to summer holiday visits and occasional, strained Christmases. Now, we spoke on the phone, and it was a distant, removed kind of relationship, like that I may have had with a vague aunt, if I'd had any aunts. Which I didn't, my family had gone in for only children with an almost state-sponsored dedication.

It was a horrible age. And embarrassment was felt so acutely then. My cheeks burned now with a kind of sympathetic mortification at the thought of explaining to the ghost-busting crowd that the lad had only seen a waitress stopping for a bit of a think, not the rapidly-developing legend of a pregnant maid who'd drowned herself in shame, which was nascent on the floor below.

Edmund stuck his head out of his office. 'What's going on?'

I explained, in a low voice because I didn't want the people below to hear, and Edmund looked thoughtful.

'Is Monkpark Hall haunted?'

'Not as far as I know,' I replied.

Edmund twisted his mouth, thinking, and casually flipped his glasses off so that he could fiddle with the arm. I had the feeling that he thought it was a sexy thing to do, and wondered why he would waste it on me.

'But it would be good for business if we were ...' He sounded as though he was talking to himself, rather than me now. 'Look, can you slip down the back stairs to get out? Without anyone seeing you?'

'I can go the way I came in, yes.'

'Then do that, please. And, when you get to the cafe, I'd be grateful if you and Julia would close up for the rest of today. If that little boy is taken for a glass of milk to get over his shock, I wouldn't want him seeing you and being upset, d'you see?

And if he, or anyone here at the moment, realises that he saw you, rather than a ghost ...'

'All right. But—'

'We'll say the cafe is closed due to illness. It won't affect your jobs.' He put his glasses back on again, but I noticed a gleam in his green eyes, as though he had a burning idea. 'And, in future, err ... Amy, if anyone asks about the ghost of Monkpark Hall ... if you could just *mention* that we may have one?'

'Do we?'

We both stood, listening to individuals checking out the spot where I'd been standing. 'Definitely colder here,' said someone. 'Like a residual energy thing. Seen it on *Most Haunted*.'

'We do now,' said Edmund, firmly.

Chapter Six

Josh

I finished the morning flying and put the birds away. Bane hadn't flown, she was looking a bit sulky, inasmuch as you can tell with a falcon, and she took a nip at me when I went in to check her. Old cow. But, like I said, they're not pets, not domestic animals and they don't do affection, not as we think of it. To her I'm just this big thing that's too stupid to guard its scraps of meat; something she can use to guarantee a good meal. She doesn't love me or anything.

Once I'd got it all done and tidy, I headed down to the cafe. Thought I might be able to bum a sandwich off the girls, or some tea or something; there's no fridge in the van and this weather stuff goes on the turn really quick, so I don't bother keeping food. There's a freezer up in the yard where I keep the birds' stuff, sometimes I bung a few burgers in there, but usually I just nip through the cafe and pick up anything they've got lying round the place that looks lonely and like the flies have had a go at it. Besides, I wanted to see Amy. Not for anything, I just wanted to see her. There was something about the way she kind of moved, something about her hair – I dunno. Just a thing, nothing I was going to be doing anything about, but she made me feel like I was noticed, somehow. So I wandered down, but the doors were locked, which was weird.

'Closed due to illness, the sign says,' some bloke in creepy shorts said. 'Bit of a nuisance, we'll have to drive to Pickering now.'

'And some lad saw a ghost on the stairs, did you hear?' His wife I'd guess, unless he had a thing for picking up middle-aged lasses. 'Someone said they're going to get that programme off the telly to come and do a "special".'

Right. So, Amy's poorly and we're going to be 'Ghostbusted'. I sat down on the old mounting block in the yard, tried not to remember the feeling of her hands around my waist this morning, riding up the drive, or the way she grinned at me when she got off the bike with her hair all round her face so she looked like a happy dandelion clock. Bugger. No buns and no Amy, well this had all the makings of a shit day, so I went back to sit with the birds for a bit. I can talk to them, they don't judge. Well, Bane does, she's got this way of tipping her head even when she's hooded, like she's that Horus dude, like she knows she's a god and she's just putting up with me. But they're mine, I raised them from young, and I love them, kind of. At least, I think it's love. Never really had it, never felt it, but this warm sort of feeling at the back of my eyes is nearest I can get.

So there I am, sitting on the floor in the bird barn, up to my arse in shit and feathers, trying to work through stuff in my head, and then I looked up and there she was.

'Hey, Josh, there you are.'

'Thought you'd gone.' I got up but I was all covered in sawdust from the bedding and I had cobwebs in my hair. 'Cafe was shut, said you were ill.'

'Oh, that.' Amy made a face and took off her hat thing, started poking it around in her hands. 'No, Julia and I had to go and talk to Edmund about some dinner party he wants us to cater next week, and we shut the cafe, well ...'

Then she told me about some kid seeing her on the stairs and thinking she was a ghost and I couldn't stop laughing until she smacked me on the arm.

'Shut up. It's not that funny, poor little chap, he looked so frightened, and then I didn't know what to do so I went and hid upstairs. Now Edmund thinks it's a good idea to put it about that the Hall is haunted.'

'Maybe it is,' I said, but really I'm thinking is it a good thing that she smacked me? Does it mean that she reckons I'm enough of a mate now to get a good clip for being out of line? Then I don't know how I'm meant to feel about that. And over it all there's that feeling again, that she really sees me. I'm not just that bloke with the birds to her, I'm Josh. And the birds have all gone quiet, listening to this new voice in their barn, there's a kind of stillness that you only get in a room full of beasts that are all waiting for something. A breath-holding kind of potential that makes even the most everyday thing seem like it's full of something important, and she felt it too.

'It's strange in here.' She'd been standing in the doorway next to me, but now she walked in. 'Sort of peaceful.'

The birds watched her, but not one of them baited up off their perch, not even Bane, who's a right madam with strangers, or Fae the kestrel. Skrillex sort of shuffled about a bit, but he's an owl, they do that.

'I've never been in here before.'

'No.' I hung back. Didn't want to upset the birds by giving them too much to look at, and Amy was quite enough to look at in her own right.

'Is it all right? Me being here? I mean, they won't all get disturbed or anything?'

'You're all right if you don't poke 'em.' I was watching her, all bustled up in that black frock thing, and trying to get the webs out of my hair while she wasn't looking, and get the shit off my jeans and everything. There was a lot I wanted to say but I couldn't find any words for it; the thoughts were there and everything but it was just going to come out all banal and thin and stupid, so I kept my mouth shut while she moved slowly round looking at the birds and the birds looking at her. 'You want a lift back?' Pretty much the only thing that came to mind.

'Mmm? Oh, yes, please. If you're finished for the morning, I mean, I don't want you to have to stop doing stuff just to take me home – it's Thursday and Gran's usually early home on a Thursday because the bus goes all the way into Thirsk today.

She goes over to Julia's mum to wait for me. It'll be nice to have an afternoon off with her for a change. Might go for a walk or something.'

Okay. Bus. Gran. Save those things up to ask about later. Maybe I could ask Julia about it? Scrub that, Julia's got a look on her like she'd eat me up and spit out the bones. Could ask one of the lads in the garden, James, he likes the birds, he'd tell me what he knows about Amy. 'I'm done, 's fine.'

'They're amazing.' She walked round in a great circle so all the birds got looked at equally. 'Beautiful killers.'

And that's when I knew. That's when it *really* hit me. She got the birds, she knew, deep down in her heart, what they were all about. They weren't here for us to patronise them, all 'look how good they are, with their little claws and wings' like humans are something special because we invented knives and guns. These guys can kill their food with pretty much their bare hands.

'Yeah. If Bane was six foot two, we'd be dead by now.'

'And this is Bane?'

I nodded. 'Lanner falcon. Not native here. And this is Fae.' I waved her on to the next perch.

'She's tiny. Oh, look at her markings!' Sounded like Amy was half holding her breath when she talked like that.

'Yeah. Female kestrels have more black on them than the males. Males have a kind of grey head.' Urgh. I'm like Wikipedia, but I had no idea how else to talk about the birds. 'Malkin here, he's a common buzzard. Like you see over the hills.'

Amy did a little stop and looked at me with her head tipped. 'You didn't catch him, did you?'

I looked at her looking at me all sideways, and then at Malkin, who was half asleep. 'He's captive bred. They all are, except Skrill. You can't take a wild bird and get it to fly for you, it'd be like … I dunno, taking a wolf and expecting it to lie on your feet at night.'

She made a face, like saying sorry. 'Skrill, is that the owl?'

'Yeah. You can stroke him, won't hurt his feathers. He can't fly anyway.' And I showed her Skrillex, how his wings are all cut up. He closed his eyes and sort of mumbled when she stroked him. 'He likes you.'

'So he should, I'm adorable.' But she said it like she was taking the piss, like no one ever said it to her and meant it. I couldn't say anything to that.

'He can be a bit funny with some people though.' I watched Skrill nibble at her fingers. Thought it must be nice to have someone touch you. Hold you like you mattered. Cleared my throat. 'He's great. Mind you, watching him bring up a pellet is enough to put you off your dinner.'

She laughed and my heart went so fast I thought I was going to throw up. Without that stupid hat she looked good, a bit wild even in the prison dress, and she'd got a sparkle in her eyes that made me feel like smiling back, but I just stared at my feet and waited for my chest to stop going like a turbine in a gale.

'I'm sorry the cafe was shut. Look, if you like I'll make you something at home. To say thanks for the lifts? It'll have to be quick, because Gran ... well, she doesn't like people coming in the house, she gets a bit sniffy. And you'll have to get back for the afternoon flying anyway, won't you?'

Okay. That'd mean inside, wouldn't it? In the house? Small house too, not all wide and full of air like the Hall. Blank that bit, maybe we could work round it. My stomach rumbled loud enough for the birds to start getting antsy and I felt the hunger go right through me. Made my teeth ache. 'Yeah. Great.'

'Right then.' She went past me again, heading outside now, and her hair trailed a sort of smell of fruit. Peaches and stuff like that. How do women get their hair to smell like that? Mine just smells of hair, whatever I wash it in. 'Where's the bike, down in the yard?'

What with the smell of her hair, the way she looked, the

way she was with the birds – that was it, I was all out of vocabulary. So I just jerked my head, I'd left the bike up here, behind the shed. Had some idea of riding down to the cafe today, sitting there in the stable yard with the engine ticking over and my leathers on; I've seen the way the girls go for that 'bad boy motorcyclist' thing, thought I'd have a go.

'Oh, brilliant.' She blew and her hair lifted up off her forehead. 'You have no idea how hot this outfit gets in this weather. I'm not sure I can walk another step. Come on then, we'll just have time to get a sandwich before the bus gets in. I might even stretch to a cup of tea.'

Indoors. But indoors with Amy. Would it make a difference?

Chapter Seven

Amy

Josh rode steadily down into the village, for which I was grateful. I've never been one of those girls for thrills and speed – when Gran let me have riding lessons I wouldn't go any faster than a trot – and the breeze was lovely and cool.

'Come in.' I held the door open but he hesitated on the step, staring into the passageway. 'It's all right, we don't have a fierce dog or anything. Gran doesn't hold with pets, and we're out all the time so it wouldn't be fair.'

He shook his head. His hair, which hung straight and a sort of muddy blond onto the collar of his jacket, did a kind of shimmy round his head. "S just a bit … dark and … you know.' He made a bit of a tunnel with his hands, as though indicating a small box.

There was an incongruity to this: Josh, a tall bloke in a leather jacket, jibbing at the darkness of our hallway like a horse refusing to go into the back of a trailer. 'I'll put the light on, is that better?' I switched on the bulb, which didn't really make that much difference, Gran will only go for the 40 watt equivalents. 'You're not going to be reading a book in the passage, are you?' she'd say.

He stepped inside and turned. 'Thanks.' His eyes were wide, a bit panicked, and it occurred to me that this was the first time I'd really looked at him properly. Maybe it was because he was in my house and I felt more comfortable, but I realised that my eyes had always sort of slid across him before, rather than taking him in. He was taller than I thought, over six feet, broad shouldered but narrow waisted, a body that looked as though it was built out of hard work. He had long fingers, nervously playing with his jacket zip, with that untidy mass of hair the colour of old hay hanging to his collar. His eyes were large and dark and kept gravitating to the toes of his boots.

'Come through in here. It's lighter and there're chairs, although I warn you, Gran doesn't hold with comfort, so sit down slowly.'

I smiled at him and he smiled back, a slow, considered sort of smile that looked as though every muscle thought about it independently before letting it loose on his face. It made his eyes spark.

'I'll get you a sandwich and a tea.'

When I got back into the living room from the kitchen, Josh was standing at the window. 'You left it open,' he said. He was under the gap, looking as if he was trying to breathe the fresh air coming in from outside.

'Gran doesn't hold with stale air either.' I handed him the plate with a cheese sandwich on. 'Or air fresheners. That window stays open, winter and summer, but it's fine because there's no noticeable heating in here. We light the fire in the back room when it gets cold enough, by which I mean when Gran has to put a second cardie on.'

He looked around the walls, eating the sandwich so quickly that I hardly saw his mouth move. I wasn't even sure he *was* chewing. 'Burglars?'

'Don't be daft. We're overlooked by every house in the village. Try climbing in through there and you'd better have a really good explanation or the sprint skills of Usain Bolt. I locked myself out once, and Gran came home to two police cars and a lot of local embarrassment. Have some more tea.'

''M okay.' He was eating and drinking very fast, almost nervously.

'It's all right, there's no rush. Even if Gran catches you here, I'll explain and she knows who you are, after all. Well, by sight.'

'Gotta get back. Stuff to … you know … do.' He folded the last sandwich in half, poked it into his mouth, wetted it with a last swig of tea and then headed for the door. It was like watching a chased deer. 'Thanks for the stuff.'

'Any time.'

Now he was on the doorstep he looked more relaxed, as though the sky somehow kept him docile with its weight of clouds. He stopped and turned and then looked as though he'd lost the train of thought he'd been following, shrugging up his shoulders and pushing his hands into his pockets.

'Thanks for bringing me home.'

'Need a lift tomorrow?' he asked.

'No, my bike's fixed. I should be fine, thank you.'

'Oh.' The shoulders came down under the leather and shifted about. 'Okay.'

'But come into the cafe after lunch and I'll see if we've got any spare panini – it'll only be wasted otherwise.'

He smiled again and it struck me how attractive he was. Oh, not Julia-league attractive, not like Edmund with his city style and loafers and narrow-shouldered designer jackets, but good looking in a shy sort of way that crept up on you until you noticed how long his eyelashes were and how his slightly stubbled cheeks had the sort of planes and angles that could have featured on the front of GQ magazine, if his eyes hadn't been so often downcast and his nicely shaped shoulders so often dipped inwards.

'Thanks. I will.'

And then he was gone, slipping out into the afternoon sunlight as if it belonged to him. I watched him walk over to the bike and start it up, ramming his helmet on with one hand while he steered the bike onto the lane and then picking up speed and his feet to shoot off up the hill back the way we'd come, to ride, presumably, back to the Hall.

I shook my head and went inside to obliterate all traces of his presence before Gran got home.

A couple of weeks later the news started filtering around the staff that Edmund had ordered six hundredweight of sand and co-opted three of the gardeners to be in charge of spreading it on a little patch of pebbly riverside to make a beach. A local supplier brought a van full of buckets and spades and Wendy printed off and laminated a load of health and safety notices, which James put up on trees beside the river. The next thing we knew, there were groups of children from the local nursery having a teddy bears' picnic on the 'beach' and we were up to our eyes supplying coffee to the long-suffering adults accompanying them.

I wanted to tell everyone that it had been my idea. Wanted to ask Edmund how it was going, to see if I could manage to squeeze the merest hint of gratitude out of him. Even an acknowledgement that I'd given him the suggestion would have been something, but nothing was forthcoming, apart from increasing numbers of adults, wide-eyed with terror at trying to stop their children from falling in the water, and drinking extra-strong coffee as if it was gin. And then one day soon after, Julia made me jump by slamming down the local newspaper on the counter. I was waiting for a batch of cakes to finish cooking and had been staring out of the window onto the walled garden. It was still early, Monkpark didn't open until eleven, and Josh had a couple of the birds out on their stands, getting some sun on their feathers. James was cutting the lawn with the ride-on mower, probably preparing for the local dance school's performance of vignettes from Shakespeare. Edmund was wringing every possible drop out of my ideas, but at such short notice he'd clearly had to resort to taking what he could get in the thespian stakes. Next year he'd probably be aiming for the Royal Ballet and trying to get Dame Judi Dench to be a room guide. And I wasn't quite sure if I felt angriest at his appropriation of my ideas without so much as a hint of a 'thank you', or the way he was laying it all on so thickly.

'Well, you made the *Gazette*.' Julia sounded a bit accusatory.

'What? How did I?' I dragged my gaze back inside.

'Here. They've done a big write-up of the "ghost" sighting in the Hall.' She folded the paper so that the article, which covered a whole page, was uppermost. 'I know there's not much that happens round here, but you'd think, wouldn't you, that some bugger would have the sense to do some local history. But, no, they've swallowed the story right down. You'd only have made bigger headlines if you'd been Champion Heifer at the show.'

I pulled a face. 'I didn't do it deliberately, Jules. Like I said, I only kept quiet so the poor lad didn't get the piss ripped out of him.' I scanned over the article. 'Wow. You know, psychologically this is really interesting ...'

'Oh, yes, you with your degree, you'd know.'

Julia had always been bitter that Gran had wanted me to stay on in education. Her family had wanted her earning as soon as she was sixteen, and she'd only been able to go to the local college to do her BTEC in Food Hygiene when we started this place up. Gran had been very keen on self-improvement and had carried on working well past retirement age so I could go to uni. I think she'd been a bit disappointed that I'd chosen to do a degree in Business Administration, but at least it meant that we could keep the house; it was either that or Horticulture, and I don't think Gran would have let me study anything that had Hor in the title. She could be a bit sensitive about that sort of thing sometimes.

'No, look ...' I didn't take it personally. And besides, Julia had 'lived' far more than I had, even though she still lived at home with her slightly raucous family and had never travelled further than a hen party to Ibiza. She had the looks, I had the brains, and we'd learned to live with it. I read: 'The ghost was seen by Stephen Myatt, eleven, who said, "It was horrible, just this shape all dressed in black and only holes for eyes. I could see right through it, and it felt like it was coming right for me." Just goes to show what a bit of elaboration will do for a story.'

'And now, apparently ...' Julia scanned down the page with her finger, then tapped the relevant part. '... Monkpark is haunted by the ghost of a pregnant maid who, unable to live with her shame, drowned herself in the river.'

'"It is said",' I added. 'I'd love to know who it's said by and how long they've been saying it, because I've never heard that one.'

'Me neither. Oh, cakes, Ames.'

The pinger was going off on the oven, telling me that today's batch of White Chocolate and Raspberry Brownies were done.

'Miss Knowles, a word, if I may ...' Making me jump for the second time in five minutes, Edmund had come into the cafe, silent in his leather brogues.

I waited, expectantly. *This is where he finally says 'thank you'. Gives me a bit of credit for my ideas. Maybe tells us the cafe is safe?* But nothing about Edmund's expression or entrance seemed to hint at 'well done Amy, you're great'. It all looked a bit more 'you've really done it now'. 'It's about tonight.'

'The food is all sorted.' I spoke as I took the brownies out of the oven. The heat covered my rising blush at being spoken to directly. 'I've got the starters prepped already and in the fridge, and I've done an extra batch of these for dessert.'

Edmund came over. Since the house wasn't open yet, he wasn't wearing his 'official' clothes, but had his jacket off and no tie. There was a studied kind of elegance about him, as though he was used to using his looks, although to what ends I wasn't sure.

'No, this is something else,' he said. And, with Julia looking daggers at me, he took my elbow and led me outside into the yard. 'It's about the piece in the paper.'

The whole 'ghost' thing was such a mistake and so ridiculous that I didn't know quite what to say. 'I could ring them up and explain ...'

'No, no, you misunderstand. As I said the other day, I

think it goes well with the character of Monkpark Hall, the "essence" if you will, to have a ghostly resident.' Edmund looked around quickly, as though to check if anyone was listening, but because it was early there was nobody much about, only James now moving some planters around the yard. I found myself leaning slightly away, Edmund's aftershave was stinging my nose. 'We're not defrauding anyone, there's no evidence, after all, that we *don't* have a ghost, is there? It's simply another string to our bow, if you will.'

'Do we need another string? We've got the cafe and the birds.' I found myself gaining a slightly sarcastic tone. 'And the pretend seaside and the Shakespearian what-not. Monkpark is pretty nearly always busy.' I felt a bit defensive, he was thinking of closing the cafe and now he wanted us to have *more* attractions? The cafe, being the nearest cup of tea and slice of cake for seven miles, was a huge draw. We already wore full Edwardian dress, we couldn't *be* more attractive, at least, I couldn't. Jules could always serve in a bikini, but then that might attract a rather different crowd to our 'tea and scone' fraternity. Monkpark was far more shooters than Hooters.

'Well. If you could refrain from mentioning that occasion on the stairs.' He leaned in even closer now, ignoring my question. 'Particularly tonight. My guests are a little, um, *sensitive* about Trust property and publicity. I would be awfully grateful.' Now he'd lowered his voice to a deep whisper that was making me slightly uncomfortable. 'Just remember, no cafe, no job; no job, no house. You're a clever girl, Amy, you can work it out.' He gave me a wink that made my mouth go all bitter and dry. 'I'll see you tonight at the dinner party then.'

And, with another look over his shoulder at James, who had dragged the pots quite close to where we were standing, he was gone, evaporating into the shadows that the morning sun was laying thick and long in the yard, leaving me with blood receding from my cheeks and a sense of panic that was making my pulse almost audible.

Julia was leaning idly against the counter, ignoring the steaming pile of brownies next to her. 'What did he want?'

'Not entirely sure.' I took the brownies off the rack and put the coolest under the glass dome. 'He seems to think our being haunted is an extra selling point for Monkpark Hall, like we need one. It's almost as though he's trying to turn us into Longleat or something. It'll be lions on the lawns next, that'll give your mum's old tabby something to think about.'

'You used to love those ghost stories when we were kids, Ames, remember? I'd have thought Monkpark having a spook would be right up your street.' Julia wiped the counter free from crumbs in a desultory way. 'Remember when we used to borrow Aaron's tent and camp up in the woods, and the time you told me that story about the ghost with its mouth sewn shut and I had to go home?'

She was carefully not mentioning that she'd left me, alone in the woods, to pack up the tent, having terrified not only her, but myself. But that was Jules for you ...

'I know, but it's a bit dishonest, isn't it?'

'So is all that stuff in the brochure about the twelfth century foundations! Come on, Ames, everyone knows there's nothing under Monkpark but mud.' Julia threw down the cloth. 'And, let's face it, Edmund is dead cute and also in charge of us. He's not going to do anything against the estate, is he?'

'Cute? Is he? He's a bit too ...' I made flappy little motions with both hands, as though I was tracing Mister Jelly. 'Don't you think?'

There was a narrowing about her eyes that made me wonder if she really did have more of a 'thing' for him than I'd guessed, but then, of course, he ticked all her boxes, with his label clothes, his Range Rover and his carefully cultivated air of 'not being a local'. But Jules always said that she didn't want to settle down until she was at least thirty, so she'd got a couple of years of wild oats still to grind into porridge.

'No. He's cute, Ames. Sometimes I worry about you, you

know ... Unless *he* has a thing for *you* and that's why he's doing this ... chance to get up close and personal ...' She gave a small, unflattering snigger at this, but it was one with which I wholeheartedly concurred. I mean, *obviously* he didn't fancy me, how could he, with competition like tall, blonde Julia, giggly busty Sally who manned the ticket office, cute little Wendy in admin, young, impressionable Imogen in the gardens or ... well, pretty much any of the women who worked here.

And then I thought about his half-veiled threats about my job, my *home*. His lack of acknowledgment that the whole beach-by-the-river-and-Shakespeare thing had been my idea. 'Yeah, pretty sure that's not the case, Jules.'

She began sorting through the cutlery tray, checking that we had equal numbers of knives, forks and spoons. 'Come over tonight, Ames. We could borrow Ry's car and go into Thirsk or something. Have a night out. We never have nights out like we used to any more.'

I raised my eyebrows at her. 'Because nights out always tend to be followed by mornings in, and we've got to keep this place up to scratch, even more so now that it could be on the line. Look, it's not long until the end of the season, then we're closed on Mondays, we can go out then, all right?'

She pouted at me. 'S'pose. But that doesn't help me *now*, does it? Honestly, Ames, being here is like living in the nineteen thirties, and *this* doesn't help.' She flipped her black, serge skirt. 'And I'm too old to be sent to boarding school.'

'Tell you what.' I felt sorry for her. It wasn't so bad for me, I got ignored in any group gathering anywhere and usually ended up talking to someone who was very earnest on the subject of trains, so sitting in with Gran every evening was a positive improvement. 'I'll come over tonight, once Gran's in bed, and we can go and drink cheap cider and swing on the gates. It'll be like old times.'

Julia looked at me, slightly mollified, but not much. 'That's not old times, Ames,' she said. 'That's *all the time since we were ten!*'

'Take it or leave it,' I said with a sniff and turned away to turn the hot water boiler on. 'There's a *Pointless Celebrity Special* on tonight, so I'm good either way.'

She bent to get crockery out of the washer and muttered a bit under her breath, but I'd spent all my life with Julia, and was already working on what excuse I'd give Gran for going out this evening.

Chapter Eight

Josh

Edmund Evershit. That's what I called him in my head, prancing about in his stupid bloody shoes that look like slippers and ordering everyone about like he owned the place ... Monkpark Hall Administrator it says on his door, not Monkpark Hall Is Mine so Know Your Place, which it looks like he'd rather have. But he's in charge, however much of a prat he might be, and I need this job. Need somewhere to live, somewhere to keep the birds where they're safe and they can fly without being shot out of the sky by some farmer who thinks they're after his lambs or a gamekeeper protecting his pheasants. All we need, that. Somewhere quiet. Somewhere with no threats.

So I turned up at the Hall on the Friday night, as agreed, and Evershit was waiting. 'Ah good, there you are. I've hired a suit for you, so go and put it on, and you might like to just tie your hair back or something, it's not very hygienic as it stands, is it?' And he handed me this big bag thing.

'Dunno. Never been a waiter before,' and I sort of let the bag trail down on the floor because I knew it would freak him.

'It's very simple, just bring the dishes through from the kitchen to the Little Dining Room and place them on the table. We'll be serving ourselves from there on, we just need them carried in and the dirty plates taken back out. Can you do that, do you think?'

'Think I can manage to carry a couple of bloody bowls and plates around, yeah.'

'Good, good.' Shitfeatures gave me one of those smiles, the ones that only involve the teeth. Looked like he was going to go for my throat. 'I'm dining with some people who I hope are going to become supporters of the Hall, financially. So if this all comes off successfully, well ...' He sort of trailed off as though he was trying to think of the thing that he could use to make me behave. Could have told him, he just had to work backwards through the things I couldn't stand to have taken away. 'Maybe we'll be able to afford to bring in a couple more birds for you.'

That wasn't it. I've got enough birds. Bane and Fae, and Malkin. Skrillex won't fly but he still needs care, so that's my lot. Stupid sod. But he was paying me extra to be here, and Amy had already given me a grin when she saw me turn up, so, you know, swings and roundabouts and all that.

I changed into the suit in the staff toilets up on the office floor. Sluiced myself down while I was there too, had started to smell a bit ... well, moist. Usually just wash in a bowl in the van, but this was proper hot water and soap and all, had to use hand towels to dry off, but that was cool. The suit fitted, far as I could tell, trousers stayed up and the jacket didn't stop at my elbows, and I did a bit of a tidy up with soap and a razor round the face just for the look of it. Nearly didn't recognise myself in the mirror – clean, shaved and in a suit, bloody hell.

Didn't see too much of the girls at first. They were cooking over in the cafe and bringing the stuff through to the Old Kitchen for me to serve from; guess it was a bit heavier on the 'ambience', bringing the food through from there rather than just serving it in the cafe. Evershit had got half a dozen blokes and their wives in, all sitting round the table in the Little Dining Room, which was still bigger than most people's flats. It was all done up like an Edwardian room, with lots of wood and pictures on the walls of blokes on horses, and this posh shiny great table all laid up with the house silver and stuff. I had a lick of some of the food as it went through, some cold soupy thing for starters, posh fish and chips and then those little cakey whatsits that they sell in the cafe for pudding. Nice.

He hadn't said what to do while they were eating, and I had to take the empties out, so I just sort of stood around outside in the hall, sat on the stairs for a bit. Then I could hear them talking about the estate, so I went in to check that they'd stopped eating and collected the plates really slowly; they just carried on talking like I wasn't there, proper upper class, pretend the servants don't exist. They were talking about the 'ghost'.

'So, what did the lad see, eh? Some shadows or something?' An older bloke, glass full of red wine, with a lady next to him wearing something like a carpet. At least she smiled at me when I took her plate.

'Oh, I don't know. Maybe the place really does have a ghost.' Shitface gave me a look I recognised from back over the years. 'Stay quiet, say nothing.' I wound him up by pretending not to notice, and managed to get a little bit of the soup slopped on his shoulder.

'Of course, if we *are* haunted, it could be good for business.'

'You don't want that *Most Haunted* lot coming round.' Young guy, beard. 'The Heritage Trust wouldn't allow that sort of thing, it's against the guidelines.'

'Good Lord, no! Nothing so ... overt. Just a mention from the tour guides, maybe a bit in the brochure, get the word out ... The Americans will love it.'

There was a lot of muttering and what sounded like agreement. I took the empties out and nearly ran into Amy in the kitchen.

'Hey, Josh ...' She looked me up and down. 'Wow. You look amazing!'

I looked down at myself. No idea why, already know what I look like. 'Just clean, 's all.'

Her eyes were wide. 'No, I mean, with the suit and everything. Very smart. So, he's got you on plate duty, has he? What did he use, blackmail? Tempt you with riches beyond your wildest dreams?'

I shrugged. 'Money does it. How about you?'

'Oh, we're in fear for our jobs. Plus, trying to keep on his good side generally, but we've got a bit of an upper hand there, what with me being a ghost and everything.'

There was a bit of a pause. 'You look nice too,' I said, eventually, not really knowing what else to say, and anyway it was true. She wasn't in the whole 'maid' get up tonight, but she'd got a different frock, something sort of silky. Green. Folded around her front and tied up at the side like an advanced bath towel.

'Bit late, but thanks.'

Now she looked down at herself, and sort of pulled the dress a bit at the sides. Made it go all tight and I could see the straps of her bra and it made me think things ... *feel* things that I really didn't want to. God, I really need to get out more ... 'Hey, Amy?' Trying to keep the talking going, not wanting her to walk away. 'Didn't you say that Mr Big there told you to keep quiet about the whole ghost thing?'

She shrugged and the dress shrugged with her, rippling all down the front. Made me think of water, which made me think of Amy in the bath and take some deep breaths.

'Yes, he did.'

'Well they're in there now rabbiting on about how it could be good business for the Hall if they mention it in the brochure.'

She closed her eyes and scrunched her face up like someone had taken something away from her. Then she did another one of those shake things and smiled, only it was a smile that looked as if it had been knocked onto her face. 'Well, that sounds about right, doesn't it?'

God, she was lovely. Behind us Julia banged down a tray, and Amy sort of jumped and gave me a proper grin. 'I'd better go and get—'

'Oh. Yeah,' I said. Over my shoulder I could hear Shitface trying to call me without doing anything as lower class as raising his voice, so I left it just long enough to rile him up, then went back through.

'Ah, Mister Scott, there you are. Plates, please, if you'd be so kind.'

Dick.

'You just can't get the staff these days, can you?' Laughter.

Fucking dick.

Chapter Nine

Amy

'"Monkpark was built in 1503 by Lord de Courcy, who is rumoured to haunt the entrance porch, which was created from the Hall, the oldest remaining part of the house. There are tales of a phantom coach which careers up to the gates, driverless, and the ghost of a maid, who, legend has it, drowned herself in the river that runs by the estate, has recently been seen on the old Servants' Staircase." He didn't waste any time, did he?' Josh wrinkled his nose and put the new brochure down on the table. 'Six weeks and suddenly we've got more spooks than the Ghost Train at Blackpool.' He ate the end of a leftover baguette and flipped through the pages. 'Nice picture of Malkin.'

'It doesn't do any harm, if people want to believe in it,' I said, and wiped the crumbs off the counter. 'And if it makes people more interested in the history of the Hall, well, it's a good thing, isn't it?'

'Still fake though.'

Josh was looking better these days. When he'd arrived at Monkpark, just before the season started properly, John, who'd been in charge back then, had taken him in more out of sympathy than because we needed another attraction and for months Josh had just been the rather grubby guy who'd arrived with a bunch of birds that he flew three times a week in the walled gardens. But gradually, slowly, I could see he was coming out of his shell. He came into the cafe more, not just to pass through in the hopes of a stray muffin, but before and after the visitors arrived. Okay, yes, he did still scrounge food, and you couldn't leave him unattended in the vicinity of a full teapot, but Julia and I had got used to him being around. Occasionally, like today, he'd have a bird on his wrist.

'You're contravening Health and Safety you know,' Julia told him, ostentatiously wiping around him with the pink spray that we used to clean the tables, and which would strip the fingerprints off you if you didn't wear gloves. 'Having that in here.'

'It's fine,' I said, although I wasn't totally sure it was. 'He's only walking through, and it's not as if the owl gets off and goes for a wander, is it?'

Josh looked down at the slightly miffed ball of feathers on his glove. 'Wouldn't dare,' he said. 'He's too stupid. Get stuck under a table or something.' And then he touched the top of Skrillex's head with one finger, just gently, as if apologising for his rudeness. The owl closed his eyes briefly at the touch, in acceptance. 'Anyway, he likes Amy. We're socialising.' And he gave me one of the quick smiles that made him look as if he was really enjoying life. They were brief and infrequent, but made him light up from inside.

'What happened to him?' I wondered if I dared stroke the owl, but decided against it. Josh had told me before that the birds' feathers could be easily damaged, and besides, Skrill might like me but he had a tendency to chew. He had a beak like a billhook and I didn't really want to spend the rest of my time cooking with blue plasters like some kind of mosaic all over my hands.

'Hit by a car. He was only a chick.' Josh moved his hand and brought Skrillex up to his face so he could look him over. 'Broke both wings and a leg.' The smile had gone now, in favour of a look so gentle and tender that it made me go a bit wobbly inside.

'Still unhealthy. All those feathers.' Julia wiped again, a bit more enthusiastically. 'Anyway, Ames, it's getting on for six, are you off?'

I jumped. I'd lost track of time *again*, it was one of the problems with Josh popping in, we'd all start talking – mostly, if truth be told, about Edmund and his plans for Monkpark, but other stuff too – and before I knew it it was time to head home. 'God, yes, I'd better dash. You not off, Jules?'

She gave me a slow grin. 'Just thought I'd pop up to the office and pick up Edmund's tea tray ... you know, like a good employee.'

'You're not *still* trying to seduce him, are you? He's been here, what, two months, and he hasn't succumbed so far, maybe he's immune?'

'Or gay,' Josh added, peering through the brochure again.

'I've got hopes.' Julia wiggled her eyebrows. 'Plus really sexy underwear on. Although in this get-up anything more adventurous than a quick blow job is a bit too much like hard work.'

'Don't say it like you know, Jules, please.' I gathered my stuff. 'Right. I'm off.'

Josh closed the leaflet. 'Want a lift?'

'I've got my bike.' Although I did have to admit it, even if only to myself and only during the darkest parts of the night, there was a certain frisson to be had from riding on the back of Josh's motorbike. The feel of his waist as I clung on, the smell of his leather jacket when I dipped my head down behind his shoulders to keep bugs from hitting me in the face and the hot throb of the engine under my backside – I'd come to the conclusion it was the closest I was going to come to sex these days, unless I took Sam up on some of his artichoke-based offers.

''S okay, leave it here. I'll bring you down in the morning.'

I looked outside. Today it was overcast, promising rain would soon fall through the heavy, humid air. The thought of cycling the mile and a half home was just a bit daunting. 'Thanks, then, that'd be nice.'

'I'll just put Skrillex away.' Josh raised his gloved hand and the owl flapped a bit to get its balance. One wing was clearly only half feathered. 'Meet you outside.'

Julia gave me the eyebrow treatment after Josh had closed the cafe door. 'He fancies you.'

'No. He doesn't. He's just a nice guy, that's all.'

She nudged against me. 'He so does. All those lifts he gives you, all these cosy chats ... blokes don't do stuff like that without having an eye to someone's knickers. So, why don't you invite him in tonight? Show him your etchings.'

I hadn't mentioned Josh's strange reaction to coming into the cottage. His fear of the dark hallway and his standing underneath the open window, as though the whole building was full of smoke. And besides ... 'Don't be daft, Jules. He's got transport, he's heading my way and he's a nice guy. All there is to it, honestly.'

'You're not holding out for Edmund, are you? *Seriously?*' Julia shook her head. 'I know he's being all friendly and stuff but ... somehow I don't think you're his type.'

I didn't like to say it aloud. *If I say anything about the ghost, Edmund will close the cafe. And Gran and I would be out of our home and on the streets.* As if putting the words out there would somehow make it real, as though Edmund were Slenderman or Beetlejuice. But I thought it, especially when I woke up in the narrow, metal bed that I'd slept in since I'd moved out of a cot; the bed my mother had slept in before me and, for all I knew, had tortured generations of our family before that. Okay, I had qualifications, experience, I could probably get something else in York. But Gran only had her pension, and living was so expensive these days, I'd barely earn enough to cover the rent, even if I had two jobs we'd struggle. He needed me to keep quiet, not reveal the ghost was a fake, but he held all the cards.

'A girl can dream,' I said, to wind her up. Edmund was giving her remarkably little attention, given that she also knew about the whole phoney ghost thing and nobody could accuse Julia of not trying. Although, on his part, he'd been incredibly busy lately and every time one of us had taken his afternoon tray up, he'd been on the phone, covering the mouthpiece when we arrived and not speaking again until we left.

'Dream on. I'm off to take him a French Fancy and see what happens.' She gave me a wiggle and set to putting a tray of tea things together.

I couldn't blame her. Julia was the girl that feminism forgot and tended to define herself by means of her boyfriends, which was why she was loathe to lower herself to go out with men who drove Ford Fiestas and a combine harvester. She'd been the same at school, so I could hardly blame cultural conditioning, although I did regard her mother with some suspicion. 'I'll see you in the morning.'

Josh was waiting in the yard, with the bike running. When he saw me coming, he swung something up off his lap. 'Got you this.'

I smiled. 'You shouldn't have.'

He smiled back. Not one of his dazzling smiles, which seemed reserved for the birds and, sometimes, me. This smile was a cautious thing, as though he was expecting someone to shout at him. ''S only a helmet.'

I tugged it on. It pushed all my hair forward and down, so from the outside I must have looked like Cousin Itt, but it had been bothering me that I'd ridden without a helmet, so it was nice of him to bother.

We rode, sedately as ever, to the cottage.

'Would you like …?' I said, as I always did.

'Better get …' He waved his arm at the road, indicating the way we'd come, the way he'd have to go back to the caravan. As he always did. Apart from that cheese sandwich moment, he'd always refused to come into the cottage, just did the same thing, waited for me to get off and then raised a hand in farewell and shot back off up the hill. Of course he didn't fancy me, Jules was just obsessed with the idea that any man who uttered more than three words to a woman he wasn't related to must want her naked.

I grinned at the thought, and then wondered what Josh would look like without clothes. It was an unwanted thought that made me blush such a deep crimson I felt as though I'd been painted. Thankfully, Gran's bus pulled up at just that moment, to spare me from further imaginings, and I watched her gather her bag to her chest for the journey down the steps to the verge, as though she was disembarking the *Queen Mary*.

'Evening, Gran.'

She looked at me suspiciously. 'What are you so perky for, madam?' Then she was off, unlocking the cottage door and performing her nightly round of tweaking at the curtains. 'Someone's been in again. Look at the state of the place.'

As usual the living room was immaculate. I felt an odd mixture of irritation and affection, which burned away in my chest, flaming all other emotions, all other feelings, into powdery ashes. 'It's fine, Gran.'

'Someone's been at these spoons. You had someone in here, Amy Knowles? You been entertaining?'

'Gran, I haven't been entertaining since 1994,' I muttered. 'Playgroup nativity, I was a dancing snowflake.'

'Don't lie to me, young lady. I can tell you've had someone in here, the curtains are all over the place.'

I sighed. 'Yes, all right, I had a couple of guerrilla interior designers come round and put a hit on the Dralon. Come and have your tea.' Fill the pot. To the spout. 'How was the club today?'

She grunted. 'Full of bonkers old biddies who don't know what day it is, same as usual. That's too much water in that pot, tea will be weak as your gravy.' She flashed me a grin that showed her wobbly top set of teeth and I tried not to take her remarks to heart. I *always* tried not to take them to heart. She didn't mean it, any of it, it was just that a brusque and dismissive manner had got her through life and now she couldn't stop it.

I remade the tea, watched *Pointless* with her, and two lots of early evening programmes, which floated through my head without registering. Then I gave Gran her tablets and the usual reassurances and waited until I heard her get into bed, with the associated muttering and creaking of bedsprings, after which I went outside, walked up the hill to where the Monkpark driveway started its curve down towards the old house, and screamed.

After that I cried for a bit, and then I sat down on an old log and hated myself for the obligatory half hour. Hated the ingratitude that reared inside me like a horse too tightly reined. Hated my impatience with Gran, she couldn't help the way she was. Hated the fact that I was five feet nothing and a size fourteen if you were generous, that I had square cut features that no amount of creative hairdressing disguised, that my nose was a blob that looked like someone had stuck a doorhandle above my mouth and my cheeks were the kind of pink roundness that used to be called 'bonny', and now just got me called 'fatface'. The only boys who ever sniffed around were those who thought I should be grateful for their attentions. Except at university, and the least thought about that the better if I wanted life to carry on as it did.

Most of all I hated that I felt like this. I had a job I loved in a place that had always been home. A roof over my head at a minimum rent, Gran had her 'club' in a nearby town, paid for by the NHS and my best friend worked with me and lived opposite. I'd got a good education and qualifications, I wasn't dying of some obscure disease, I wasn't about to go bankrupt and be thrown onto the street. I'd got the cafe, which wasn't exactly what I was qualified for, but it had been the only job that had come up at Monkpark after university, and, what the hell, I could make cakes, couldn't I? I was lucky.

I had another quick screaming fit, but by then I'd started to feel a bit silly. Letting the rage and anger out was fine and all very cathartic, but it could only go on so long before it started to feel self-indulgent, and self-indulgence was one of those things, along with vanity and wearing the same underwear for more than one day, that Gran had nagged me out of by the time I was fourteen. So I sat back and breathed in the stillness of the late summer evening.

There was a background whirring that told me the combines were still out working, and the smell of corn dust in the air competed with the smell of hot tar from the road. Somewhere along the road I could hear a couple of cars moving at speed, but no other traffic. The sun was still warm and tingled along my arms, the breeze puffed into my face until, if I closed my eyes, I could almost imagine the breath of a lover, gentle on my forehead. I kept those eyes closed and imagined a face close by mine, a prick of stubble against my cheek. A hand cupping my chin, raising my lips …

The cars were close now, roaring up the far side of the hill towards Monkpark; they crested the hill and braked suddenly, as though taken by surprise. I opened my eyes to see two hatchbacks, both filled with people, hesitating in the middle of the road. A window wound down.

''Scuse me, love, is this Monkpark Hall?'

It was on the very tip of my tongue to say, 'No, we're positively littered with historic houses round here,' but I didn't. 'Yep, down the drive, about a mile on your left. Can't miss it. But it's closed now.'

The face at the window grinned. 'Ta, love. It's okay, we're expected,' and the car began to turn over the cattle grid. Plastic boxes in the boot jumped and wriggled as the car passed over the narrow metal bars and then the cars were away, sending spurts of loose gravel up as they headed out, disappearing around the sharp bend in the drive, and leaving nothing but dying puffs of dust to show they'd ever been there.

Chapter Ten

Josh

Someone had been in with the birds.

When I got in next morning, they were all hunched. All kind of huddled, like they shouldn't be first thing, when they should be all relaxed. Bane screamed at me when I went over. She never makes that much fuss, but today she was in a right state. I went back out and checked the lock on the door, it hadn't been forced or anything, so it hadn't been someone after stealing them. That happens sometimes, not that often because birds aren't like dogs. You can't just tell them they're part of a new pack now, they have to learn to trust you and work for you, to know that you mean no harm and there will always be food, even if they bugger off and spend four hours in a tree somewhere.

But someone had been in.

I calmed them all down. I'd take them up for a fly later, exercise and all, but it wasn't one of my demo days, although I often took Skrillex out on the fist and talked to some of the visitors, amazing how many of them don't realise what can happen to an owl if you don't watch out when you're driving at night. Just as well I didn't have to get them out in public though, Malkin was proper aggrieved and a buzzard in a shit mood is not something you want to be on the other side of.

Or maybe I'd upset them? I'd ridden in slower than usual, just enjoying the feel of Amy on the back of the bike. She doesn't sit so rigid now, she leans in more and it's ... I dunno. Like we're in balance. So maybe I'd come in a bit fast, a bit of a different shape, because she makes me more upright, like I feel like a real person when I've been with her.

Whatever it was, something crap had happened. I settled them all back down and went on through to the cafe. Smells great first thing, when they've got the ovens on and all the stuff in cooking; there's flour everywhere and the air is warm and full of that oily sweet smell of cake. I remember back when I used to love that smell. Back in the day, when it was just Mum and me before – yeah. Before. And now those memories kind of stained the back of my mind.

'Hey, ten minutes, you took your time.' Amy was setting stuff up on the counter. 'Jules, I owe you fifty pee.'

I just looked at her. Felt a bit weird, the birds all upset and her being just as normal, like I jumped over some crack in the middle where things joined together.

'We had a bet. Amy said three minutes, I said seven.' Julia came in from the kitchen. She'd got her hair all up under her cap, like she'd got horns under there. 'She obviously rates you hungrier than I do.' She gave me a look. Dunno what that was all about, but women have so much going on that we're supposed to get and I never do.

'Someone's been in at the birds.'

Amy stopped. 'Are they all right? Nothing's been taken or anything, has it?'

'Nah. They're just ... fussed.' I sat on the edge of a table. 'Even Skrill and he's really hard. No imagination, owls.' But I was glad she'd thought about it.

Amy started staring at her hands. 'I wonder ... last night I saw a couple of cars, they were heading down here ... But it was daylight, and they said they were expected.' Then she looked at Julia, who'd got a kind of hawk face on her. 'Did Edmund say anything to you about expecting people?'

Julia did a thing. She kind of half-shrugged, half-shook herself, like she was trying to get rid of something stuck on her back. 'No. He helped me bring the tea things over here and then told me to get home.'

'No nookie then, Jules? Are you slipping?' Amy started giggling. I dunno why, it wasn't that funny.

'Said he was "busy". But I did see him looking down the front of my dress, so, you know, I think I'm starting to win there.'

'There's only me and him have a key to the birds,' I said. 'Why would he let some blokes go in there? Apart from him being a shit.'

'Hey, Josh.' Amy did that girl-touching, putting her hand on my arm and then rubbing it a bit. Couldn't feel a thing, still had my jacket on, but hell, and she was all pink from the oven and smelled of burning sugar and I had to start looking at the floor. 'Maybe it was a mistake. Like you said, nothing was taken and the birds weren't hurt or anything, so ...'

I did some deep breathing. Had the feeling if I said anything my voice was going to be all bust up like when I was thirteen. So I just kind of raised my eyebrows and stayed looking at that floor and she kept her hand on my arm and all smelling of cake and holy hell I couldn't talk if you paid me.

'Here. Try this.' Amy had something in her hand and I was a bit afraid to look, because that floor was nice and steady. 'We're working on a new recipe, what do you think?'

'It's a bun.' Well, voice was okay, even if my brain had cut out on me and my body was ... well, yeah.

'It's Earl Grey and rose petal. We thought it might go down well with the teatime crowd, didn't we, Julia?' The oven 'pinged' in the background and Amy went off to do something in the kitchen, carried on calling through. 'If we want to keep the cafe then we have to make sure we're all up-to-date with stuff, we don't want Edmund saying we're old-fashioned.'

I looked around for a second. At the white-clothed tables and all the fancy dishes they had on this cupboard thing in the corner. 'Yeah.' I cleared my throat, but the voice was still holding up. 'I can see how you wouldn't want that.'

'Oy, this is atmosphere! We don't want our menu to get dated. So many of these places just serve the same old tea, scones and sandwiches year in year out, we want to be a bit more ...'

'Twenties,' Julia said. It made Amy laugh.

'I'm hoping we're going to knock a century off, at least.'

I hadn't eaten since ... what, yesterday's panini, and the

cake smelled good. Fresh and a bit like perfume. I held it under my nose for a second. There was a bit of something lemony there but then ... *roses*.

'We got the idea from the rose garden.' Julia pointed, no idea why, I knew where the rose garden was, I just never needed to go round there. Never wanted to, I mean, flowers are okay but they don't do much. But the smell on this cake was like no roses I'd ever smelled from the gardens. It was ... it was softness and hugs and a hand pushing my hair back off my face and all those things that I couldn't think about any more. All those things that had got buried under the memories of tight, dark spaces and hurting.

I dropped the cake.

'Oh Josh ... never mind.' Amy picked it up, no fuss. Like she could see that it made me feel weird, didn't want to push it. 'Look, have one of the orange drizzle ones. Then you'd better get going, we've got a load of baking to do this morning.'

I was back looking at that floor again, but I could see her out of the corner of my eye, sort of at my shoulder.

'Come back after five and we'll probably have some sandwiches left over,' she said.

'You shouldn't encourage him.' Julia was dusting stuff on the cupboard.

'It's just wasted stock otherwise,' Amy said. 'And besides ...' she sort of trailed off and it was like the first half of a conversation.

Had to go anyway. Birds wanted cleaning out and weighing, got to know what they weigh so they'll be hungry enough to fly tomorrow. So I stood up and went to take the bun, which had a kind of orangey shiny top thing, but Amy didn't let go. She kept hold, and looked at me with her eyebrows up and her mouth a kind of sideways line. Not quite a smile but more like she was asking me a question with her face.

Trouble was, it was a question I didn't even want to think about, let alone answer.

Chapter Eleven

Amy

It was my turn to take Edmund his tea tray. Julia seemed to be caught up in mixed feelings, as though she was slightly afraid to let me up there alone, and yet didn't want to go herself. I wondered if she'd made an actual pass at him and been turned down, but then, why worry about me going instead? As she pointed out, it wasn't as though Edmund was going to prefer me to her, was it?

We'd been instructed to cover our dresses with the big white coats we wore when we did messy baking. Edmund wasn't taking any chances that someone might see me or Jules on the stairs in our maids' get ups and put two and two together, so I pulled mine down off the hook, put the tray together and, checking that we didn't have a queue stretching round the block to overwork Julia, I headed through the yard and into the house.

It had been a bit of a chilly morning. Autumn was beginning to tint the air, only faintly, just brushing the leaves of the big sycamores with a dusty brown stain and I knew, after six years' experience of running the cafe that the crowds would start to tail off any day now. Monkpark Hall was open all the year round, and we'd start picking up the Christmas crowds in November, but it was nice to have a couple of months to try out new recipes and new baking ideas on the smaller and less pressurised number of tourists who came at the back end of the year. I stopped for a second and looked around the yard at the staggered roofline of the house and the buttery stone of the stable buildings behind me. Imogen was sweeping leaves away from the back door, talking to Sam over her shoulder, and one of the room guides had popped out for a cigarette, I could see the smoke trailing up over the yew hedge. All comforting, routine stuff that sort of settled itself around me, as though I was at the heart of a world separate to the wider one.

I'd grown up here. Played in this yard before it was all refitted and done up as a cafe; it had been an overgrown and derelict area where the gardeners kept their tools and the compost bins. I'd learned to ride my bike up and down the drive while Mum and Gran had been at work, wandered around the estate poking into barns and sheds and pinching apples and pears from the trees as if they were in my own garden. Knew every stone of the place. Had banged my elbows and grazed my knees on most of them.

I would not have it taken away from me. Not by some bloke who just wanted to make his mark on the place – turning the stables from a cafe into an 'education room' was pretty short-sighted anyway, we already had the old butler's pantry full of dressing up clothes for school visitors, and there was the summer house at the top of the garden for outdoor activities. And what would people do for a cup of tea and a sit down when they'd been round the house? No. This was my domain and I would keep it, even if that meant turning the tables on this whole 'ghost story' rubbish – threatening Edmund that I'd tell the truth if he tried to close the cafe down.

With a new determination weighting my steps, I carried the tray up to the office on the top floor. Edmund seemed to have opened the sliding windows, there was a breeze blowing all the way down the staircase, carrying a slight top note of something that smelled like oxtail soup, which was a puzzle. We didn't sell it, Wendy was a vegetarian and was tapping away at her computer with no signs of any kind of soupular comestible having been eaten. Anyway, she had to get home before lunchtime to pick up her small daughter from playgroup, and she came down to the cafe for anything she wanted in the morning so she rarely ate at her desk. Maybe Edmund had started bringing in a flask? But his desk, when I plonked the tray down, was bare of any bowls or cups.

'Have you made any decision about the cafe yet?' I asked Edmund, who was flicking through a ringbinder file full of newspaper cuttings. 'Only, I was thinking, the whole ghost thing—'

To my utter astonishment, Edmund stood up. 'Amy ...' he said. 'Have I told you how much I value your input into the running of Monkpark Hall?'

'Er.' I'd been spending so long in my state of ire at his lack of any kind of gratitude that I felt completely wrong-footed and a bit disappointed. There were so few things that I was allowed to feel actually, genuinely angry about that I'd rather enjoyed sucking all the resentment and infuriation out of the situation with Edmund. To have him suddenly show appreciation, particularly when nobody else was around, was rather annoying. 'Really?'

'Really.' He took his glasses off. 'Would you ... I mean, is there any chance you'd be free for dinner tonight?'

I was glad I'd already put the tray down otherwise I'd have dropped it. 'Seriously? Dinner? Me?' My voice rose up the scale with each word, until I was practically squeaking. 'But ... Julia said ...'

'Julia ...' He came around the desk to my side. '... is a little bit *obvious*. Oh, she's attractive, but you ...' He came closer. '... you are something else.'

Yep, that 'something' would be plain, I thought.

'Wendy!' Edmund called through the open door to the next office and I heard the sound of the stuttering typing stop. Wendy was usually a lot faster and more fluent with a keyboard than that, she must have been listening.

'Mmmmm?'

'What's the name of the hotel that, err, what's her name, room cleaner ...' He clicked his fingers at Wendy as though trying to call a disobedient dog. 'You must know. She works there in the evenings.'

Wendy looked at me and widened her eyes. 'Do you mean Tegan? She works at the Cock's Head.'

'Yes, yes.' As though it had been his own memory and Wendy had interrupted him. 'Book me a table for two, would you? She speaks well of the place – should be good enough, wouldn't you say, Amy?'

There was a moment's silence, in which I tried to focus only on the desk and imagined Wendy's expression.

'Er. Yes, fine, okay, what sort of time?' She sounded about as stunned as I felt.

'We'll say seven, shall we, Amy?' I wished he wouldn't keep using my name. It was a little bit as if he didn't keep saying it, he'd forget what I was called.

'Er ...'

'I'll pick you up. You live in Oak Cottage, yes?'

I nodded. He'd done his homework all right. Did that mean he knew about Gran? She'd been pensioned off from her job helping out with housekeeping for Monkpark when it became obvious that it was all getting too much, and the estate had made it clear that they wouldn't kick her out of the house right away. They'd give her a chance to find somewhere, maybe nearer to town, they said. Somewhere more convenient, with shops. They'd even help her to look, act as guarantors, loan her the down payment for the advance rent and bond. But then I'd come back from university, all qualified up and keen to start my own business, and they'd just finished renovating the stables and ... well. Gran had been able to retire. But she'd worked here for sixty years, give or take, so Monkpark must have had records on her. And it wouldn't at all surprise me to find that Edmund had been right through the personnel files.

I wondered what he'd found about me.

I headed back down the stairs, with the kind of stunned feeling I'd only had once before, when I'd stood up too quickly underneath an open cupboard door. Edmund. Wanting to take me for dinner. *Why?* Julia was going to kill me.

There was only one couple in the cafe when I got back, and Josh, who was sitting at the corner table nearest the counter.

He'd got the Monkpark brochure open in front of him and a plate that had clearly once held a cheese toastie.

'Edmund's asked me out to dinner.' I didn't see any point in prevaricating. The way gossip travelled around this place, they probably already knew.

Julia's face set. 'What, you? When?'

Josh didn't look up, he just flicked pages over with his finger. 'You can ask him who he let in with the birds.' His mouth seemed a little harder, as though he was biting his lip, but where I couldn't see.

'Tonight. Seven. And, yes, I do intend to ask him what those cars were doing driving down here yesterday. Maybe he just had some friends round for another meal?'

'He'd have got us to cook like last time.' Julia still looked amazed.

''Sides, Trust doesn't allow the Hall to be used for private parties. Says so here.' Josh poked a finger at some text. 'Not even weddings. So he was on dodgy ground even having his mates over the other night.' There was a definite tightness in his voice now.

'Hadn't you better get home then, Ames?' Julia was loading up the dishwasher. 'I mean, you are going to need all afternoon to get ready!' She started to laugh. Josh, I noticed, didn't join in. 'And don't forget I can see the front of your house from my window, so no sitting there snogging when he drops you back.'

Josh stood up and gathered up the brochure, shoving it into his pocket. 'Thanks for the sandwich,' he said, and wandered off out without looking back.

I stared after him. I wanted to tell him, to explain that I seriously doubted that Edmund wanted anything more from me than to make sure I wasn't going to blab about ghosts, but then, taking me to dinner was a bit extreme. After all, he'd got the whole cafe thing to dangle over us and I wasn't going to do anything to jeopardise that. But then, despite what Julia kept saying, Josh had never given me any indication that he wanted to be anything more than someone who sometimes gave me a lift to work. And ate our leftovers.

'So.' Julia slammed the dishwasher shut. 'What are you going to wear?'

'Jules, I don't think it's *that* kind of dinner.'

Her mouth moved into a wry expression. 'Probably not. But even so, shouldn't you at least be making him think that *you* think it is? I mean, it's kind of blackmail really, isn't it – he knows that you know and you know that he knows you know and all that crap, so he's trying to buy you a bit, so you should really take him for everything he's offering, and to do that you've got to wear a proper frock.'

'You've got a point.'

We gave one another slightly cautious grins. I remembered … she probably didn't, why would she? But it was okay. I was okay.

Chapter Twelve

Josh

I took the bike up onto the moors. Wanted to be a long, long way away. Somewhere it wouldn't hurt. It still did though. But then, what did I expect? I'd never said, never *done* anything that would make Amy think I thought of her as – whatever I thought of her as. Even I didn't know. Knew what I'd like her to be, but didn't have the balls to say anything.

Up there the sky went on and on and a couple of sparrowhawks were hunting, the air smelled clean and washed and I didn't have to think about her having dinner with the dick. Shit. Shit dick. Over the moors I went, and then down over to Whitby, where the abbey was all dark and jagged on the headland; it looked like I felt, so I parked up and sat on the wall next to it.

I sat there while the sun set. Lights came on, in town first and then the houses further out and then the farmhouses scattered round the moor, and the sea was this big, black heaving thing down off the cliffs. Too dark. Like the air getting thick around me. I checked my watch. Half nine. Would they be done yet? If I shut my eyes I could see her, sitting in front of a table with a candle on, nice glass of wine. Smiling that smile through the flame.

When I came back through Pickering, the supermarket was still open. Something kind of hopeful in the light shining through the windows, so I went in. Seeing people moving around, shopping helped a bit. Stopped me focussing on what might be going on with Amy, made life feel a bit more real, somehow. Didn't want anything, just wandered up and down a bit, then saw some flowers near the checkout. Big yellow flowers, like little bits of the sun cut off and wrapped in paper, making me think of Amy. The way she smiled at me was like that, like someone took a bit of something big and bright and gave it to you, all wrapped up in her. So I bought a big bunch.

Got back on the bike and rode home slowly, checking out all the cars as I went. Didn't want to run the risk of riding past them, but I'd know his shit mobile anywhere, poshed up Range Rover, too shiny to be real and it wasn't on the road anywhere I was riding. And I certainly wasn't going in through the village, so I rode over the high top and down to the Windmill field, where my van sat at the bottom like the edge of the valley had gone rusty and peeled back. Pulled up and let the engine idle. Did I really want to go in there, sit on the bed and breathe the damp air, thinking about Amy and how she looked when she smiled? Times like this I wish I'd got a telly. Or a radio. Anything to put a bit of background noise up between me and what I was imagining. But there was nothing down here, just me and the van and the quiet, so I gunned up the bike, rode down to Monkpark and let myself in with the birds.

It's not a big barn, not much more than a shed really. But a proper one, built of stone and with a roof that keeps the rain out, keeps the birds dry and secure and keeps the light out so they don't get all uppity. Big enough that it doesn't feel like … I can breathe in the barn, it's okay. And it smells of the sawdust I use on the floor to keep it clean, of moulted feather dust and old stone, almost like the smell of a beast. It was dark, so the birds were sleeping, or at least quiet, even Skrillex who technically should be just getting started, but he's adapted to life as a day bird.

I sat on the floor and listened to them. Just the odd feather-ruffle, occasional stretch or shift up and down a perch, noises that let me know they were alive. And mine. It was dark, but if I kept the door open just a crack then the light from the moon came in and it wasn't so bad, not as suffocating as the dark in a house or …

Yeah. Forget it. Forget all of it. Forget the past, forget the future, just live for the now. And the now was here, on this floor, with my back up against the wall of the barn and my feet in the wood shavings that smelled all acidic and the birds just shuffling and clacking away. Being alone has never mattered before, and I should never have let myself think that things were going to change. Just because I liked her, because I thought she liked me – well, she needs to watch out for herself, like I do. Because, really, when it comes down to it, we've only got ourselves.

I looked at the bunch of flowers I'd brought in with me, and they looked stupid now. Like clown faces with smiles painted on. Fake. How could I ever have thought Amy would like them? Edmund might have given her flowers tonight, and he'd have got a bouquet, all properly wrapped. Lilies, probably. Something expensive, something to show off what kind of man he was, all about money and flash, he wouldn't have picked flowers that reminded him of Amy, he'd have whatever cost the most in the shop. And I looked at those daft yellow flowers and felt like an idiot. Shoved them in the corner where I didn't have to look at them. I took my jacket off and kind of wrapped it round me. Lay down in the sawdust with my head on my arms and fell asleep, with my birds around me.

Chapter Thirteen

Amy

The food was good. Fresh, well prepared and nicely presented I couldn't help noticing, as the evening turned into one of the strangest 'dates' I'd ever been on, and I'd once been on a date with a bloke who turned up dressed as a horse. Edmund started off talking about the Hall, about how the finances weren't great and how we needed to find new revenue streams. About how 'his' ideas for events in the gardens were just the start of bigger things.

'I hope, Amy, that you realise I appreciated your attempts at ideas for the gardens. Obviously, those were unworkable, but they corroborated some plans I'd already put in place.'

I smiled a closed sort of smile. If my ideas had been unworkable, then how come they were pretty much exactly what Edmund was doing? But what could I say?

'And I'm hoping that my latest idea, that of the "ghost", will attract more visitors keen on the more psychic attractions.'

'But we don't have any,' I pointed out, pouring myself another glass of wine. It was going to my head a little bit, alcohol being one of the many things that Gran didn't hold with, and when I went drinking with Julia she'd down three to my one and end up throwing up halfway through the evening, so getting the chance to down more than a glass and a half was pretty novel.

'Come on, there must be stories about the Hall! Anywhere that old is bound to have some kind of folklore, surely.' Edmund looked around us at the restaurant. It was quiet, the couple that had been in earlier had gone and the waiting staff – one of whom was Tegan – were circling us like bored sharks.

'Well, I suppose I could ask Gran, she knows everything

that's ever happened there since before Noah got hold of his first Screwfix catalogue ...'

'That would be fantastic.' Now he lowered his voice and raised his glass. He'd been drinking carefully measured little splashes of wine to my glugs. 'Anything you can do to help, Amy, *anything* ...' He lowered his voice even further. '... and I will be terribly grateful.'

Tegan came over and recited the dessert menu at us, giving me very wide-eyed looks. She was clearly finding Monkpark's administrator taking the cafe girl to dinner about as odd as I was. 'What about getting one of those TV programmes round? The "ghost hunting" ones? Getting Monkpark on TV would be a guaranteed tourist magnet.'

'Sssssshhhh!' Edmund hissed at me, under cover of smiling at the waitress. 'The Heritage Trust doesn't allow that sort of thing,' he said, through a thin sort of smile. 'Or I would. No private parties – our dinner the other evening was Trust sanctioned, of course. Local bigwigs are exempt from the normal rules.'

'But we can do stuff in the gardens?'

He gave me a strange sort of look. It was the kind of look you get when your boss is assessing your intelligence level, wondering perhaps if you might be a lot cleverer than you look. 'Yes. But haunted houses tend to be just that. I don't think the BBC would be interested in making a TV programme in a garden, particularly when the ghost was seen in the house, do you, Amy? All our attractions must be outdoor based.'

'The birds are all right then.'

He gave me another look. 'The birds are very much an attraction. I've been delighted with the public reaction to them.'

I swallowed the last of my wine. The bottle, I could see, was empty now, but Edmund didn't seem keen to order another. 'So, you're not allowed to have people in the house, except for Heritage Trust visitors, is that right?' I was slurring a bit and it took me two goes to get 'Heritage Trust' out. 'Why?'

He looked down at the tablecloth and began fiddling with the alignment of his cutlery. 'When the Hawtons handed the Hall over to the Trust they wanted to continue living in the house. So there was a rule that there were to be no private tours, no visitors after hours, to enable the family to live as normal a life as possible. After Lady Hawton died, the rule stood, for the protection of the interior of the house.' There was a glib speed to his reply, as though he'd read up on it. 'Several other Heritage Trust houses have the same stipulation, it isn't just us.'

'Does that mean you too? You can't have monum ... momuntn ... massive parties in your flat? Even though that's your home?' My head was spinning a bit now. Definitely time to slow down on the wine consumption. The thought of facing Gran in the morning with a hangover was enough to make me fill my glass with water from the jug on the table.

'I'm afraid so. Although, obviously, I am allowed to entertain small numbers in my own private accommodation, anything else would be against the rules.'

'Yesterday I saw a couple of cars heading down to the house ...' I said, slowly.

He gave me a narrow-eyed look. 'Just a few friends of mine popping over to see my new place of work. In the area on holiday, touring around, I invited them ...' Now his voice was little more than a whisper. 'As I said, nothing against the rules.' He seemed irritated. Annoyed that I'd seen his visitors? Or just snippy because I'd questioned The Rules? Hard to say, with Edmund. He had one of those smooth faces that don't show much emotion of any kind, his smiles only seemed to get as far up as the end of his nose and displeasure was limited to under-brow staring. I wondered if he'd had Botox.

From there on our meal lapsed into complete silence. Edmund kept looking around the room and I half wondered if he was going to make a break for it and leave me with the bill. He kept beckoning Tegan over, to ask a question about the food or to order a coffee, and whenever she approached our table he'd smile at me, or murmur something so quietly that I couldn't hear. It was disconcerting to say the least, it felt a little bit as though he was trying to sell me to her or something.

I drank some more water, quite quickly.

We finished our meal and headed back to Monkpark. I sat beside him in a sweat of terror. He wouldn't try to kiss me, would he? I mean, my lack of interest in him physically must be plain, unless he was so self-absorbed that he thought every woman had to fancy him. But then Edmund didn't really seem to recognise me as female; apart from his momentary gratitude earlier on he might actually have thought of me as a particularly realistic robot.

We drew up outside the cottage. 'Thank you for a lovely evening,' I said, my mind on semi-automatic pilot as I watched him for indications of intent.

'Yes, it's been most ... pleasant.' He was facing front pretty hard. Nothing about him gave any sign that he wanted to kiss me goodnight.

I opened the door and slithered down onto the grass beside the road and he just kept looking beyond the windscreen as though he was measuring distances. 'Thank you,' I said again.

'Goodnight, Amy.'

His face was a pale smudge at the window as the Range Rover passed me, heading off up the hill. Despite the fact that he physically gave me the shudders, and the resolutely impersonal nature of most of our conversation, I was counting this as a dating success. Or, at least, a date; despite Artichoke Sam's sporadic and somewhat off-putting efforts, any kind of romantic interlude had been a bit lacking for quite a while and at least he had come human-shaped and not legged it during dessert or anything.

Gran was downstairs. Sitting in her nightie in her chair in a slightly '*Psycho*-esque' way. 'You went out,' she said, accusingly.

'Yes, I told you I was going for a meal with Edmund, the new boss.' I helped her stand up. 'And it's not late, look, it's barely ten.'

'I'll not have you ending up like your mother.' Gran flapped about inside the nightie like a thin, annoyed spectre. 'Out till all hours, with men old enough to be your father.' My *actual* father remained something of a mystery, to my mother as well I got the feeling.

'Gran, I'm twenty-eight.'

'Not too old to be taken in by some loose-living man who just wants ... well, never you mind what he wants. I know his type.'

I sighed. 'Come on, Gran, back to bed.' I ushered her through to the stairs, pausing only for her to tweak at the curtains as she passed.

'Place is a mess.'

'Yes, Gran, I'll tidy in the morning.'

The next day was Sunday. Gran didn't go to her 'club' today, instead she went to the local church with Julia's mother, even though Gran wasn't notably religious and I had the feeling that her prayers were more like a one-sided slanging match with God. So I left her getting ready to go over the road and headed off to work. I wanted to show Edmund that I was a professional, that his taking me to dinner didn't mean that I was going to take advantage and start rolling in to work at all hours. Even though I had a monumental headache.

As I wheeled my bike over the cattle grid and into the yard, I noticed something odd. The door to the barn where Josh kept the birds was ajar. Just a crack, hardly even noticeable, but after yesterday's panic I thought I'd better check, so I propped my bike against the wall and went to peer in through the gap.

Josh was sprawled on the floor, wrapped in his jacket, fast asleep. He looked pale and his face, relaxed in sleep, had lost the perpetually wary expression that clouded his eyes and puckered the fine skin round his mouth when he was conscious. The birds were all awake and eyeballed me furiously as I pushed the door a little more open and went to check they were all still tethered.

'Sssh, it's all right,' I whispered to them, their heads moving to keep me firmly in sight as I moved down the line, making sure they were all present and correct and nobody had interfered with them in any way. 'It's just me.'

Bane wasn't reassured. She shuffled from foot to foot and let out a piercing 'mew' of a cry that made me jump.

'What's going on?' I heard Josh's voice, sleepy but also sounding slightly threatening. 'Leave the birds alone.'

'Sorry, I … I thought someone had been in.' I turned around. He was propped against the wall now, his jacket on the sawdust beside him. 'Were you here all night?'

He slumped a bit. 'Hey. Didn't recognise … dark in here. Yeah, I …' A moment's pause. 'Wanted to make sure nobody tried to get in last night.'

'The birds look fine.'

He'd bent his knees and put his chin down so he was practically huddled. 'Worked, then.' He sounded tired. Even in the gloom I could see his eyes looked shadowed and he kept avoiding my gaze, glancing up quickly and then back down at the toes of his boots, which were buried in the bedding.

'Are you all right, Josh?'

A sigh. 'Yeah.' Now he extended an arm. 'Give us a pull.'

I grinned and caught at his hand. As I did so he closed his fingers around mine and his skin was so cold that it made mine tingle. 'Feels as though you'd better come in the cafe and have a hot cup of tea before we both get started. You're freezing.'

He used me to draw himself up to standing. In the half dark of the bird barn he looked taller and his hair, messed up from sleeping on the floor, kept raining little bits of wood shavings down onto his shoulders. 'Cold, yeah.' He kept hold of my hand.

'Josh ... if you're worried ...' His cold touch and immobility were starting to alarm me. 'I spoke to Edmund last night and your job is safe. You're quite an attraction, apparently.'

His hand fell away but the cold stayed, as though he'd somehow freeze-marked me. 'Attraction, yeah.' Then he cleared his throat as if his voice had fallen. 'Yeah. Thanks, Amy.'

'No worries.' I'd been about to turn and lead the way out to the cafe, but something about him, the birds, the half-dark of the barn kept me there. Outside I could hear James getting the mower started, sparrows were kicking around the dust in the yard with plaintive cheeps, but in here it was heavily silent as though the air was weighted with unsaid words. 'Are you sure you're all right?'

He was just looking at me. Big, dark eyes under a fringe of floppy, dark blond hair and a mouth that I could see was surrounded by fine lines that he was too young for. A face that knew things I wasn't sure he would ever share. 'Yeah.' A huge sigh that rocked his body against me for a second. 'Yeah, fine.' He smelled of the wood shavings, as though his clothes had been dried by time rather than warmth. It was a lonely smell. The smell of a man who does only what he has to to keep himself together, a smell that doesn't care.

I went to lead the way out of the barn and then stopped. Leaning against the wall just behind the door was a bunch of sunflowers. Slightly droopy from being out of water, but fresh and wrapped in cellophane, like a presentation bouquet. I bent over and picked them up. 'What on earth are these doing here?'

Josh went very quiet at my elbow. Almost as if he wanted me to forget he was there, but I kept waiting for an answer, the flowers laying their heads gently across my arm. They smelled of autumn and outdoors and there was something lovely and optimistic in their open yellow faces.

'I bought them for you.' His voice sounded far away, even

though he was actually touching me. 'Then I thought how stupid that was.'

'*Josh.*' I lifted the flowers to my nose and inhaled that sweet earthy smell. 'That's a lovely thing to do. Why would you think it was stupid?'

'Because I don't know what I'm doing around you.' He was keeping his head down, his hair falling forward so I couldn't see his eyes. His words were heavy but quiet. 'And I wanted you to have something nice, but then it all felt wrong.'

I wanted to throw my arms around him then. Tell him that nobody had ever bought me flowers before, I wasn't the sort of girl that inspired that kind of sentiment in men. If they ever bought me anything it would be something practical, something robust and useful, not a riot of colour and ornamentation, good for nothing but decoration. I wanted to kiss him, hug him to me and press myself against his body to try to leech some emotion from him. But one quick sidelong glance told me that would be a bad move.

'Come on then. And I'll tell you what Edmund told me over dinner. He wanted me to find out if there's ever been any ghost stories about Monkpark Hall.' Practicality was the best way round this. Treat him as though nothing had changed.

'Oh. Okay.' Once we were out of the barn, Josh carefully locked up the door. 'I'll see to them in a bit. Y're right, I'm cold. And hungry.' He kept his eyes averted from the flowers and I carried them in a nonchalant, floppy-headed way, as if they didn't matter.

He sounded more like himself now, he'd lost that cautious note from his voice, as though he'd been bracing himself for a slap.

'I asked Gran this morning, and, apparently, there's a priest hole in the Library somewhere. She can't remember where it was, but she said they used to keep the Hoover in there.'

'Wow.'

'But no ghosts.' We'd walked through to the cafe by now

and I unlocked the door and turned on the hot water machine. 'Honestly, all this history and we can't even rustle up a headless dog or a groaning lady.' I plopped the flowers in a jug and tweaked at the stems to make them all stand up. When I turned around, he was sitting on the edge of one of the tables, watching me with an oddly intent expression. I wondered for a second if Jules had been right, if he did fancy me, but he didn't look like a man who fancied me. He looked cold, hungry and a little bit lonely. I was not the sort of woman on whom fantasies are built, unless the man in question fantasised about efficiency with a tax return and the ability to make seventy-five cupcakes in under an hour. But the flowers stood there on the counter, nodding their heads in the warmth as though they were silently committing our conversation to memory. He'd bought me sunflowers. 'Here. Have some tea.'

I poured him a mugful. Bone china and teapots clearly weren't going to cut it with a young man who looks as though his bones have frozen.

'House is closed tomorrow,' he said, when half the mug was gone and he'd eaten an old scone that I'd put aside to feed to the chickens that roamed up under the plum trees in the village.

'Yup. Monday, lovely Monday.' The house closed on Mondays and Tuesdays, except Bank Holidays and August. Now we'd edged into September things eased off a bit.

'What do you do? On Mondays?'

'Housework, usually. Gran doesn't go to her club when I'm off, so sometimes we go for a potter around the place. I read a bit, check out some new recipes.' Sleep. Shave my legs when I can be bothered. Stare into space and wonder if this is my life until I die. I didn't say any of that though, plenty of people think that life around a big house is idyllic, what with our cheap rents and all that space. Maybe it is. I know I found life hard in Leeds for the three years I was there, all that noise and all those people, but it was nice to have shops that stayed open all night and places to go that you didn't have to drive fourteen miles behind a tractor to get to.

Josh pulled a face. 'I could do with a hand. Need to get the bird shed mucked right out and dusted for mites. Any chance I could borrow you?' Then he gave me a smile that made his eyes shine at me through the tea steam. 'Sorry it's not glam or anything.'

'Can I bring Gran over to see the birds while we do it?'

He tipped his head on one side, it made him look a bit like Bane. No, more like Skrillex, with those big eyes and that thoughtful expression which carried a hint of wariness. 'Why not. Long as she doesn't upset them.'

'She's a seventy-eight-year-old woman, not an eagle. Although, given her ability to spot dust or curtains out of line there's not a lot in it.' His grip around the mug had lost some of its tightness, I noticed, and there was a degree of relaxation in his body now. He'd stopped perching and was slouching, much more as though he belonged here. 'Then, all right, I'll come over and help you.'

'Cheers.'

'Right, now bugger off. Jules will be here in a minute and we've got a load of batch baking to do before we open.'

Josh gave me another smile and put the mug down on the table. 'Buggering off now. See you.' And he was actually whistling when he went out, but Julia was going to kill me over the amount of sawdust he'd trailed in his wake all over the floor.

And the sunflowers stood on the counter, still nodding.

Chapter Fourteen

Josh

I imagined Amy's face. While I was walking round with Skrillex on the glove, I tried to think what she'd look like if I told her why I lived in the van. Why I was scared of the dark, of small spaces, why I lived this little life with my birds. But I couldn't. Couldn't fix an expression onto her face when I tried, when I said the words all quietly so the bird wouldn't panic, just to try out how they felt; all I could see was a kind of blur where her face should have been. Like my brain couldn't even begin to imagine her reaction.

Thought she'd be okay. Thought she'd be kind, but when I tried the words and they sounded kind of weak and stupid, I thought maybe she'd think I was weak and stupid too. After her having a dinner with Shitface, I was never going to look a good bet, was I? Just this bloke, with birds. No designer gear, no fancy car, no flat in Monkpark Hall – yeah, I went up with James when John was moving out to give a hand with furniture, that place is sweet up there under the eaves. But she seemed to like the flowers. More than like them, somehow, as if they were more than just flowers to her, so I'd stopped feeling such a dick about buying them. And then even the words went, and I couldn't even make the sentences to tell her why I was here, but I did whisper out why I liked her; that smile, the way she seemed to care, the way she was funny and serious at the same time, all that. Until Skrill started looking at me with his head turned down and I had to stop because if it was bad enough to disturb him then it wasn't something I wanted anybody to catch me doing.

"S too late anyway. Shouldn't've let Shitface get a look in.' I should've ridden in there and done whatever it is that these heroes are meant to do, swept her off her feet or stuff. But it's hard to imagine Amy being swept off her feet, she's pretty grounded, looks like she knows what's going on, I reckon most of what he's got is just the designer gear and the car. Not that she's shallow, fuck, no, but I've seen where she lives and all, and she's got a bike and he's got leather seats. I mean, I'm only one step up, my bike's got an engine, saves you having to pedal, but it's still a bastard in the rain. So maybe she's looking to make a future. She's, what, twenty-five, six? Little bit younger than me and living with her gran, so maybe she's looking for a place of her own, family, kids and all. Stuff I've never even thought of, let alone wanted.

Because. Because family isn't always cosy homes and buttered toast. Not all that stuff they put in the ads on TV. Sometimes family is trying not to be seen, keeping out of the way. A strap across your back till you cry and then a smack in the face for crying. A shove and the door shutting, and that cold, airless place with no windows. Crying for someone who never comes.

I let some little guys stroke Skrillex, showed them how to be gentle and not break his feathers, showed them his claws and his beak and then showed them what had happened to him when the car hit. Could be that they'll remember when they get cars of their own, remember to watch out when they drive at night for young owls just taking to the wing, bit clumsy, not up to avoiding a huge travelling hunk of metal. Poor bugger. Skrill was lucky that I found him, that I knew what to do, otherwise he'd have been fox food, and one less barn owl in the world.

When the kids moved off, I found that my heart felt like it was full of something, sorrow or some kind of pain that I couldn't save them all, all the injured owls, all the birds that got taken and kept in cages and never allowed to stretch their wings.

Can't save them all though. Can't do anything much. Just sit in the van and wish that I'd got the guts to ask Amy out or at least make something of my life so I wasn't a target for people like Shitface. But at least I've got her as a friend, I've got a place to live and I'm earning, so it could be a lot worse.

I'm so good at spinning a situation.

Chapter Fifteen

Amy

'So, where was this priest hole then, Gran?' I shovelled another load of woodshavings into the barrow, while she sat on a nearby bench, Skrillex perched next to her. It was a hard call to know who was watching who.

'I said, in the Library. I don't remember where exactly, I never had anything to do with it. You'd have to ask Joan, she was head of housekeeping back then, she'd remember, she was the one who used it to keep stuff in.'

Joan had been dead for ten years, so, short of a séance, it looked like that was a closed avenue.

'We could look.' Josh popped his head out of the barn, where he was puffing louse powder in the cracks. 'Today. While it's closed.'

Gran pursed her mouth at him. But being outdoors seemed to dilute her usual antipathy towards people she hadn't known since they were foetuses, and she'd actually managed not to insult Josh at all, although she had sniffed heavily at the sight of his leather jacket. He'd taken that off now, and there was something about his tautly muscled arms under rolled up shirtsleeves that had rendered her unable to do much more than pull faces.

'Isn't the house locked up?' I picked up the barrow, ready to empty it down on the shavings heap by the compost. 'I suppose we could ask Edmund for a key … say we wanted to get something from the Old Kitchen …'

'He's out.' Josh jerked his head upwards, indicating the little skylight to the flat where the Hall Administrator lived. 'Car's gone.'

'Well, then.'

Gran tutted. 'Amy Knowles, how long have you lived here? And you haven't found out how to get in without a key?'

I set the barrow down. 'You mean you know how to?'

Gran started to laugh. It was a sound I didn't hear much these days, as though laughter had been eroded out of her over the years and left her with the cracked bark that she'd turn out when I did something she considered really stupid. But the fresh air, the sun that was flashing at us from behind the thickening clouds, and the presence of Josh, all seemed to have combined to make her thought processes a little bit more coherent today. 'When the house was still in the family, no one ever locked the doors.'

'Yes, Gran, social history is all very well, but it would be nice if we could actually do something practical today.' I glanced at Josh, who'd got louse powder in his hair, but was grinning at me. 'If we can find the priest hole, then we've got something we can use. I can sort of hint at it to Edmund but not tell him where it is, unless he—' A quick look at Gran's face. 'Well. It might come in useful.'

'Plus, you know, could be fun.' Josh turned the grin to Gran now, and she actually got a little bit pink in her cheeks. He really had a way with the septuagenarians. 'Adventure.'

I wheeled the barrow down to the heap and tipped the last load of sawdust, then wiped my forehead with my arm. It was nice working alongside Josh, he'd emptied out the old barn with a quiet efficiency and, louse powder notwithstanding, there was something about the way he looked that made me smile to myself while I shovelled. Neither of us had mentioned the flowers again, but he seemed somehow a little bit less reserved towards me since then. As though he'd shown me a side of himself that he'd thought I would brush off or laugh at, and, because I hadn't, he felt a bit more relaxed in my company.

'Okay then,' I called back as I dug damp bedding out of the recesses. 'Let's do it.'

Gran didn't answer, and, when I turned round I found that Josh had taken his shirt off to shake the powder off it, and she'd got a lost, distant look in her eyes. She was obviously watching another man take his shirt off for manual work, somewhere down the ages. A small secret smile crept around her lips and she looked down at her hands. At her wedding ring, worn thin with age and hard work, and I saw her give it a little rub.

'Gran?' This was practically an emotional outburst from my grandmother. 'Are you all right? Not too cold?'

I was astonished when she glanced my way and gave me a little wink and a nod of her head towards Josh. 'Just thinking,' she said, but there was a lightness in her voice as though she'd lost about forty years. 'Just thinking.'

We left the barn empty to dry out, the birds on their perches in the intermittent sunshine, and followed Gran round the outside of the house. All the doors we tried were locked, even the small side door that led to the office suite and Edmund's flat that was often just left on the latch, but Gran didn't even bother to stop, she just kept walking until she got to the damp and ferny steps that led down to the storehouses underneath the Old Kitchen. 'Down there.' She pointed.

'What? It's not even part of the main house,' I said.

'You get in through there, then down the corridor. It leads to the butler's pantry, comes out in the back of the big cupboard. Then you jiggle the latch and Bob's your uncle.' She began to head back round the house again. 'You can let us in the front door, I'm not climbing about in cupboards at my time of life.'

Josh gave me a look, clearly torn between not letting my grandmother disappear and not wanting me to go in alone. 'I'll …' he dithered.

'You go with her, I'll open the doors.' I headed down the slippery steps, where water was dripping, heard but not seen. I knew where I was, but I'd never thought that these stores connected to the main house, although it made sense. Food

92

could be kept cool, or alcohol, since the house didn't have a wine cellar, and the butler would have had access without having to go up and down these deathtrap stairs.

I let myself into the store, then down the bare brick corridor to a big latched door, where, as instructed, I jiggled until the latch loosened and I fell into darkness. A moment of fumbling and I'd let myself out, found my way up through the hanging fancy-dress clothes and fallen out into the room, like a refugee from Narnia. All the internal doors were shut but not locked, so I could easily get through, up the flight of servants' stairs and into the main hall, where I could see Gran and Josh pressing their faces to the side windows.

'I'm impressed, Gran,' I said, letting them in.

She sniffed. 'Place is a mess,' she said, almost reflexively, glancing around. 'Joan would never stand for it.'

Like the oddest Scooby gang ever, we made our way to the Library, going in through the lower door rather than from the Gallery.

'Where do we start?' Josh looked around at the bookshelves that alternated with oak panelling all round the walls. 'Is it in one of the walls?'

Gran sniffed again. 'Unless those priests could levitate. Joan couldn't even lift a Hoover above her waist, so it must be.'

I walked around the room one way, Josh walked the other way and we met in the middle of a glass-fronted bookshelf full of leather bound books. Gran sat stiffly on one of the side benches, hands on her knees.

'All looks solid to me,' he said.

'But it would, wouldn't it? Otherwise the priests would be sitting targets, and the householder would be outed as a Catholic,' I whispered back. The rumoured historical Catholicism of the Hawton family was something else Gran didn't hold with, although having a priest hole made the matter pretty much cut and dried, I'd have thought. 'Gran? Any ideas?'

'They've changed the curtains,' she said, darkly. 'I don't like them.'

'About the priest hole, Gran.'

'Oh, I think it was over there, somewhere. Never saw it.' She waved a hand at the wall opposite the big windows.

'Makes sense, probably the thickest wall.' Josh began a slow pace along the panelling. 'Anything ... odd ...'

I looked at the bookcase. The one in the corner wasn't glassed in, it was just an ordinary set of shelves built into the wall and filled with massive editions of *History of the French Revolution*, all covered in beige leather. 'You would have to be seriously bored to start reading one of these,' I said. And then I saw, three shelves up, just above waist height, a book without the gold lettering down the spine. A book whose cover looked a little more worn, a little less pristine than the interminable tomes below. I stared at it. 'Josh?'

He came over and moved the book I pointed at. Behind it, and standing slightly proud of the wooden back of the shelf, was a carved roundel, as though a Dalek had landed hard against the wall. 'What d'you reckon?'

'Try pressing it.'

Josh pressed, there was a click, and about three feet away a small section of panel moved a fraction. 'Hey ...'

'Wow.' I went closer. 'It really is a priest hole. Or something like that, a hidden room anyway.' I glanced up at Gran, but she'd fallen asleep, leaning into a window alcove. 'How far back does it go?'

'It's a bit ...' Josh swung the door wide and peered in, but wouldn't step forwards. When I looked I saw why, the room beyond was pitch dark, set within the thickness of the wall between the Library and the Hall. It smelled of dry wood and old newspapers and a little bit of spray polish. His eyes had gone wide, as though there was an equivalent small dark room opening up inside his head.

'I'll have a look.'

'Be ...' Josh started, jerking away from the panelled opening as I went closer. 'Careful,' he finished quietly.

I wasn't really sure what I was supposed to be careful of, nobody I'd ever heard of had died of the smell of old cupboards. Cautiously, just in case I was about to be the first, I leaned my head and shoulders in. The smell of old boxes and dust intensified and further back in the gloom I could just make out the lines of something leading upwards into the darkness. 'I'm going to have a look,' I said, but Josh grabbed my arm before I could step inside.

'Don't. Please,' he said. There were dark circles of contained panic under his eyes and the skin looked tight across his cheekbones. 'Might not be safe. Woodworm in the floor, that kinda thing.'

I looked into the musty depths again and then back into the depths of his eyes. His hand still gripped my wrist. 'Okay,' I said, slowly. 'You could be right.'

His relief was obvious in the way his head stopped looking as though someone had anchored it to the floor. 'Yeah.' Gradually his fingers unwound from their clasp.

We stood for a second or so longer. He couldn't even bring himself to look at the gap where the panelling stood open, as though a bite had been taken out of a dark toffee. 'What happened, Josh?' I asked, quietly. 'Why are you so afraid of the dark?'

A flick of his head that made his hair trail up across his face. 'What?' Hands went into his jeans pockets now and his shoulders had come up in a cross between stress and defence. He looked like a hunted thing.

'You're so ...'

He stepped back, away from me, turning his back. 'That's the Range Rover. Quick, close the cupboard, we don't want him to know what we found, do we?'

'He's not Hannibal Lecter, you know.' But I helped to shove the heavy panel back across and watched the roundel click into place, locking the secret away again. 'But let's keep quiet about this for now ...'

Okay, so he clearly didn't want to talk about his fear of the dark, well, that was fair enough. I could think of a few things that *I* might have trouble discussing with someone I hardly knew too.

Although ... as we crossed the Library back to where Gran was slowly waking up, I couldn't help wondering about this man whose feet barely made the polished wooden floor creak, despite his boots and height. Tall and quiet, with that shaggy-cut hair that looked as though he'd taken to it himself with a pair of scissors; those long legs outlined in jeans. Josh was a good-looking bloke, really, it suddenly occurred to me. But he wore his looks like a burden, kept his cheekbones hidden under a layer of stubble and those calm dark eyes averted, his well-formed body draped in a succession of workmanlike clothes. I remembered how he'd looked the night of Edmund's dinner party, in that borrowed suit, like a cover model almost afraid of the way he looked.

'Is it time to go home yet?' Gran got stiffly to her feet. 'I don't want to miss *Countryfile*.'

Then we all froze, hearing the sound of the Library door swinging open, standing in attitudes of guilty shock even though we hadn't been up to anything, not really.

'Oh, bugger,' breathed Josh.

'What on earth are you doing in here?' Edmund stood, perfectly framed by the mahogany doorway, like an eighteenth century painting. 'And how did you get in?'

Gran opened her mouth, and since, with Gran, I could never quite be sure what was going to come out, I rushed to talk over her. I didn't want Edmund to suspect that she knew about the secret way in, didn't want to give him any tiny little lever that he might be able to use against either her or me, and I had the horrible feeling that prosecuting an elderly, and somewhat confused, lady for breaking and entering wouldn't be entirely beyond him.

'The small side door. It wasn't locked.' It was the most logical place I could think of.

Edmund pursed his mouth. 'Hm. Wendy must have not shut it properly yesterday. I'd better have a word with her about it tomorrow, that sort of thing could lead to—'

I panicked, staring around me for inspiration. 'I've been thinking about the "ghost" thing,' I said, trying to distract him. I didn't want Wendy in trouble any more than I wanted him fretting about Gran, but I couldn't see anything around me that was more inspirational than shiny panelling and the slightly agitated Josh. There was one of the new Hall leaflets lying on the bench that Gran was sitting on, bent open to the picture of the 'haunted' porch. 'About, maybe, doing a Halloween entertainment around Monkpark. You know, build on the whole "ghost" thing, get some people in costume, bit of spooky noises and suchlike. It can be outside in the gardens, so it wouldn't break any rules. We came over to the house to ask you about it.'

'Spooky happenings in the shrubbery,' supplied Josh. 'Good thinking,' he said, very quietly.

I made a complicated face that I hoped summed up my views on our lack of ethicality.

Edmund ran both hands through his hair, looking half exasperated and half considering. 'Well,' he began.

'Who's he, then?' Gran said, staring at him. 'Is he the new boss?'

'Er, yes, Gran, this is Edmund Evershott, the new administrator for the house.'

She sniffed. 'Doesn't look like he knows his arse from his elbow.'

Again I waded in with words that hadn't been properly considered. 'You could get the staff to dress in costumes, maybe do a late opening, have pumpkins on the lawns and a spooky treasure hunt for children.' I breathed in, and carried on, crossing the Library and grabbing Gran's elbow as I talked.

'It would be great as a lead up to Christmas, something to help keep the numbers up in the quiet season and it would build on our ghostly thing so people would remember.' I'd managed to hustle Gran to the door, with Josh manning the other elbow. If she'd resisted I had the feeling that we would have picked her up by the arms and just carried her out, feet trailing.

'Well, that all sounds …' Edmund was sort of following us, obviously trying to keep me in earshot without looking as though he was trailing behind our cartoonish exit, Gran rigid in between our hurrying bodies as though we were manhandling a mannequin. 'Like an excellent starting point for some ideas,' he half shouted as we got into the hall. 'We'll speak about this tomorrow!' His voice carried behind us, echoing between the stone flags and the wooden panelling as though it funnelled down the centuries. We hit the outdoors and kept going, not even slowing down until we got out onto the driveway, where Gran finally got control again.

'That young man is *not* a gentleman.' She shook my hand off her arm and ostentatiously brushed herself down. 'Lady Hawton would have offered us tea. I cannot believe that a member of the aristocracy could be so … *abrupt*. I've got a good mind to tell Her Ladyship.'

Josh looked at me over Gran's head, and raised his eyebrows. I made the tiniest sideways motion and he gave a small smile. 'I'd better escort you ladies home,' he said. 'You can't trust the gentry round here.'

Oh, Gran … 'Yes, let's go home and I'll make you a pot of tea,' I said.

'I'm not an invalid, young lady,' Gran said, sharply. 'And I've a good mind to go back and give that man a piece of my mind, chasing us off the property like that. Who does he think he is?'

'God,' said Josh and, to my astonishment, Gran laughed. Properly laughed, not that harsh bark she used on me, but something that was almost a giggle.

'No, God and I have an understanding, I don't bother him and he doesn't bother me.' Then she hesitated, caught, it seemed, in a conflict of time zones, when she wasn't quite sure where she was; but, Gran being Gran, she wouldn't let any weakness show, which tended to make her rude and difficult Thankfully Josh jumped in.

'Don't know about you, but I could murder a cup of tea.'

Gran's thought processes were derailed. 'I suppose you'd better come back to the cottage, then. Madam doesn't believe in opening the cafe today.' She shot me a fierce look. 'I keep telling her, in the old days we used to work seven days a week, with half a day off a month, but apparently it's "different now".'

She set off surprisingly quickly, up the gravel towards home, only the scuffling drag of her footsteps giving away her age as she went.

Chapter Sixteen

Josh

Why did I do it? Why suggest tea? To stop the old lady from panicking, I suppose. That look on her face, all pulled up, like something was dragging at her from the inside, like half of her is in the past and she's trying to stop the rest of her getting jerked back too. But it was my idea, so I couldn't chicken out.

'You don't have to,' Amy sort of whispered in my ear as we got to the door. 'Pretend you've got to go off and do something. Gran always thinks men are fickle anyhow so she won't worry.'

'I'm not fickle,' I said. 'Anyway, what's fickle?'

'You know, unreliable.'

I stared at her. 'Yeah, maybe in the nineteenth century. You sure you both haven't fallen through a wormhole?' And then I smiled, 'cos falling back into the past isn't something funny, not something you joke about. Seen a fair few visitors to the Hall in that way, brought by people who think it might help, or sometimes just to get them out the house. Who am I to say? Sometimes you see the old ones sort of smiling, when there's something familiar, one old guy talked about the proper way to rake hay for half an hour, it was kinda nice, in a weird way.

'All right, so you're not fickle. But ... you know, inside ...?' We were still hesitating on the doorstep. Indoors I could hear the complaining noises.

'I'll get by. You'd better put the kettle on.' I gave Amy a little nudge and she smiled at me, suddenly, and it made her whole face change. The little line between her eyes opened out and she was looking as if she enjoyed being with me.

'You're a lovely guy, Josh,' she said. 'Thanks.'

Then she went inside, which was great because it gave me

the chance to cool down a bit before I followed her. Everything I was wearing had got a size too small and felt like it was made of steel wool.

'Well, come on in, you're letting the heat out.'

And I had to go in. I mean, I'm proof against most things, but little old ladies? I don't stand a chance. But that narrow hallway, that feeling that there wasn't enough air, that the dark had squeezed everything breathable out … The door slammed behind me and I jumped. Ran through to the room where I knew the window was open and stood underneath it, sucking down that trickle of fresh air like the house was a vacuum. Amy was in the kitchen, clanking crockery, but her Gran looked up from where she was doing something with some spoons.

'It's all right, I don't use air freshener,' she said. 'Won't have the stuff in the house, good real air should be enough.'

Took in another few lungfuls before I could answer. 'Just don't like being shut in.' Kept my eyes focussed on the view outside the window, the tree dropping its leaves carefully, one by one like autumn was rationed. There was a magpie in the branches; I met its eye and my heart calmed down.

There was a noise that sounded like 'hmph' from the old lady. Couldn't tell if it meant she was annoyed or sorry or what, but I kept my eyes fixed hard on that black and white bird until it swept up off the branch and away and I had to look back into the room.

Amy had brought a tray in with a teapot and cups and saucers. 'Yes, Gran,' she said, without anyone asking anything. 'Up to the spout.'

'Good.'

Amy looked at her Gran. It was a look that said she was half annoyed and half fond, the kind of look that I've seen mothers give their little kids when they do something sticky, a look that says 'you irritate the hell out of me but I love you anyway'. An everyday kind of look, something that sits on a face without the wearer knowing it's happening and I felt my arms itch and twitch as though they wanted to go around her and give her a hug.

'So, now we know where the priest hole is, what do we do?' Amy poured the tea, chittering the cups onto the saucers like her hand was shaking.

'Why not keep it quiet? I mean, you might need the leverage one day. Or somewhere to hide.' I stayed under the window, took a cup. Didn't know if I could drink it without suffocating, but for Amy I'd try. 'Good idea about Halloween though.'

'It was a bit spur of the moment, but it could work.' She handed her Gran a cup, carefully. 'It'll bring in some more business and it might be fun. I quite fancy dressing up in all that vampire gear, all corset and bustles and stuff.'

'You will do no such thing.' The old lady raised her eyebrows. 'You can keep your corsets and make-up for when I'm dead and gone, I'll not have you got up like a trollop or a slut.'

I thought about Amy in a corset. That was an image I'd carry with me like a photo in my wallet, but I couldn't unpack it here, it was too dark, too constricting. I had a gulp of tea. 'I think you'd look great.'

The old lady looked at me with her eyebrows raised and her eyes a bit narrow. Didn't want her to think that I thought of Amy as a trollop though, but couldn't see how anyone could think that, not really. 'Better head back,' I said. 'Finish the birds.' Wanted to be outside, wished we could have this conversation out of doors, so I could hear more about her plans for fancy dress, chat about what happened with the priest hole, all without worrying that this room was going to press the air out of my lungs.

'Josh …'

'Let the boy go.'

I wouldn't want to cross her Gran. Voice like someone used to being obeyed instantly, but not like Evershit's little weedy whiney command. Hers was proper 'do as you're told'.

'Show him out and then come and pour some more tea, although I don't know why you bothered, this stuff is like cat's widdle.'

Amy did the complicated face again, and I put my cup down, squared myself up for that hallway. One last breath from the open window to keep me going and then I followed her down and let my breath out when the front door opened. 'Gran doesn't mean ... She's all right really, most of the time,' Amy said, standing on the inside and fiddling with the handle.

'Yeah.'

'She's had a hard life and I think that makes her a bit controlling sometimes. She likes to have everything just so.'

I shrugged.

'And she's lovely really, when you get to know her, she can be a laugh sometimes, and she knows so much about the life at Monkpark in the old days, it's really interesting to listen to her talk about—'

'Don't want to buy her,' I said. There was a pause and then Amy laughed.

'Sorry. I'm so used to making excuses for Gran, it's second nature now. Seriously though, thanks for everything today, Josh. I think she enjoyed seeing the birds and getting out, and even all that business with Edmund will give her something to talk about at her club tomorrow.' She leaned forward. I'd gone out and down the step so we were almost level, and her lips hit me on the cheek before I knew what was coming. 'Thank you.'

It was one of those moments. Like when I took Skrillex in, when things could have gone either way, destruction or life. Sickness or health. Deep breath. 'Okay,' I said. Turned and walked away, back to my birds. 'Okay,' I said, all the way. 'It's okay.'

Chapter Seventeen

Amy

Edmund called a staff meeting the next day. Jules and I tossed for who went and who manned the cafe, and I either lost or won depending on which side you looked at it from. She gave me a saucy grin and retied her apron to make her waist look smaller. 'Wonder what he wants?' She hoiked up her skirt to show a bit of ankle. I was about to point out that, these days, a glimpse of ankle wasn't quite the turn-on it had been in the nineteen hundreds, but kept quiet. It was Julia, if anyone knew a turn on when they saw one, it was her.

'Probably about the Halloween thing.' I carefully iced another cupcake. There was another hour and a half before we opened and I'd got forty more of these to do yet.

'What Halloween thing?' Under the mob cap, Julia narrowed her eyes at me. 'Have you been cooking something up with Edmund?'

I sighed. 'Just go and find out, all right?'

She 'hmphed' at me, sounding so much like Gran that I almost laughed.

'Well, what with you and Edmund and you and Joshua, you're like something out of *Hollyoaks* these days, Ames. I can't keep up with you.' Julia adjusted her skirt again and I felt that chill down my spine that I so often got when she said things like this.

'You know very well that Josh is just a friend and Edmund … I'm really not sure what the hell he's after.' I squirted an unnecessarily large blob of icing onto another cupcake. It made it look a bit like a boob labouring under an enormous nipple. 'Now, you'd better hurry, the meeting starts in five minutes.'

Julia straightened up. 'Talk of the devil,' she said, nodding towards the far door, where Josh was just coming in. 'Not coming to the great meeting?' she asked him.

'Nah. Find out what's going on later.' Josh leaned against the end of one of the tables. 'Got any spare buns?'

Julia came out from behind the counter but stopped before she left the cafe and gave Josh an appraising look. 'Talking of buns ... you know, you'd be really good looking if you actually ate some proper meals and had a proper shave,' she said, consideringly. 'Get yourself a decent car and I might give you a go.'

Josh stared at his feet. 'Er, yeah, no.'

Julia did one of her smiles, tossed her head and checked her apron again. 'Right, I'm off to make an entrance. Don't do anything I wouldn't do, you two,' and she flicked out into the yard in a swirl of Edwardian enthralment.

I shook off the cold feeling that had gripped at my innards as soon as she'd started looking at Josh in that measured way. 'I'm not sure that leaves much,' I said. 'Don't worry, Josh, it's just how she is.' But I squeezed at the icing bag so hard that the last cake vanished under a glacier of buttercream.

He was still staring down at his scuffed toes, now ruffling a hand through his hair as though to make himself look less attractive. 'Why d'you do it?' he said, eyes suddenly flicking up to meet mine. 'Why d'you always make excuses for her?'

I shrugged and took off my all-enveloping white coat. 'She's my friend.'

'Yeah. But why? You always give in to her, you're always ... like ... keeping the peace. She calls you fat and you just apologise, she hits on me and you're all "she doesn't mean it". What's it take for you to stand up for yourself, Amy?'

He sounded more forceful than I was used to from Josh. And when he came over, with his head tilted on one side as though he wanted serious answers, my heart did an odd trippy thing, almost as though I was afraid of him. 'I don't ... I mean, why rock the boat?'

'Because she's a cow, that's why.' Josh leaned on the counter between us. 'Why *are* you friends with her? Just because you live in the same place – I live with a bunch of silverfish, but I'm not inviting them on nights out, am I?'

His new angry tone startled the truth out of me, past the double beat of my heart and the clogging in my throat that I usually kept all the fears locked away behind.

'Josh, look at me.' I fixed my eyes, very hard, on the tower of muffins under the glass cake cover. I could only see his hands and forearms resting along the counter, long fingers slightly curved inwards and mirrored in the glass surface so that it looked as though he had several sets.

'Yeah, what?' The hands vanished from my field of vision but I didn't look away from the cakes to see where they'd gone. Only my very rigid stare was stopping me from crying.

I took the cloth and began polishing the cake dome. 'My mum left me when I was ten and I've only seen her a handful of times since, she's got a husband and a fancy job and I think she's practically forgotten I exist. I have no idea who my dad was, and I'm not even convinced that Mum knows either, so it's me and Gran, and it has been for years. She's nearly eighty, Josh. It could happen any time now, anything, a fall, a stroke ...' My cheeks ached from their immobility. 'And then I've got nothing and no one.'

Josh was a voice to one side. 'That's not always so bad, y'know.'

'It's bad for *me*.' Now I looked at him. Under his jacket his shoulders were hunched and his hands were in his pockets. 'I always kind of hoped ... don't laugh ... that I'd find someone. That it wouldn't be quite so bad when Gran ... went, because I'd have someone.'

'I'm not laughing, Amy.'

'No, I know you aren't. But ...' I put the cloth down and moved out from behind the counter. It felt wrong keeping the barrier between us when I'd just let him into my life like

106

this. 'I'm looking at spending the rest of my life on my own. Working here, at Monkpark, because I can't afford to live anywhere else, cooking or whatever until they pension me off and I have to find a housing association house somewhere I can live with the twenty-five cats I don't have at the moment but, hey, I'm looking into it.' I felt the tears move up my throat. 'And Jules and I have grown up together, she's practically my sister in all but blood. She's hung around with me, stood up for me when the girls at school called me ... well, there's a whole series of names for overweight girls, I think there's a reference book somewhere. And if she's all I've got standing between me and a future of working until I die, alone, and if that means keeping the peace with her so she doesn't go storming off to ... Birmingham or somewhere, then that is what I will do, all right?'

We were standing side by side now, in an awkward way, as though we were queueing for something. 'Amy ...' Josh said, and then shook his head as though he had no idea what to follow up with.

'And I know I'm plain! I mean, look at me, I'm dumpy and podgy and I've got a face like a goblin, do you really think Julia is telling me something I don't already know? Men don't look twice at me, they only try to get me into bed because they think I'll be easy because I'm desperate – and you think I don't *know*?'

I had the horrible sensation that I was saying too much, saying things that he didn't want or need to hear, but it was too late now, I wanted to say them. 'And Jules will marry some Porsche-driving, Ralph Lauren-wearing bloke from the city and head off to a cosy little cottage and a few kids, and, if I'm lucky, I might get invited round for Sunday lunch once a month or so, to appreciate how great her life is, but at least it will be *something*. And I'm sorry if this all sounds self-pitying and pathetic, but that's how I feel right now.' I sniffed and gave a half-laugh that was full of snot. 'And that makes it sound as though all anyone needs is a bloke to make life all sweetness and light, and I know it's not like that, and I know I'm happy on my own and I've got my own business and everything but, do you know what?'

'What?' he asked, somewhat cautiously, and I didn't blame him, I sounded *fierce*.

'I'm *jealous*,' I said, and put my head into my hands so I could cry without him observing how it made my nose run and my eyes swell, and my lips go all pinched and sore, until it felt as though my face had become one huge area of raw skin.

He was six feet of hesitation. I could feel him wavering beside me, but I didn't really care what he did, whether he hugged me or walked out on me. The whole confession thing had been for my benefit right now, not for his. Sometimes everything got so dammed up, so clogged and bitter that I had to let it out, although I didn't usually have an audience while I did it, unless you counted some rather baffled sheep, or the odd, uninterested cow. Every so often I boiled over like an unwatched pot. Unwatched. Unconsoled.

'Amy,' he said, and then repeated my name until I looked up. 'Here.'

He'd bunched a handful of paper napkins into a tissue-fist and thrust them into my hand. I took them as a reflex action and hid my face against the soft, cake-scented wodge. Wiped up and down and tried to get all the little snotty bits off my cheeks, while Josh stood by.

'I'm sorry,' I said, when I'd got enough control to speak without my voice going all self-pityingly whingey on me. 'It's nothing. Just stupid stuff and you happened to be there.'

When I lowered the various soggy bits of napkin, I saw he was staring out of the window, looking towards the birds on their perches over near the walled garden. His face had a curious expression on it, almost neutrality, and I didn't know if it was because he was embarrassed or because he didn't know what to do or say. Or whether he just, genuinely, didn't care.

'Not nothing,' he said, still with his eyes focussed on the outdoors. 'Nothing doesn't make you cry.'

'Okay, not nothing exactly, but nothing anyone can do anything about. Ignore me, Josh, I'm probably just hormonal or something.'

'You hurt.' And now he did look at me. There was something in his eyes. I couldn't tell what it was, something like an inward stare. Almost as if it wasn't me he was seeing in front of him, draped in the unflattering Edwardian gown, but someone else. 'Something hurts as bad as that ... it needs to be out.'

He didn't touch me. Kept both hands in his pockets, and didn't so much as brush against me with his shoulder, but the way he was looking at me was so personal, so intimate somehow, it was as though his eyes had got inside me and were seeing my tawdry little horrors from my side.

I gave a half-stifled laugh. 'I'm not usually as hopeless as this,' I said, still wiping vigorously. 'I've got a lot to be thankful for, and I know it and, yes, Jules can sometimes be a bitch queen from hell but I'm not always exactly Miss Cuddles to live with myself so, you know. Life.'

He was still looking at me. 'So why don't you go somewhere else? You're qualified.'

I thought about the village, about the cottage with the oak tree outside all the windows like a sentinel. About the routines of life. 'Well, there's Gran, and I like running the teashop, and Monkpark is a nice place to live.' Then I heaved in a breath. 'Besides, so much of all this ...' I waved a hand at my face to indicate the tears and, I could see reflected in the cake stand, a scattering of bits of napkin stuck to my cheeks. '... is down to stuff that I would just take with me wherever. My mum and not being exactly model material, all I'd end up doing is what Gran would call "cutting off my nose to spite my face".'

'You're not.' Josh picked up one of the cupcakes from the counter and considered it. Brown eyes, lined with lashes so dark he looked as though he'd put on eyeliner, Julia was right, he was only a couple of good meals and a wash down from being model material himself.

'I'm not what?' I scraped, using the reflection from the counter and cake stand to clear the sulphurous yellow bobbles from my face.

'You've not got a face like a goblin. You look like Skrillex, all eyes and your face is kind. Dunno why women always want to look all thin and sharp, makes them look like they don't want a bloke to love, they want one to disembowel.'

Then he gave me one of those half-shrugs, peeled the paper off the cupcake, and wandered off out of the cafe, taking bites as he went.

'Josh, you are an odd bugger,' I said to myself, taking the opportunity to go into the kitchen and swoosh my face off with water, then gave my skin a firm rub down with the somewhat austere paper towels to remove all traces of my meltdown. I didn't want Julia to even *suspect* that I'd had a bit of a 'moment', she could be even more practically-minded than Josh had been if I got a bit self-indulgent. In fact, even Gran was more sympathetic than Jules, who would point out, very matter-of-factly, that I could go and work anywhere. Put Gran in 'a home' and get a live-in job in a hotel had been her suggestion last time I'd got a bit droopy about my life being so Monkpark-centred.

And the awful thing was, I knew she was right. Knew Josh was right. I could go. I could take Gran, rent a house in a city somewhere, work in almost any catering establishment – with my qualifications and my experience, I didn't have to be here.

I tidied the kitchen, sorted out the till and checked the tables and had filled up the ice machine before Julia came back. She was carrying a piece of paper, which she shoved under my nose. 'He's hiring costumes for us, we're late-opening for Halloween. It's going to be all torchlight and ghost stories in the gardener's hut, honestly, Ames, we're only two weeks away, he's going to have to go like the clappers to get this pulled together in time.' She tugged her apron straight. 'Oh, and he wants to see you in his office at twelve o clock.'

'Why?'

She did a kind of turning-away shrug. But I'd known Julia since we were babes in prams. We'd fought through nursery, sat together on school buses and whispered together during sleepovers, I could read her like a Janet and John. She knew exactly why Edmund wanted to see me and she wasn't happy about it.

'Sounds like fun though,' I tried to appease her. 'You could dress as one of those Brides of Dracula, you know, all Victorian Gothic, velvet and lace and fangs.'

Knowing Jules as well as I did, I knew that would cheer her up, picturing herself as a photo opportunity. It worked.

'Ooh, yes! All floating around, wafting out of the bushes and "whooooooo"!'

'It will look great in next year's brochure, if this one takes off.'

'What will you go as, Ames?' Julia began getting stuff out and laying it on the counter.

'Maybe I'll just pull a sheet over my head and go as an unmade bed.'

Julia laughed. 'Hey, though, Ames, don't you think I've got a point about our Bird Man out there?' She jerked her head at the walled garden. I should have known that I couldn't keep Julia's mind too far away from men for very long. 'Now he's wearing some decent gear and everything, he's actually proper good looking.'

'Josh? He's a really nice guy.'

'Yeah.' Julia tapped her teeth with a spoon. 'I wonder what he does at nights down in that old van? Maybe I should drop by one evening, take him a packet of chips and see what happens.'

'You haven't bothered with him in the last nine months,

why are you suddenly deciding that he's dating material?' I felt my grip tighten on the handle of the cake slice. She couldn't be serious, surely? Not *Josh*. No. 'He's not really that kind of bloke, I don't think. He's quite happy with his birds and the odd plate of leftovers, he doesn't really seem to want company.'

'Oh I don't want to *date* him. Just a shag would be fine. I want to know if he's as cute without his clothes on, that's all. Come on, Ames, if you're not going to make a move then I will, he's obviously lonely, that's why he keeps hanging round in here. Maybe I could offer him conversation and some consolation.'

I wanted to. I *so* wanted to face up to her and tell her, 'Don't you dare.' I wanted to tell her that Josh wouldn't welcome that kind of advance, that he'd send her away with a polite dismissal and a slammed door, I wanted to tell her that she couldn't do this, she couldn't wade in every time a man seemed to like me or want to talk to me. The words rose up in my throat, I could feel them heating my spine and prickling across my shoulders like an itchy scarf. But, as usual, I bit them back down. Distracted her. 'So, what's that paper?'

'Oh, it's just a timetable of events. Edmund listing out who's going where and all that. He asked me if we'd volunteer to do something as well as the cafe.'

'And you said …?'

'Well, I said yes, of course. Still got to worry about our jobs, haven't we? Besides, if I'm going to be got up in one of those nightie-things, I'm not being stuck in here. Your gran will be fine, won't she, once you've got her to bed?'

'Yes,' I said, slowly, various slightly wicked thoughts creeping through my mind. 'She should be all right …' *And she'll never know what I'm wearing.*

'And don't forget to go and see Edmund,' Jules said, getting spare cutlery out of the washer.

'I'll go now.' I tidied my hair up under my cap and pulled my white coat down from its peg again.

'He said twelve,' she reminded me.

'Well, tough.' My outburst to Josh, combined with having to suppress the desire to tell Julia to leave him alone, had given me a kind of inward seethe. It was a bit like being driven by steam, a low boiling that made me not care about being early. 'Edmund will just have to deal with it. Besides, we're quiet now, we might be busy by twelve.'

'Ames, it's October. We'll be lucky if we have to put the second boiler on.'

But I was powered by buried emotions, and I just waved a hand at her, and headed out up to the offices.

Chapter Eighteen

Josh

The gardening lads were all humpty about the Halloween thing, chatting about it while they swept leaves off the lawn. Big James was up for it, he's got kids so he was going to dress up anyway, and some of the younger ones were keen, but Sam just gave evil looks and muttered that he wasn't getting all dolled up like a gay boy, not for anyone. I put the birds out on their perches and put Fae up a couple of times, couldn't really see what the fuss was about.

'You getting all dressed up then?' James stopped by on his way to morning break. He gave the birds an approving nod as he went, he used to fly Harris hawks in his younger days, so he knows what he's looking at. 'Should be a bit of a laugh. Might get Ruth to bring the kids over for the evening.'

'Probably go as one of them bloodsucking ladies in a skirt.' Sam wrinkled his lip at me. According to Sam, any bloke who isn't giving one to every female under the age of sixty is probably gay, so I'm like double gay. I ignored him, but he was going to push it. 'That right, Josh? Going to borrow a frock off one of your girlie friends, are you?'

'Hey, man, tone it down,' James said. He's not bothered whether I'm gay or straight as long as I look after my birds right. 'He can wear whatever he wants.'

Sam wasn't getting any back up, but that didn't stop him giving me the eye. 'He's a queer. You want to watch yourself, James, he'll have you too if you're not careful. Probably only hanging round the cafe to get make-up tips. Wouldn't bother, mate, one of them's had everyone round here and the other one is too ugly for make-up to make a difference. Eh? Am I right?'

I muttered at him, hoped he'd give it up and go away.

'What's that? You haven't noticed?'

There was a bit of an audience gathering, the outdoor blokes all coming through on their break, smelling a bit of trouble in the air like sharks picking up a blood trail, slowing down as they went past us to the shed where they left their bait boxes and flasks. All drooping their heads, dragging their steps as they tried to listen in, see what the trouble was without going slow enough to get drawn in.

'Hey, lads, shall I tell him about young Julia and how hot she is for a man with a real job, or how little Amy's mum couldn't stand her ugly face any more and buggered off to London?'

Right. I'd given him the chance to back off. I'd tried ignoring him, but that was the second time he'd insulted Amy, so I carefully put Fae back on her perch, tethered her down, and then swung up and out, caught Sam right on the jaw and laid him down there on the grass in front of his mates. It wasn't a hard punch, just a warning, and I'd started to walk away when he scrabbled himself to his feet and came after me.

He tackled me down to the ground and sat on my chest, started flailing at my face, but I rolled, and doing the artichoke beds isn't any kind of preparation for the real kind of fighting. He'd done a bit, at school maybe, maybe later, and he'd got proper muscles from gardening but nobody had ever really taken him on. Could tell, the way he sort of swung around, losing too much energy making the effort. Wanting a crowd, wanting everyone to see him fight; it's no real way to take someone down.

I'd learned from dirty scrapping. Where a bloke might pull a knife on you if you took your eye off him, where you didn't try to pin someone down because his mate might be right behind you with a razor. You keep up, you keep moving and you bloody well fight with everything you've got because if it's not him then it's you, and life might not be much but it's all you've got and you want to be last man standing.

So Sam didn't know what hit him. Leastways, he knew it was me, I made sure of that.

Chapter Nineteen

Amy

I'd surprised Edmund by being early. He was in the middle of a telephone call, I could hear him talking as I made my way up the servants' staircase.

'Yes, I agree, Halloween would be a perfect time. But it will need to be late, we've got an event ... oh, yes, of course, midnight will be fine.' A pause, during which I moved more quietly and slowly, listening hard. 'Oh, yes, a record of very active paranormal activity, a ghost was seen in September on a staircase, so, very recently.' Another pause. 'So, how many people are we talking about? Ten? So, that would be two thousand for the usual, four for an overnight vigil.'

I stopped just short of the top of the staircase, with my mouth open. *Edmund is pimping out the Hall!*

The door at the bottom of the stairs opened with a bang and I turned to see Wendy shrugging herself out of her coat as she started up towards me.

'Oh, hi, Amy!'

From above came the sound of a ringing silence.

'Morning, Wendy,' I said, too late now to try to pretend I hadn't been here.

'Are you coming to see Edmund? You must have got an early start this morning! I'm a wee bit late, Sasha was so overexcited at nursery drop off, wanted to show me all the Halloween stuff they've been making and I couldn't get away.'

There was a clearing of the throat from Edmund's office. 'Amy? Can I see you in here, please?'

Wendy and I exchanged a quick look. She was an astute, if somewhat chaotic, girl who travelled in from York every morning to do Edmund's paperwork and field the telephone calls. When John had been in charge I'd sat in for her sometimes when her daughter had been ill and she hadn't been able to get childcare or when she'd been on holiday, and it had given me an insight into the workings of Monkpark, which stood me in good stead when it came to making decisions about the cafe. She pulled a downward mouth at me. 'He sounds a bit cross,' she said.

'Yeah.' I finished my ascending of the stairs with Wendy just behind me and we emerged onto the office landing to see Edmund standing outside his office. He'd taken his glasses off and the top two buttons of his shirt were unbuttoned, which gave him a kind of 'off duty orthopaedic chair' look.

'Into my office, Amy, please. Wendy, would you mind popping down to Housekeeping? There's a problem with one of the windows in the Old Kitchen and I couldn't get through on the phone earlier, so if you could go and ask them to get it looked at?'

'But it—' Wendy began.

'Thank you. Left hand window, nearest the range.'

Edmund swept into his office, clearly expecting me to follow, which, of course, I did, and then he closed the door very firmly behind us. It was obvious he knew that I'd overheard his phone call, and equally obvious that he wasn't happy about it. I rubbed my palms down the front of my floury white coat, dusting both hands with a coating of self-raising.

To my surprise, he didn't immediately raise the subject that I could feel pressing both of us to the walls with its weight. He perched himself on the corner of his desk and, because the room was quite small, this meant he was right in front of me, his knees almost brushing against me. 'You're early,' he said.

His tone was reassuringly soft. I'd been preparing myself for irritation, even anger, so I was momentarily confused. 'Err. Yes, I ... worried we might ... the cafe, you know.'

'Very commendable, Amy. I actually asked you over here to discuss your ideas for the Halloween night, but now I feel ...' He moved even closer. Not enough to make me feel oppressed, but within my personal space, and he'd got that aftershave on that got right up my sinuses. 'You overheard me talking to some people who want to perform a ghost hunt on our premises.' He held up a hand to forestall any interruption I might be about to make, even though I couldn't think of anything to say. 'Now, I know that you're about to tell me that it's against Heritage Trust rules, that any kind of gathering of that sort contravenes Monkpark Hall guidelines.'

To my surprise, he reached out and flicked at the shoulder of my coat, brushing a coating of flour from its surface. Also, incidentally, encountering a rogue blob of icing; I had no idea how that had got there, it was probably a result of my somewhat forcible cupcake decoration earlier. It made him hesitate.

'Well, it is,' I said, feeling that I had to take some part in this conversation, otherwise it was just going to be Edmund monologuing me into compliance.

'Yes. Yes, it is.' Edmund still had his hand on my shoulder and was obviously trying to work out how to deal with the icing blob. 'Amy, I'm about to tell you something that you absolutely must not repeat to anybody, do you understand? And I'm only saying this because I know I can trust you completely, you and I share a ...' He shook his fingers. '... an outlook, I feel. We both have the best interests of Monkpark Hall at heart.'

I turned my eyes to the carpet. It was the same practical brown cord as the carpeting in the rest of the house, although the public rooms had sisal flooring to add to the 'historic nature' – even the most uninterested visitor could work out that cord carpeting probably wasn't sixteenth century.

'Mmmm,' I said, working on sounding as neutral as I could.

'Amy, Monkpark is in trouble.' He dropped his hand away from me now. 'Real financial trouble. That's why I seized on your Halloween idea, even though it's going to mean a very quick turnaround time to get everything organised. That's why

I've been so keen to implement new attractions. We need ... and I cannot stress this enough to you, we *need* to cover a serious financial shortfall. When John left ...' He stopped and cleared his throat, then raised his head so that he was looking out of the high window, out towards the tree-studded horizon. 'Did you know John well? My predecessor?'

I thought of the small, grey man who'd always been bustling around 'doing' something.

'Not very well. We worked together for five years or so, he was the one who got the stables done up and turned into a cafe, so he interviewed me to run it.'

'Ah,' Edmund murmured, and he sounded a bit relieved. 'Well, John left the finances in a bit of a crisis. Now, I'm not saying "mismanagement", I'm sure he did all he could, but, you know, straitened financial times, they've made an impact on us all. And to keep Monkpark running, to keep everyone here employed ...' He squinted up at the sky. '... including young Joshua and his birds, as well as yourself and Julia, we need to make some money, very quickly. Otherwise we're looking at the Heritage Trust possibly being forced to sell.'

I thought of Josh. Of his face when he flew the birds, so composed and focussed. Of the fact that he lived in that rusty old shepherd's van. Of Gran and her obsession with the spoons. If Monkpark closed, if it turned into executive flats or some posh hotel, where would that leave them? And if I rang the Heritage Trust and told them what Edmund was doing, where was the guarantee that they wouldn't sell up immediately, cut their losses and turn the place into private housing? And where would that leave all of us? *All* of us, the gardeners and the girls who cleaned and kept the place up, the room guides ...

'Okay,' I said, carefully. 'So you're making people pay to come and look for the ghosts which we don't have.'

'*Might* have, Amy, might have.' Edmund seemed to have relaxed a bit now.

I put a few things together. 'Those cars, the ones that were looking for Monkpark back in the summer? Were those ghost hunters too?'

He shrugged. 'A small reconnaissance unit. I wanted to find out what the market was for that sort of thing.' He really was standing ridiculously close. I could see where he'd nicked himself shaving that morning, a small patch of stubble in the point of his jaw that he'd missed, growing like a conifer plantation in a reaped field. 'I knew you would understand, Amy. I knew that you were different from the others here, you have more ...' He waved a hand as though the end of that sentence was implicit.

The only thing I could think of that I had more of than anyone else was poundage, so I didn't finish it for him.

'I realised, from the moment we went out to dinner that night ...'

Yep, still poundage. But he'd got such an earnest expression, looked as though he meant every word. There was a crease of concentration at the corner of each eye that somehow accentuated the colour, and I didn't think he was aware of the way he was moving his hands, transferring that sticky icing from finger to finger as though it were particularly persistent Sellotape. I was looking at him out of the corner of my eye, keeping my head dipped as though that carpet held the secrets of the universe.

'You and I, Amy, together we can really make something of Monkpark. We can pull it up out of the doldrums and turn it into the go-to venue for days out in North Yorkshire.' Edmund was still talking. He was doing that repeating-my-name thing again that made me so uneasy.

Deep breath. 'Right. So, these ghost hunting bods are going to pay a fortune to sit around Monkpark in the dark, are they? With nothing happening? It's going to be quite a short-lived way of making money then, isn't it?'

Edmund cupped his hands around the back of his neck.

I hoped he'd finally lost the icing blob, otherwise he'd just moved it to his hair. 'Results aren't necessarily ...' he began, and then stopped. 'I mean, absence of evidence isn't evidence of absence, is it?'

I could suddenly feel the little ridges from the carpet through the soles of my pumps. It was something to concentrate on and I did so, fiercely, while the implications of what he was saying came in and gave my conscience a kicking. *Just keep quiet. Just a little pretence. More groups like this mean more money for the Hall, meaning more stability for all of us. Come on, Amy, you've done it this far, just keep your mouth shut for a bit longer and our futures will all be secure.*

'But it's all a lie!' I couldn't stop myself eventually. 'People are paying for a lie!'

Edmund sighed and leaned against the desk. 'Amy,' and his voice was very, very quiet. 'Maybe there are ghosts, maybe there aren't. For all we know, the Hall is riddled with spirits that nobody has ever seen yet. This isn't a lie, it's more of a ... slight bending of the laws of physics, that's all. Nothing illegal, after all, they aren't coming on a definite promise of finding some proof of otherworld existence. Look on it as ... an entertainment, yes.' And now he reached out and touched my hand, very lightly, running a finger down from my wrist until all the hairs on my arm pricked and twisted. 'You and me, Amy,' and he was whispering now. 'We can do it. For Monkpark, we can do it.'

I *should* have pulled away. But it was so nice to be touched as though I was important. It was something I hadn't felt for so long it felt almost as though I was hungry for it, my skin so starved of sensation that it didn't care what occasioned it, it just wanted it to go on. 'Well ...' I began, my voice as quiet as his. 'It ...'

And then he moved in. Leaned across the space between us, his lips pursed up as though he was expecting something bitter at the end of the lean. Was he ... he was trying to kiss me! Okay, yes, being touched was nice, Gran wasn't exactly Miss Cuddles and Jules normally only hugged me when she was extremely drunk so ... All right, I'd admit that having someone stroke my hand was pleasant. But kissing? Whoa, no, that was a whole heap of personal interaction that I wasn't sure I was ready for, particularly from a man who looked as if reading a book made him want to wash his hands.

'Um.' I sort of wiggled, so his lips missed my face and hit the side of my neck, making him lurch forward under his own impetus and grab at my arms to stop himself falling. There was a moment of half-embarrassed silence, then Edmund let go of my arms and straightened himself up. He'd cleared his throat, about to say something, when suddenly there was a tap at the door.

'Edmund.' It was Wendy. 'Sorry to bother you, but there's a bit of a fight going on down in the walled garden. We're only ten minutes from opening and it's all going to hell down there.'

Edmund gave me a slow smile, and moved towards the door. There was a sprinkle of flour dust all down his front. 'What sort of fight, Wendy?'

As soon as he opened the door, Wendy looked at his floury frontage, and then over his shoulder at me. 'Sam and Josh are down there beating seven kinds of cr— pooh out of each other,' she said, raising her eyebrows. 'I don't know why.'

He sighed. 'For heaven's sake. I'm trying to get this place back on its financial feet and this sort of thing happens.'

'*Josh* is fighting?' I asked. I didn't know why it amazed me so much, perhaps because, in contrast to the burly physicality of the other lads who worked around Monkpark, Josh seemed separate, almost ethereal in his isolation.

'Yeah. He and Artichoke Sam.' Wendy kept her eyebrows up but made her mouth go all tight, probably going for 'anticipation of trouble' but mostly getting 'badly carved pumpkin'.

'For heaven's sake,' Edmund said again, and started off

down the stairs, with me coming along behind, trying to rub away the feeling of his lips against my neck with the back of my hand.

By the time we got to the walled garden, the fight was over. Sam was standing in one corner, stifling a nosebleed with the aid of a large handkerchief and Josh was in the opposite corner, sitting on an upturned flowerpot. Both men were accompanied by a couple of the gardening lads, and it looked like a boxing ring between rounds. I half expected someone to ring a bell.

'Josh?' I went over to him. He'd got a bruise appearing on one cheek, but apart from that he looked untouched. In contrast, Sam, as well as the bleeding nose, had a big red mark on his forehead and what looked like the makings of two black eyes.

Josh just looked up at me in silence.

Edmund was getting the inside information from James, the de facto foreman of the gardening squad, and I was mildly reassured, James was practical and straightforward and wouldn't manipulate the facts as he saw them, unlike some of the others who would have grafted a UFO and full ninja attack force onto the situation given half a chance and an interested audience.

'What happened?' I asked, quietly.

Josh just shook his head and looked back down at the ground again.

'Does it hurt?'

Now I got a breathy kind of laugh, the kind of dismissive snort that should speak for itself, but he followed it up. 'Nah. Had worse.'

'Right, you two. I want you both to go home.' Edmund looked from Sam to Josh and back again. 'Take the rest of today off, come back to work tomorrow, and if there is any repeat of this then you can both leave the premises for good. Understand?'

'He fookin' started it!' Sam shouted from the corner by the old walnut tree. 'Bloody nutter.'

Edmund raised one eyebrow. 'Home. Both of you.'

'I need to see to the birds,' Josh said, quietly. 'First.'

'I'll help,' I said to Edmund. 'We can't just leave the birds sitting out all day.'

Edmund sighed. He took his glasses off and pinched the bridge of his nose, as if all this was just one thing too much. Although, given that he'd led me to believe that Monkpark was teetering on the edge of financial ruin, maybe it was. A falling-out between the staff was not exactly indicative of a smoothly running institution. 'All right. Amy, you and Josh get the birds sorted out, then Joshua, you may leave. Sam, I am assuming that the artichokes can mind their own business for the rest of today, so you go now.'

Sam opened his mouth, probably to reiterate Josh's insanity and his own lack of responsibility in any of this, but Edmund just repeated, 'NOW,' and he slunk off, hanky still clasped to his nose and a slight limp becoming evident as he shuffled out of the garden.

Shaking his head, Edmund left.

'Pull?' Josh said.

'No, he just tried to kiss ... oh.' When I looked down I saw his extended arm and grabbed his hand to drag him to his feet. 'Are you sure you're all right?'

Josh was very pale. It made the dawning bruise stand out on his cheek, a red blur gradually darkening to scarlet along his cheekbone. 'Yeah.' He shook his head quickly as though to force his thoughts to line up.

'Look, I'll take you back to the van. You shouldn't be on your own in case you pass out.' I kept hold of his hand, it had gone a bit clammy. 'James, will you tell Julia that I'll be back with her later on? She should be able to manage, unless a busload arrives and we usually only get coaches on a Thursday.'

James gave me a raised hand of assent and went off in the direction of the cafe. He'd probably chat up Jules and score a couple of buns while he was there, but since he and Jules already had 'history', he was married with kids, and drove a ten-year-old Citroen, he was safe enough.

I helped Josh put the birds back in their barn. Neither of us spoke. When Malkin, as the final bird, was back in, Josh picked up his leather jacket from the grass and yanked it on. 'I'll be okay,' he said. 'See you tomorrow.'

'You can't go back on the bike! What if you pass out or something?'

Josh stood next to me. His hair was dishevelled but his face was very composed. 'Amy. It's not the first time I've been in a fight. I'll be okay.'

'What was the fight about?'

His head came up and the wind tugged randomly at bits of his hair, so they feathered around his face. He looked like Bane. 'Stuff. Bloke stuff, you know.'

He was lying. I could tell it in every line of his body, the way he'd shuffled himself down further into his jacket and the way he wouldn't meet my eye, but I wasn't going to challenge him on it, it was something he'd have to tell me himself.

'Look, I'll ride back with you to the van, check you're all right and then I can come back to work over the fields.'

It wasn't just that I was afraid he'd pass out. I wanted to talk to him. Despite my promise to Edmund that I wouldn't tell anyone about Monkpark being in trouble, there was something so quiet and controlled about Josh that I knew I could tell him anything without the risk of it being spread through the neighbourhood. He was diametrically opposed to Julia, on the wheel of life. And I wanted to tell *someone*, wanted to talk over the implications and general legality of it all, and there really wasn't anyone else, apart from Gran, who'd listen impassively while I told her, then tell me to complain to Lady Hawton if I didn't like what was happening. While I supposed that standing in the local churchyard yelling at a tomb might be therapeutic, I didn't think there was much Lady Hawton could do from the Other Side.

Josh hesitated. His eyes flickered.

'It's okay, I don't care what state the van is in. Julia's got three brothers, I'm pretty well immune to dirty socks, topless posters and the Himalayas of unwashed dishes.' I slapped at his arm to get his attention. 'Come on.'

Still seeming reluctant, Josh went over to where the bike was propped on its stand round the side of the bird barn. 'It's not very …' he began. 'The van. It's not …'

'Like I said, three brothers. *And* they all shared a room, in which I swear the curtains were only opened for twenty minutes a day. I thought her eldest brother was a vampire for three years.' I threw my leg over the bike, a movement which had almost become second nature now. 'There's not a lot you can have over there that will surprise me, trust me.'

Chapter Twenty

Josh

For all she'd said the van wouldn't surprise her, she was still surprised. I could tell from the way she stopped in the doorway and just stared. 'Might as well come in.' Knew I sounded sour, but couldn't help it.

'But …' She followed me in. '… there's nothing in here!'

I shrugged. 'Got a kettle.'

'This place makes minimalism look overcrowded.' She looked at the walls. 'Where do you sleep?'

I didn't look up from lighting the gas, just pointed. My sleeping bag was rolled up and strapped closed, tied to a bit of old string hanging from the ceiling.

'What are you, a bat?'

'Got to hang it up or the rats get in it.'

'Josh …'

''S fine. I've got walls and a roof. Gas burner. What more is there?' I shook the kettle, good, there was water already in it, otherwise I was going to have to dip it in the stream and, while Amy might be taking the whole 'spartan' thing well, she might not go such a bundle on potential typhoid.

'Well, sanitation, hot and cold running water, furniture, that sort of thing.' She sat down on the crate. 'Is this actually meant to be a seat or am I sitting on your fridge or something?'

'No, you're good.' I wanted to say that I never had visitors, never needed anything more than the basics; that I liked the fact that the van was as cold as the outside and it was no effort to breathe in here. 'It's nice,' was all I could come up with. There was something weird about having another person here, even if that person was Amy. I never spoke in here, okay, sometimes I sang a bit when it was dark and I wanted to hear some noise, but … no. Never spoke. Nothing to say and no one to hear it anyway.

So I made tea. Only one mug, so I had mine in the baked bean tin. Tea bags were bitty, like the mice had been at them, but I found a couple that weren't too bad, and at least the cold meant the milk hadn't gone off. Amy sat all hunched up on the crate and watched me. She had a look about her that reminded me of Bane. Watching, just watching, but with a whole aura of waiting about her. What was she waiting for? Me, to say something? I couldn't think of a damn thing, but when I turned round to pour the boiling water into the mug I could feel her there behind me, like she'd changed the inside of the van somehow just by being in it.

'What do you do when it's even colder than this?' She took the tea from me and sort of hunched over it.

'Put a jumper on.'

'But what about when it's *really really* cold?'

'Put two jumpers on.' The bean tin was too hot to hold, so I put it down and used the last of the boiling water on an old tea towel to wipe over my face. I could feel the bruise coming on my cheek where Sam had landed his lucky punch, and my teeth ached a bit, but it would go. Another couple of days there'd be nothing to show. 'You should get back.'

'I never thought of you as the fighting kind.' The change of subject kind of swept underneath me, made me feel like I'd missed something further back.

'I'm not.'

Now she was looking me over. It was a look that made me itch somewhere deep inside, a hot kind of almost-embarrassment with an overlay of a kind of half-arousal. I didn't know what I was meant to feel right now.

'Be careful, Josh. Edmund was telling me that Monkpark is in financial trouble so he might be looking for an excuse to cut the wages budget.'

She started telling me some gubbins about Evershit using Halloween to run ghost-busting nights to raise money, and all I could think of was that smug tosser in his shiny shoes whispering his nasty little secrets to her, dragging her in on his schemes until she was as deep in as he was. I mean, I could see where she was coming from and all, wanting to keep a roof over her Gran's head and not rock any boats or anything but ... seriously? She should just front up to Julia, stop taking the assorted crap that she's getting heaped on her and ... I dunno. Run away?

'John never said. When he took me on, he never said there was a problem.'

I'd got it again now, that bitter little knot in my stomach. Worry for the birds, for me; sleeping rough is easy enough but when you've got creatures to care for – they don't understand why they aren't spending the hours of darkness in a nice, secure barn. And Skrill is pretty much a walking target for all the predators out there, he can't even get airborne when things get tough. Shit. I started drinking the tea, burning my fingers on the can.

'I know the Trust wouldn't approve, but Edmund is just trying to do what he can to keep it all running.' Amy was sort of swinging her knees side to side, jiggling about like she was wanting to make me see how urgent this all was. 'I know I used to think he was an idiot, but it sounds as though he's just trying to do what's right for us. What do you think?'

What do I think? What I think is that he is on some major rip-off, not sure how he's working it but there'll be more to it than he's told Amy. But if I say that ... it's going to make her think I think she's stupid, and I don't. I don't, really, I think she's lovely. But, let's face it, I'm a guy who lives in the domestic equivalent of this baked bean can, I've got nothing. And Shitface is showing her little bits of a world that she wants to be part of, yeah, I didn't miss her saying that he'd tried to kiss her. So that's how he's working it, draw her in, make her think he likes her, make her this kind of willing slave who'll cover his back. 'Yeah,' was all I could say. 'Sounds good.'

'Why don't you ask Edmund if he can find you somewhere

to live that's a bit more … well, *more*?' Amy looked around the van again. 'There must be somewhere, the old gardener's cottage where the lads have their breaks, it's got electricity and heating and stuff.'

I just looked at her. I thought she understood, but maybe she didn't. But then, who could, really? 'I like it here,' I said, carefully. Didn't want her to see what was underneath. 'If I didn't, I wouldn't stay.'

'Yes, but …'

I leaned in and took the mug from her hands. 'You should go.'

Hoped she wasn't going to argue. If she did, I'd fold, I knew it. That part of me that I've ignored, the part that really likes Amy and knows that I could trust her and tell her everything and make some kind of normality with her, it was hovering like Fae on a still day over a hedge line. One tiny bit of encouragement and then … what? I'd pour it all out about how crap my life had been, how I'd grown up being belted and locked up all for what, being a kid? How I'd run, how tough it had been? How would she look at me if I told her all that stuff?

'All right.' She stood up and I didn't know whether I was disappointed or not. 'Jules will probably be incandescent by now anyway, and it's not much fun being snapped at all day by someone dressed like a funereal Mary Poppins.' She gave me that grin again, the one that always bypasses the guards and goes straight for the heart. It makes me excited, despite myself, and I hate that my body betrays me like that. 'Just keep your head down today and, by tomorrow, it will all have blown over.'

I couldn't speak, on account of that grin freezing up my vocals as much as it heated up my groin, so I just opened the van door for her and watched her hop out. She gave me another grin and a wave, and I watched through the moss and the condensation of the little side window as she hitched up her long skirt and began picking her way through the damp grass back towards the Hall.

Chapter Twenty-One

Amy

It was a scramble, but we made it. Edmund ordered the costumes from somewhere in York, a theatrical costumier I think, and, between Wendy and I, we got the publicity into the local press and onto the radio, so people knew it was happening. Julia and I baked as though our lives depended on it, freezing small portions of every day's batch so there would be enough spare for the late opening.

And then it was Halloween. The house had been quiet all day, so we'd closed up early to give the house staff time to get the themed decorations up and the grounds all torchlit. I went home to sit with Gran.

'This place is a mess.'

'Yes, Gran.' I'd picked out my costume when they'd arrived yesterday in the back of a white van that looked as though it usually delivered vegetables. It was something I knew Gran would disapprove of, so I'd left it over at Julia's. I was going to pop over there to change before she drove us both in.

'And you'll be back before midnight? You know what I say about staying out after midnight?'

To hear Gran talk, no baby had ever been conceived during the hours of daylight, and any girl who was dressed up and out after the witching hour was 'no better than she should be'. I had a little frisson of wanting to be no better than I should. My costume was scarlet and black, fitted and slinky, a sort of witch-cum-vampire outfit, and I was, for this rare event, going to wear heels. I'd got my make-up in my handbag and a pair of stockings and suspenders in a carrier that I'd also left at Jules'. I was either going to pull, or appear in *Rocky Horror*. 'I'll be in, Gran. Now, what about *Pointless*?'

We did the TV, tea and bed routine as usual, I gave her her tablets and waited until she'd got into bed, then skipped over to Julia's. She answered the door got up like an evil angel.

'Wow. You look corrupting.'

Behind her, in the kitchen, her mum was washing up. Jason, her eldest brother was making sandwiches, he was a night guard at a factory in Malton, and the two other boys were watching TV in the living room with their girlfriends. It was warm, chaotic and homely, and crowded with the paraphernalia of daily life, unlike Gran's cottage, which was mostly crowded with china shepherdesses and half-used cans of Brasso. But I'd got so used to the contrast that I hardly noticed it now, except at times like Christmas, when their six foot real tree from the Monkpark estate made our eighteen inch artificial one look a bit pathetic. But real trees dropped needles, and Gran couldn't be doing with needles and all that hoovering, even though I did it these days, and so I'd got used to it all.

Julia's mum flipped a sudsy hand at me in greeting. She'd always treated me with a kind of warm distance, I could never have described her as a 'second mother' or even a replacement for the first one, but she was unfailingly accepting of my presence. Mind you, with three large sons, she probably welcomed me as an attempt to level up the oestrogen content in the cottage.

As I wriggled into my costume and we sat side by side at Julia's dressing table, I felt the echoes of all the other times we'd done this bouncing off the walls around us. 'D'you remember doing this for the night of the school prom?' I asked, carefully making up my eyes. 'You went with Danny Prior and he ended up being sick around the back of the geography block.'

I'd gone to the prom alone, of course. It hadn't been a problem, I'd not expected to have a date, and I'd had a perfectly nice time. Better, I think, than Jules had, when Danny, school heart-throb had turned out to have feet of clay inside vomitty shoes.

'Hmmm.' Julia reapplied her lipstick. It was some dramatic shade, halfway between purple and red and made her look like a Twenties starlet that's been at the Merlot.

'What, hmmm?' I laid on the eyeliner a bit thick. My eyes, so everyone said, were my best feature, and I wanted them to stand out tonight. Although, it had to be said, they had severe competition from my bosom, which was being pushed up and out by the costume's bodice, so that I appeared to be wearing a life jacket that had prematurely inflated.

'Just wondering about tonight. Why Edmund has decided to put us all through this at such short notice, and why you're wearing those eight inch stilettos when you know last time you couldn't even stand up in them for more than ten minutes without, and I quote "feeling like your feet were being eaten off at the ankles by hyaenas".'

I couldn't say anything. I knew that Edmund was really using the Halloween entertainment as a distraction; keeping the place open late meant he could have the ghost hunters on the premises without anyone wondering about the lights and general activity, he could just say that they were helping to clear up after the festivities, or some other ... lie.

'Oh, come on, Jules, I don't get to dress up much. Just thought it might be nice, especially since these buggers cost me sixty quid.' I wiggled an ankle. It hurt already. 'So.' I stood up and put my hands on my hips. 'How do I look? Suitably scary?'

'Well, you frighten me, I hope there's no children of a nervous disposition there tonight.' Julia adjusted her halo to an angle indicative, if not of fallen angel, then certainly one slightly unsteady on its feet, and pouted at herself in the mirror.

'Gee, thanks.' I'd half hoped for some expression of, if not amazement, then at least being impressed, but I should have known better. 'Well, *I* think I look great.' I turned sideways, trying to see myself but only having bits become visible in the gaps that Julia left as she checked her mascara.

I was wearing a black and red bodice, tightly laced down the front, trailing sleeves of chiffon and lace. The skirt was long and flatteringly flared, black with a red panel down the front. Red flashings of chiffon fluttered from the waist and around the hem.

'You look like a distress flare.' Jules reapplied her lipstick again. She'd got so many layers on that she'd be able to eat a toffee apple without worrying. 'Right. Are we ready?'

I could really have done with another half an hour alone in front of that mirror, smoothing the edges and checking that I really did look good, but Julia was already grabbing her coat and opening the bedroom door. 'We're manning the soup and coffee stall, is that right?'

'Yep.' I pouted my lips at myself one more time. 'And selling cakes.'

'Well, that'll be a change from the day job,' Julia said, darkly.

'Come on, it's going to be fun!'

Julia looked me up and down. 'No, it's really not,' she said.

She was kind of half right. It was fun, watching all the overexcited children chasing around the gardens hunting various spooky things, seeing the house all lit up and glowing against the dark sky like a huge version of the pumpkin lanterns that were dotted around the grounds. I stared at the golden windows, wondering whether this was what Monkpark had looked like in its heyday as a real house, lived in by people who'd moved through its rooms searching for a book, or lost glasses or eating dinner in the Small Dining Room.

Julia nudged me. 'Looking good,' she said, nodding her head across the yard.

'What is?'

'Bird boy there.'

I followed the direction of her nod, and saw Josh, dressed in a black frock coat, a floppy-fronted white shirt and knee breeches. His hair was tied back with a black ribbon, which made him look austere, and he had fake blood smeared on each side of his mouth. He was stalking around the outskirts of the herbaceous border, looking as though he had been forced to attend at knifepoint.

'You're right, he does look good.'

Julia gave me a look out of the corner of the eye. 'I have no idea why you haven't made a move on him yet, Ames,' she said, pouring herself a cup of hot chocolate. 'He's obviously up for it, and you've been playing the "friends" card for way too long now.'

Julia didn't know. She didn't know about that cold, ascetic furnitureless van, about Josh's hatred of being shut in and his seeming distrust of anything and everything. She never really bothered to have a conversation with him, just raised her eyebrows and ogled whenever he came into the cafe.

'I don't really think he is "up for it",' I said. 'He's nice and he's kind and we like to chat. That's all.'

Josh still came through the cafe and scrounged the odd bun, but since our time in the caravan he'd hardly spoken to me. I didn't know if it was because he didn't approve of my going along with Edmund's misuse of the house, or whether he felt a bit exposed because I'd seen the way he lived, but I couldn't ask. Even when I did see him, he had a bird on the glove and his eyes had a wary expression; neither were exactly conducive to heart-to-heart chats.

'Well, that's just a waste.' She drained the cup. 'Okay, here comes Mister Big, look busy.'

'I hope you're using Mister Big in its figurative sense,' I whispered as we tidied the front of the ranks of cakes, watching Edmund get closer and closer, and I tried to look as proactive as was possible in a corset. 'Or have you got a lot closer to him than you're letting on?'

Julia made a sort of duck face at me, all pursed lips. 'That would be telling,' she said.

But, if she and Edmund had shared more than a Raspberry

Crunch, he wasn't giving any sign of it. 'Good evening, ladies,' he said. 'How are things going?'

He was dressed in the full Dracula, long black cape, black wig and top hat. He looked a little bit like an undertaker off for an evening at the opera, I thought. But the white face make-up made those green eyes stand out, and they were fixed on me, not Julia, despite the fact that most of her charms were visible in that Angel getup.

A trio of small children ran past giggling, illuminated briefly by the circle of light from one of the torches stuck in the ground, then off into the darkness again, like sprites.

'It looks pretty successful,' I said. 'Quite a good turn-out, given that it was all a bit short notice.'

'Yes. But I'm very pleased, overall.' Edmund smiled to reveal a pair of fangs. 'This is the sort of thing Monkpark needs, events on special occasions, I'm thinking of something for Midsummer, and possibly some kind of Easter egg hunt or ...' he trailed off.

I waited for him to congratulate me on having the idea in the first place, but, yet again, he didn't. I supposed I'd have to chalk that one up to another round of 'claim the credit'. It was that 'homework done on the bus' all over again.

'Again, thank you for all your hard work.' He doffed the top hat and bowed, then moved off through the night, the gravel crunching evenly under his feet as he disappeared beyond the torchlight.

'No more cosy dinners then?' Julia looked at me. I'd have taken her slightly sarcastic tone far more seriously if she hadn't had a ring of chocolate around her vermillion lips. 'Maybe he's just after your brains.'

A car drove slowly through the pools of light, weaving its way between the children and assorted adults still playing treasure hunts, screaming, waving pumpkin lanterns and generally having a good time.

Julia stared after it as it vanished around the side of the house. 'Who the hell is that?'

'Dunno,' I lied. 'Maybe the people Edmund rented the lighting off, coming to pack up.'

'Oh, right.'

'Might not be, though. Could be burglars. Very cocky burglars.' I was slightly annoyed by Jules' lack of curiosity. She'd always been like that, at least, she *did* have curiosity, but it was quite tightly focussed on men, and had meant that school hadn't exactly been her shining hour. If she'd asked, if she'd *really* questioned, I might have told her that I knew who it was, that it was Edmund's planned visitors, the fee-paying ghost hunters. Might have confessed to everything, Monkpark's poverty, Edmund's desire to earn money by whatever means, even if it wasn't strictly in line with Trust policy. My lips itched with the urge to spill it all.

But Julia just poured another hot chocolate and made eyes at a man buying a flapjack slice. I came out from behind our little flap and stood for a moment in the pool of darkness beside the tent. The air smelled of crushed grass and burning fuel, little bits of paper swept around my ankles in the chilly breeze and I could feel my heels sinking into the soft turf of the centuries-old lawn.

'Looking great.'

The voice came from the deeper darkness behind me and made me jump. Josh swept into view, lit randomly by the flickering lights, it was like being approached by a jigsaw puzzle. He looked oddly 'right', probably because his outfit was similar to that in a lot of the portraits which adorned the walls of Monkpark, very eighteenth century, if the eighteenth century had invented polyester and had a robust approach to very tight trousers.

'So do you, you look amazing.'

He looked down at himself. 'I look like Louis the Fourteenth off to play golf,' he said and raised a knee-breeched leg. 'Could've let me have proper trousers, at least.' In the intermittent light his eyes looked very dark and deep and his cheekbones very high and aristocratic. He could have been the ghost of a previous owner. Which reminded me ...

'Looks like Edmund is going through with the whole "ghost-busting" thing,' I said, lowering my voice. 'A carload just arrived and went round the back.'

Josh raised a hand to the ribbon keeping his hair in check and loosened it so that the ponytail came apart. 'Stay out of it, Amy,' he said, quietly. 'If anyone finds out ...'

'I'm sure Edmund can make a case for doing it for the good of the Hall.' I tweaked at my bodice. It kept riding up and around to one side, giving me a sort of 'uni-tit' frontage. 'Have you seen Julia? She's got up like something God might see if He was running a really high temperature.'

Josh smiled. The effect, with his hair half-loose, the hidden darkness in his eyes and the crisp cut of his facial bones, was quite devastating. 'Seen her. Fended her off.'

'She doesn't mean ...' I began, but he held up a hand. Torchlight coruscated up and down his velvet sleeve.

'Please. Don't.'

'She just likes you, that's all.' I felt duty bound to finish.

'Nah.' He sounded dismissive.

'She does, honestly. She thinks you're cute.'

Most men, on hearing that a woman found them 'cute', would react positively, but not Josh. He sort of raised his shoulders a bit, hunching himself into his coat collar. It made him look like one of the birds.

'I'm not,' he said, and his voice was heavy. Conversation killer heavy.

I decided to change the subject again. 'So, what are you doing tonight? You can't fly the birds in the dark, can you?'

The shoulders relaxed. He stroked long fingers down a velvet sleeve. 'Had Skrill out a bit, earlier, but really making up the numbers,' he said. 'Think Evershi-shott wants us all up here. Plus, he's paying, so ...'

From the yard came a fast crunch of gravel and I heard

Edmund calling me. 'Amy? Amy, could you come into the house for a moment, please?'

Josh looked at me, a very calm, level sort of look. I thought he might say something about Edmund and his activities, but he didn't. He just sort of folded off into the night, fading into the shadows. Julia, on the other hand, wasn't nearly so accepting.

'Ames, can't you stay and help me pack up?' She wiggled her shoulders. She was wearing a pair of feathered wings that had gone into decided moult, and her halo was bent.

'I'll only be a minute, I'll find out what he wants and then I'll come back out and give a hand, all right?' I tugged at the bodice again. I'd rather head into the house looking all 'vampy' and not looking like an unmade four-poster bed with an unruly bolster.

'I suppose.'

'I'm doing this for the cafe.'

'Well, that's all right then. Just as long as you aren't enjoying it.'

I made a face at her and headed off, following the way Edmund had gone, into the house through the Library door.

Inside, despite the lights, the house was quiet. All the events were taking place in the grounds, there was nobody inside apart from a couple of lighting engineers and a family trailing a hyperactive ten-year-old who'd got in through an unlocked window. Edmund was standing on the Library stairs. Apart from some of the reading lamps, the lights were off in here, the walls glowed a magical shade, like a fresh conker, and he was all in shadow.

'How can I help?' I asked, perkily for someone whose boobs were trying to inch round the back of her neck.

'Can you please show the … the group where the sighting took place?' Edmund whirled his cape. 'I need to be seen to be out and about, I daren't disappear upstairs.'

'Where are they now?'

'Unpacking in the Old Kitchen. Thank you, Amy.'

I stayed standing in the Library, he stayed standing on the stairs. 'And you're sure it's all right? The Heritage Trust aren't going to find out or anything?'

Now he did come down the few steps that separated us. In this broken light he looked taller, the pale face make-up made his face look 'flat', like a puppet. 'I told you, everything will be fine.' He was almost definitely looking down my bodice, although it was a bit hard to tell, the nearest lamp was about five metres away so whenever he dipped his head his whole face was in shadow.

'It's all right, Edmund, I won't tell,' I said, keeping my voice low. 'I know you're doing this for everyone at Monkpark.'

'Good.' His voice was expressionless. Almost as though my acquiescence went without saying, so my voicing it was absolutely pointless. As though he wasn't even thinking about what he was saying.

There was a crash and a loud sound of swearing from the Old Kitchen, so I hastened through the dark house to find the group of ghost hunters and take them up to the office staircase, where I'd 'appeared' to the young lad back at the end of the summer. It would serve me right, I thought, as I dashed down the dark corridor, if I ended up seeing a real ghost, in some kind of supernatural karmic retribution, but I didn't, just five large blokes from Newcastle and a lot of electronics.

Chapter Twenty-Two

Josh

All the fuss died down around nine. Visitors went home, I checked the bird shed but it was locked up tight, hung round a bit in case Amy might be about, but she wasn't. She looked great in that dress, a bit naughty like a little girl in her mum's shoes, and it made her walk funny too, like an S bend. But I wanted to tell her. Just wanted her to know that I liked it. Knew I never would. Even if she'd been standing there in front of me, grinning that grin, I'd never say it.

So I walked back to the van, kicking myself. Just a small thing, such a tiny thing, all I had to do was tell her she looked good. Easy. Nothing to be scared of. Unless you're me, and then it's terrifying. So deep down frightening. On the surface I could do it, if I thought about it, but then I got those images of what it all meant, how it all went, and I just knew. I'm here in the van, she's out there, probably being chatted up by Evershit who doesn't give a toss about her and how she is and how she laughs, and how her smile makes me feel that I might just have a shout at a normal life one day.

But that's my deal. If I can't tell her, she's allowed to go with a bloke who does, it's her choice. I'm not coming over all gladiator and riding in to take her away, how can I? What use would it be?

I got back to the van and lit the burner to take the edge off the cold and all the candles I had to take the edge off the dark. Somewhere in the wood a tawny owl was calling. People get freaked by that noise, it's a lonely kind of sound out there in the moonlight, but I like it. Shows there's something out there, something else in the dark apart from me. Then I sat on the old crate, thinking of Amy, thinking of how it was I'd ended up here, scared of the dark, scared of inside, having to live in this place that's like outdoors only with a roof on it. The stupid shirt smelled of garlic I hadn't eaten, and the funny little trouser-things were digging in round my knees, but I couldn't even be fussed to get changed. Just sat in the little bit of light the candles were making and listened to the owl.

When there was a knock on the van door I bloody nearly fell through the floor. First thought was, 'Amy's come over', which was stupid, I'd never asked her and she'd never been near since that other week when she made me bring her. Since then I'd not found much to say to her, thought she might be weighing me up, wondering … Long story short, I opened the door.

'Hey, Josh.'

Julia. In a lopsided frock covered in feathers, and on the outside of a bottle of wine.

'Hi,' I said, cautiously like, in case there was an emergency and I just hadn't 'got it'. 'What's up?'

'Nothing. Just, I had to pack the coffee stall away on my own, Amy went off into the house to do something for Edmund and she never came back out. So I opened a bottle and whoops, there was another one.' She pulled her hand from behind her back, she'd got a bottle in it. 'And I thought, who might still be up and appreciate a nice drinkie? And then I thought, Josh, he won't have gone to bed yet …'

Now she wobbled the bottle in my direction and winked.

'You're drunk.'

'No, no, just had a couple. Oh, come *on*, Joshua, 'm just wanting a bit of company and someone to help me put this bottle away!'

She half fell up the step to the van. I put out an arm to stop her from going face-down on the metal edging, next thing I know she's grabbed my shoulder and used it to haul herself inside. Little bits of feather fluffed in on the night breeze.

'I don't really want a drink right now,' I said, but it was too late. I heard the screw top come off and then she was looking around for something to pour into. 'It's late,' I kept on trying.

'What I want to know is ...' She'd found the mug and poured wine into it. Must have been mine because she was drinking out of the bottle. The air in the van smelled of something heavy, scent put on to cover the smell of a hot body, and hairspray. 'Why you live out here on your own in this ...' She kind of went round in a circle, those pretend wings all askew on her skinny shoulders, like a broken bird. 'Come *on* Joshie, it's like something off an ITV drama!'

Didn't pick up the wine. There was too much drunk in here already. 'I like it. And you better go.'

Julia made a duck face and sat down on the floor. 'Nope.' She started pulling at her costume, yanking one of the straps until the top came down and she was sitting in her bra.

'It's okay, I don't want a "thing" with you, not looking for a boyfriend, just want to know if you're as much of a big boy downstairs as you look. Just a game, just a bit of fun.' Her hand came up, her arm was longer than I'd thought, and she got her fingers on the front of those stupid knickerbocker trouser things.

Her. Sitting there. All white skin and her legs sort of sideways, hand on my crotch and licking her lips at me and ... oh shit, oh shit ... The hot chocolate I drank in the yard came rushing back up and my face went sweaty, my hands couldn't grip, and I ran out through the door, down the steps and heaved the hot drink back up over a nettle patch. It didn't settle my stomach. Didn't stop the cold cramps that took me chest to groin.

Heard her stumble to her feet, heard the kind of hollow crashing that the van makes when someone walks around in it. Heard her call my name and I took off, out through the little beck up to my ankles and freezing, on, into the wood where the rooks called at me and the brambles that hadn't finished dying yet got hold of me. Pulled at me, dragged like they were trying to pull me back into that van, and then I was running. Tripping, staggering, but running most of the time, with eyes I couldn't see out of any more.

Chapter Twenty-Three

Amy

Next morning, the first thing I did before I opened the cafe was to check that the 'visitors' hadn't left any trace of their presence in the Hall. Apart from a Kit Kat wrapper on the stairs up to the office, and a nipped-off bit of cable in the corridor, there was nothing, and I breathed out a long sigh.

Edmund's office door was closed, so was the door to his flat. I toyed with the idea of knocking to ask how the evening had gone, but then reasoned that I really only wanted to do that to reassure myself that nobody from the Trust had found out, so I went back down to the cafe and turned the oven on to heat up.

'God, I feel like something a sick dog might produce.' Julia slumped in through the main door. 'What the hell possessed me?'

'Hey, morning,' I said, carefully. 'Look, I'm really sorry I didn't get back to help you pack up last night, I had to help Edmund ... err ...'

Julia cupped both hands to the sides of her head. 'Please. Do not finish that sentence, last night's supper is only just under my voice box as it is.'

'Oh, it was nothing sordid, we were just doing some forward planning in his office.'

What I'd *actually* been doing was showing the burly Newcastle crew around the house, with particular reference to the especially 'haunted' parts, trying not to alert anyone to our presence, and hurting myself at the rate of once every thirty seconds as I fell over furniture, equipment and, in a couple of cases, one of the blokes, in the dark. But I couldn't say that to Julia, Edmund had impressed on me the importance of keeping this little sideline quiet.

'Right. Forward planning, is that what they call it now? Well, I hope some element of family planning was brought into the equation, otherwise you are going to have one hell of a lot of explaining to do to your gran.' Jules groaned again and moved carefully over to the dresser. 'Don't think I'm going to be much use at cooking today, Ames. Might just have a day of gentle dusting, all right?'

I didn't feel, given my dipping out on helping with the clearing up last night, that I really had any grounds for argument. 'That's fine. We probably won't be busy, anyway.' I set the food mixer going, butter and sugar, then half a dozen of the free-range eggs from the village. 'Thought I'd make some cappuccino cupcakes again, they went well last time.'

'Just as long as I don't have to smell them cooking.'

Julia began tidying the front of the dresser, lining up the genuine Edwardian tea service that we displayed there, while I finished getting the cake batter done. As I scraped it into the cake cases in the baking tray, I looked around.

'Funny. I would have thought Josh would have been in by now. Maybe he's overslept, the birds haven't been put out yet.'

'How the hell could he oversleep? He must wrap himself in cardboard just to keep warm.' Julia blew dust off the teapot.

'You've been to the van?'

Julia shrugged. 'Popped round last night to see if he fancied a drink.'

I felt my grip tighten on the oven gloves, fingers curling inside the padding. 'And did he?' I asked, tightly. *I've got no claim on him, no claim at all. Nothing. But why, why does she have to do it?*

Jules shot me a look over her shoulder. 'No,' and then she was back to straightening the napkins. 'He didn't.' She gave her hair a toss as though dismissing me.

Twenty-eight years. Twenty-eight years I'd known this woman and for as long as I could speak I'd been biting back what I wanted to say about her behaviour. But this was *Josh*, and today my mouth seemed to have a mind of its own. 'Surely, even *you* can see that he doesn't want that kind of thing from anyone? Shit, Jules, with the way he looks he could have had half a dozen of the girls here, *but he didn't!* Did it ever cross your sex-crazed mind that maybe he's got problems?'

Julia kept her back to me. 'I just thought he might want some company.'

'*Really?*' Oh, that sarcastic note made me sound exactly like Gran. 'And what was stopping him from going looking for it if he wanted it?'

'You can't shout at me. It's not fair. I was only being friendly, it's not my fault he's weird.'

I tried to say something more. Opened my mouth and framed the words inside my head. But her list of self-justifying reasons stopped me. She really didn't know what she'd done, Julia judged everyone by herself, by her own standards, and Josh, being a man, in her world meant he'd be up for a quick fumble. She really hadn't noticed that he was different.

'Just leave him alone.' My voice, this time, was completely my own.

Julia flashed me a quick look. Assessing, maybe, how serious I was being. After all, none of this was like me, I was usually kept quiet by my fear that falling out with Julia might sever some essential link, my hatred of facing anyone down.

'I mean it, Jules. Whatever it is that Josh has got going on, he doesn't need your brand of "consolation", okay?' I was going to go on, now that the bitterness had started to come, but there was a bang and rattle at the far end of the cafe, and I looked up with a cautious smile, ready to greet Josh. But it was James instead, pulling off his heavy outdoor-work gloves.

'Have you seen Josh this morning?' he asked, moving his head to include both Julia and I in the question. 'He's not turned up for work.'

'Maybe the bike won't start and he's had to walk in,' I suggested.

'Maybe, only we've got a bit of a problem. Think that falcon of his is loose in the shed, I can hear her crying and it sounds like she's up in the roof. I'm just worried that she might do herself a damage.'

'Why don't you drive down to Windmill Hill and fetch him in?' Julia asked. She'd stopped pretending to arrange the crockery and was standing with her hands on her bustled hips, her mouth drawn up into a pensive smile.

'Yeah, problem is, I sent Andy in the Transit. Josh isn't there. Van door's wide open and there's no sign of the lad.'

Julia gave a little start and began adjusting her apron as though her life depended on it. 'I saw him last night, thought he might like to share a bottle of wine and he was … weird. I mean, he's pretty weird anyway, but this was like … double weird. We were just talking, and he took off on me, legged it out into the wood.' Julia looked at the floor, examining the toes of her button boots. 'Thought he maybe just wanted some fresh air, so I waited a bit, then came home.' She threw another quick look at me, as if afraid I was going to shout at her again.

'Jules,' I breathed. I doubt she even heard me.

Josh hadn't been easy with me being in the van, he'd behaved as if the two of us together in there might tip the whole thing over, or consume all the usable oxygen or something. I could almost envisage the panic her visit must have engendered.

'Let me see if I can get Bane down,' I said. 'She sort of knows me.'

'If you think you can,' James said, cautiously. 'Shed's locked, though.'

'Edmund has a key.' I set the baking sheet into the oven and turned the timer to forty minutes. 'Jules, you stay here and take these out when they're done.'

'Oh, I don't know, Ames.' She held a hand to her stomach. 'Might not be a good idea.'

'If Josh has run off, it might well be because of something you did,' I said, sharply. 'I think we owe him. I'm going to get the key and try to stop Bane from breaking a wing by panicking in that shed, right?'

Jules stuck out her bottom lip like an eight-year-old and it annoyed me.

'For heaven's sake, you aren't a little kid, Jules! That look stopped being cute and disarming when you were five!' I fastened the front of my white coat and brushed off the excess flour, then headed out across the yard up the stairs to Edmund's flat.

He was pretty much dressed for work, just without his tie on and socked feet.

'Amy?' He looked taken aback. 'I'm sorry, what are you ...?'

'I've come to borrow the bird barn key. Josh isn't here and Bane is loose.'

Edmund had pulled his front door half closed behind him, so I couldn't see into the flat. I wondered if he had a woman in there. 'It's quite important, otherwise I wouldn't have disturbed you.'

'Well ... all right.' Edmund retreated back into the narrow hallway, leaving the door open a slice, through which I could see some tasteful art on the wall nearest me and a small oak table. I wondered why he'd left me standing on the metaphorical step; if I was good enough to try to kiss, and good enough to confide in about Monkpark's finances, why wasn't I good enough to invite over the threshold? I'd just moved a step closer to where the cheap cord carpet of the landing met the much better quality grey wool of the flat entrance, when he was back, key with its white label in his hands. 'Please return it straight after use, would you?'

So businesslike. No sign that we shared a secret. 'Yes, of course I will.'

But he was already closing the flat door in my face. The splinter of me that lived inside my chest and had been pleased to see him, hoping for some sign of mutual reliability, sank into my heart. What the hell was going on with Edmund?

I shot back down the staircase, across the yard to the bird barn. Put an ear to the door and listened, holding my breath, to the sound of flurrying wings, the half-stifled 'mew' of the falcon inside.

'Bane?'

A momentary silence. She'd heard me, but would she recognise my voice and sit quietly, or react as though to a stranger and try to fly out when I opened the door? I couldn't leave her. Josh adored Bane, if anything happened to her, if she damaged herself badly enough, he'd be devastated. So I drew in another breath to hold and turned the key in the lock.

'It's only me, Bane.' I pushed the door open a sliver and sort of slid around it into the barn. Which wasn't dark. There was a Maglite on the floor, half-buried in wood shavings, with its beam a weak, sickly thing shining a cord of light that stretched about a metre from its origin. I picked it up and looked at the bulb which was a barely glowing filament, then played it around up into the roof space, where I could see Bane as a hunched shape on one of the beams. She shuffled away from the light and stretched out her wings as though she was going to come straight at me.

'Take the light off her.'

The voice made me jump so hard that I dropped the torch, squeaked, and tried to find the door in the darkness behind me with both hands.

'Josh?'

When I picked up the torch again I concentrated on shining the beam around the walls, where it found him. He was doubled-up in a corner, his left hand encased in his falconer's glove.

'What are you doing in here? Why is Bane loose?'

The eyes of the other birds were things I could feel rather than see. Josh was huddled over behind the perches, and it was as though they were guarding him. He didn't answer me. Didn't speak at all. Just sat.

'You were locked in. We thought ... Bane ...'

He wouldn't look up. His head was on his knees, laid with his cheek against those knickerbocker trousers and he looked as though he was only half-conscious. With one eye on the perched birds, in case this was going to come over all Hitchcock, I went over to him.

'Josh? What's going on?' Then I reached out a hand and touched his shoulder. He was only wearing that frilly shirt and I could feel his skin through the thin fabric; he was *freezing*. 'Look, come into the cafe. You need a warm drink and something else on or you are going to die.'

With his head still down, he shrugged. It was a kind of hopeless gesture like the final wave of a drowning swimmer. 'So?' The word was faint and careless.

'So, if you die, what do you think will happen to the birds?' I asked, softly. Above my head Bane was hopping from beam to beam and in front of me the other three were still staring. 'Okay, so Bane and Malkin and Fae might be all right if we can find someone who wants to take on a bird that's been trained by someone else, and you told me yourself how difficult that can be, but Skrillex? Who's going to want an owl that has to walk from place to place?' I looked over at the barn owl, who blinked at me. 'And tends to bump into furniture while he's doing that ...' I muttered. 'Please, Josh. You need help.'

Now he raised his head. He wasn't seeing me, his eyes were fixed somewhere on years ago. ''S too late,' he said. There was no tone at all in his voice, no sign that he cared about anything. 'Too late for anything for me.'

I bent down beside him, but carefully didn't touch him. There was something in that inward stare that told me any kind of physical contact might break him. 'Just come into the cafe and have some tea. You're disturbing the birds being here, look.' And I raised the torch beam a little bit to show Malkin shuffling about on his perch. Skrillex was still staring, but that was pretty much all he did, anyway. 'Bring Bane down.'

Josh picked up a feather that had settled in the shavings by his feet. He looked at it, then drew it slowly across his cheek, closing his eyes as though it was the caress of a lover. 'Why do you care?'

'Because you are just about the only person in my entire world who doesn't call me fat?'

A ghost of a smile pulled the side of his mouth. 'You're not fat. You're lovely.'

'And sentiments like that cannot be allowed to leave this world. Come on.' I held out the hand not grasping the torch like a madwoman. 'Up, and call Bane in.'

He hesitated. There was a long, slow moment on which an entire life seemed to turn, and then he reached out a cold, cold hand and grasped mine. It felt as though he'd already died, his flesh was putty-like against my fingers. As I pulled and he rose, creakily, he held up the glove and whistled. As though she'd never intended to do anything else, Bane dropped from the rafters and settled on the leather, trailing her jesses. Josh released my hand, reached into his little falconer's bag and pushed a titbit of meat through his fingers, watching her lean in and tug at it. She had an air of smugness that no creature without a proper face should be able to manage, settling her feathers at me almost as if she was saying 'there, that's the way you do it, none of this wiggling about in high heels, *this* is how you get a man,' although I did want to tell her that eating raw chicken in front of him probably wasn't how you went about getting him to stay around.

We put Bane back on her perch and fastened her up. Josh couldn't seem to meet my eye, his movements were deliberate and slow and his joints seemed to hurt. I had to lock the shed back up because he couldn't manage enough fine-motor coordination to get his key into the lock; his hands were shaky and his fingers seemed to be numb. Of course, if he'd spent the majority of the night in that shed wearing nothing but an Anne Rice special, it was hardly surprising, but there was something else about the way he behaved that told me it wasn't just the cold to blame. He seemed chilled from the inside. As though his thoughts were some snowy wasteland of hopelessness, which weren't going to be helped by a pot of tea and a cake.

Chapter Twenty-Four

Josh

Amy sort of bundled me through to the cafe, like she was afraid I'd sit down and die if she didn't keep me moving. Not far from the truth. Wanted to lie down, wanted it all to stop. Yeah, Amy was great, lovely, kind with the sort of smile that stops you, makes you look and then smile back like your mouth can't help itself, but … Nothing more. Nothing more, not ever, not however much I wanted it, like this little switch in me that didn't *quite* work, didn't *quite* shut it all down, but might as well have.

Suppose the cafe was warm but I couldn't tell. Julia was in there, chatting to some bloke, posh looking git who dressed a bit like Edmund, jacket with a jumper underneath and those twatty shoes all pointy and shiny. When she saw me she sort of slithered.

'Really don't feel well, Ames,' she said and she couldn't look at me. 'Think I'll be better taking the day off.' I saw her grin and pass a bit of paper to the shoe bloke. 'And after last night, you owe me.'

Still not looking at me, like she couldn't. Like her eyes sort of slid off me.

'Yes, I suppose I do.' Amy shuffled me into a seat near the counter. 'You go home, Jules and I'll see you tomorrow.' But her voice was kind of cold too.

Julia whispered something to the bloke and he gave her one of those smiles that blokes do when they think they're on a promise. It made me start to shiver, and I realised that I'd been so cold my body had stopped moving completely. Then she went and he went and I think Amy put the 'Closed' sign up but I didn't see her do it, she just went where I couldn't see her for a bit, then came back with a pot of tea and a really big mug.

'Sorry,' she said, when I looked at it. 'It's one of those novelty ones we sell in the shop, but I didn't think little bits of bone china were going to cut it today. You look as though you need to sit in a bucket of the stuff, actually.' She poured and I felt the steam against my face, like ghosts of all those thoughts I'd had. 'You're looking a bit better already. Hang on.' Then she went again and this time she came back with one of those white coats she wears to cook in. She sort of hung it around me. 'There. That'll help you warm up.'

I held onto that mug like it was nailing me to the room. Took a couple of sips of the tea, it was hot but I was cold, so I couldn't feel how hot it was until it hit my throat. I knew Amy was sitting there opposite me, drinking out of a small cup, but she didn't speak and I didn't look at her, I had my eyes on the table top, looking at all the threads in the cloth, all interwoven and smooth. Like life, I wanted to say, wanted to show Amy how all those separate threads pull together to make one thing, how life is made up of all these events that are nothing to do with each other but all go to make one existence, but I couldn't think of the words to do it with.

So we sat and drank tea. Slowly, slowly I stopped shivering and just felt ordinary cold, not like my bones had frozen any more, but there was still a deep pit of ice in my stomach. Knew I was going to have to say something, explain. Or at least have some reason why I'd gone mental and locked myself in with the birds. Wondered if Amy knew about Julia coming in last night, then remembered the way she'd let Julia go home, no messing, so, yeah, she knew. But she didn't ask anything and only got up again to bring a plate of buns over. Just sat, all quietly, being there but not pushing it. I knew I'd have to do it.

'D'you want to know?' Still couldn't look up, couldn't meet her eye.

'Only if you want to tell me, Josh.' Now she leaned in so I couldn't *not* look at her without getting under the table. 'But I think you ought to talk to someone. If not me, then maybe a doctor?'

'You reckon I'm a nutter?' I put my mug down, nearly empty now and she refilled it from the pot.

'No. And, by the way, there's no such thing as "a nutter", so you can knock that sort of talk off right now.' She was talking half-stern, letting me know that she meant it, but half-laughing, to stop it sounding like she was angry. 'Sometimes people don't cope well with things, or they have problems they were born with – none of it is anyone's fault.' Now she reached out a hand, I saw her fingers kind of creep across the table like she wanted to touch me, but didn't.

'You think?' Now I did look up. There was something in me, something that burned behind my eyes and she could see it, I *let* her see it, that anger and helplessness all tangled up with the wishing things had been different. 'Sometimes it is someone's fault you know, Amy.'

'Okay.' She sort of breathed it out. 'Okay. Then I think you really had better tell me, because I am imagining all kinds of nasty right now and I'd like to be imagining from a position of power.' Now she did touch my fingers, just the tips, and she didn't try to catch hold of me. Her eyes stayed looking at mine. 'You know what they say about a trouble shared?'

'Yeah, it's two people having nightmares instead of one.'
'Josh ...'

'You seriously want to know? Why I ran out on Julia? Why I live in that van?'

She nodded. 'And the other stuff, like why you hate being in small spaces, and the dark, and there was something weird with that Earl Grey and rose muffin too, wasn't there?'

Thought she'd forgotten that, or not noticed. Didn't realise I was that obvious. I pushed the mug away, didn't want to smash anything. The shivers were back but they were nothing to do with the cold now. 'I dunno.'

Amy sort of rocked back her chair. 'Your choice, Josh,' she said and she sounded all mixed up. Like a bit sad and a bit angry and a bit like she was getting impatient. 'You can tell me and maybe it will make things better, although I'll take any bets on it not making things worse, or you can keep it all to yourself and keep living on some kind of edge that, one day, you are going to tip over.' Now she came back to face me across the table. 'You could have died,' she said and now her voice was just quiet. 'If James hadn't heard Bane in the barn, you could have just sat there until you froze to death. Now, if what happened to you is worth doing that over, I really think you need to talk about it, don't you?'

That cold thing that lived in my chest began to uncurl. I could feel it coming to life. 'It's ... a bad thing,' I said.

'You'd better have a bun, then.' Amy gave me a grin and pushed the plate over. 'Everything is better with a bun.'

'It used to be just me and my mum.' I started talking. Words I'd only ever said to the birds before. 'Dad took off when I was born, but it wasn't so bad.' I let myself smile. One small, secret smile for how it had been then. 'No money, but we got by. Then she took up with a tosser. Some bloke who didn't like kids who used to—' I stopped. 'If I looked at him wrong he'd hit me. If I cried, he'd hit me some more. And then he'd lock me in the coat cupboard.'

Hard to talk now. Words felt like they'd gone solid and in the back of my head all I could see was Mum, crying, hand to her cheek from where he'd clouted her one, and that door. Big, solid door, with no light behind it.

'Called me "pretty-boy". Told me some bloke would take me off, keep me like a sex slave, made me scared to even look at anyone in case – in case they noticed me. Then, on my sixteenth birthday he brought a "friend" round to meet me, turned out he was trying to sell me to the highest bidder.'

Amy's face had gone very still. There were little ridges of goosepimples on her cheeks, but she didn't say anything.

'So I decked them both and took off. Wanted Mum to come with me, but she wouldn't, she had to stay with him, she said. No one else would ever love her, *she said.*' God, I hated the bitterness I could hear in my voice. '*I* loved her. *I* would have protected her. But she wouldn't come.' Breathe. Let the air take the misery. 'Lived on the streets and in squats for years. Did stuff, had stuff done to me, learned stuff, worked in lots of different places but then at a Bird of Prey centre, got my birds, bought a car, came here. Sold the car to get the bike, it was too ...' Felt my hands make a kind of 'roof' shape. 'Can't do small places. Can't do dark. Can't do ... can't be with anyone. She let me down. I loved her and she let me down, and I'm afraid to go through that again.'

That was it. Words were out now. I'd find out now if she thought it was all disgusting, *I* was disgusting. Couldn't think of any way to tell her how much I wished none of it had happened, how much I wished I could have a normal life, date a few girls, marry, have a few kids and a settled home with a girl like her. How sick it made me feel that I'd ever let that happen to Mum and me.

She was crying. Real, proper crying, not doing a pretty-cry to show she had sympathy but tears all streaming down and her nose running, like she'd cried before, so I did the same thing I'd done then and handed her a big bunch of napkins.

'You don't need to cry,' I said. 'It's over now.'

She made a snotty, broken sort of noise. 'I'm not crying for *now*,' she said. 'I'm crying for *then*. For that poor little boy that you were, for all the innocence and fun you had ripped away from you.' She did a big sort of 'waaah' noise. 'Did your mum ...?'

'Heard police got called one day. That's all I know. Maybe he killed her, maybe she saw some sense and got him out.' I shrugged. 'Makes no difference to me. I'm alive, got the birds, got a job.' And I'd lost that feeling inside me like a bucket of ice had been put in in place of my stomach. Got so used to living with it, it felt weird.

'And the muffin?'

Shrugged again. 'Yeah. Roses. Mum ... my mum used to drape herself in rose water when I was younger. Before she took up with the shit that ... when I was young. Still can't go in the rose garden. Smells are ... it hurts, y'know?'

Amy took a very deep breath. 'I'd really like to hug you about now,' she said.

'Yeah, better not.' But I stayed sitting where I was.

'Can I just ...?' Very, very slowly, like she was handling Malkin on one of his bad days, she stretched out her fingers so she could touch mine properly. The weight of her hand didn't feel bad, not like she was trapping me in, more like a warm bedcover. 'Is it why you don't like anyone to notice how good looking you are?'

I looked in her eyes, all red and sort of swollen. 'It's why everything, Amy,' I said. 'Everything. Can't shake it, can't run from it.'

'Had you thought about professional help?'

I felt the laugh. 'They going to make it go away? Nah. It happened. I just have to deal.'

'*Josh*,' she said my name again like it was breaking her heart, and sort of cupped her hand around mine.

'Better get the birds done,' I said. 'Probably think the world's ending, with me sitting in there all night.'

She pulled her hand back, but really slow, letting me know that she was ready for me to leave. 'Why did you have Bane on the glove?'

It was almost hard to remember last night. Everything was all caught up, running, cold, Julia trying to touch me. It all seemed like a huge episode from a soap opera cut into tiny flashes. 'I was going to let them all go loose. Locked the door to stop them getting out, but I wanted ... I wanted them to have freedom in there. Sounds stupid now but … yeah. Wanted them not to feel tied down. Let Bane up but then … it was so cold and I couldn't think.' I stood up. That cold thing was still there, like I'd swallowed a plastic dragon from the freezer, but it wasn't pulling me down so far any more. 'Yeah. Work to do.'

'Thank you for telling me.' Her voice was all quiet. 'It must have been hard.'

I didn't know what to say. It had been hard, but in some ways it had been the easiest thing in the world, telling Amy. Like that was what she was born to do, listen, and I was born to tell her things. Couldn't find the words to say that either, so I shrugged again and went off out to put the birds outside.

Chapter Twenty-Five

Amy

I sat for ages after Josh had gone back outside, just breathing carefully and occasionally wiping at my face. Through the side window of the cafe I could see him, walking a bit stiffly but otherwise giving no sign of the sheer horror that dogged along behind him, getting the birds' perches out of the shed and moving each of the birds, talking to them as he did so. He'd hooded Bane and put her perch in the shed doorway, she'd obviously taken a severe hump at being disturbed last night, but the other three just preened at their feathers in the weak sunlight.

I was trying not to let myself imagine what he'd gone through, although my brain kept throwing lurid images and passages from newspapers at me. So much made sense now, his hatred of dark, confined spaces – how scared he must have been, shut in in the dark, waiting to see if he was going to get belted again. The caravan at the bottom of a field, all light and air even if most of it was sub-zero, must be like paradise. The way he seemed deliberately to make himself look scruffy and unattractively crumpled ... My heart gave another twist and the recently-banished tears made a quick reappearance. He was talking now to James outside, with Skrillex on his glove, almost smiling, but keeping a wary distance and not for fear that Skrill, the world's laziest owl, would attack. It was the past keeping him detached, he wore it like an invisible dark coat.

'Amy?' Edmund's voice coming through from the kitchen end made me jump. 'You said you'd return the bird barn key and I was wondering what ... oh.'

I gave my face one last wipe and stuffed all the used napkins into my apron pocket. 'Sorry, Edmund. The key is here.'

'And you've put the closed sign up? What is it, are you ill?' He came a little closer, eyes fixed on the ruin that was my face.

'No. I just had some bad news,' I improvised. 'I'll be all right, I'll open back up in a minute. Just let me wash my face.'

'You look …' Edmund hesitated. 'Fine,' he finished, but with a tentative upward swoop to his words that made them more of a question. 'We had an excellent report back from last night, by the way.' He was standing behind the counter now, clicking his fingernails against the glass top.

'Well, there were lots of people there and they all seemed to be … oh. You mean the ghost hunting brigade?' I shook my head clear of the visions of what Josh had been through and pulled myself up into the present. Edmund needed me compos mentis, and these ghostly evenings might be all that stood between us and homeless joblessness; knowing now what I did about Josh's past made me even more certain that we had to keep Monkpark running smoothly.

'Oh, yes. They found some "interesting anomalies" apparently. Enough to encourage them to return, and hopefully to get us a few more similar bookings.' He looked at my face again. 'I hope your "bad news" wasn't regarding your grandmother?'

What? I didn't even want to contemplate what Edmund knew about Gran. 'No, this was … something else. I'm sorry, I'll open up the cafe again now.'

'No hurry, no hurry.' Edmund came closer now, around the counter. 'Are you sure you're all right, Amy?' He touched my arm and he did look concerned.

'I'll be fine.' I sniffed hard. 'Honestly.'

'You know …' Now he was even closer. Above the smell of buttercream that always seemed to pervade the cafe, I could smell that citrussy scent he used, as cold as the air outside. 'If you do have any concerns about your grandmother … it may be possible for the estate to fund some proper nursing home care for her. Should you find it hard to cope at home, of course.'

I stared at him. 'Put Gran in a home, you mean?'

'As a last resort, obviously.' Edmund rubbed a hand over his face and then swept it up through his hair. 'I know you want to continue to care for her yourself, very admirably, obviously, but these sorts of conditions can become ... Well, just think about it. She could have the very best of care, somewhere you could visit regularly.' Almost thoughtfully, he pushed fingers through the hair above his ears, as though neatening it. 'Always assuming that Monkpark continues to be solvent, of course, but I fully support using any spare funds to make the lives of the retired members of the estate a little more comfortable.'

Okay. So, not only did we have to keep raking in the money to keep our jobs and homes, there was also the possibility that Gran could be cared for at the estate's expense when the unthinkable happened and I could no longer look after her. I was dreading the coming of that day, when her 'club' was no longer enough. I wouldn't be able to give up my job to look after her, not and keep the house, and I couldn't afford proper help. God, I was really painted into a corner here, wasn't I?

'Thank you,' was all I could think of to say.

'In line with this ...' Edmund checked his reflection in the counter. It seemed such a natural action that I wasn't even sure he knew he was doing it. 'I was wondering if you could come along in a couple of weeks and assist with another group visiting the Hall. Just showing people around, telling them the stories of the ghosts ... you have a very trustworthy face, Amy, and a capable attitude that makes these sorts of events much easier on myself.'

I thought of the alternative, an evening in the cottage, alone, with Gran upstairs asleep. TV, a good book and a cup of tea. Was that all I had to look forward to? As though I was prematurely ageing, catching up with Gran?

'Of course,' I said, and was rewarded by Edmund giving me

a fleeting smile. At least, I thought it was me he was smiling at, it could have been his reflection.

'Thank you.' He raised his eyes from the counter. 'So? You said you were about to reopen the cafe.'

'Yes.'

'That's good.' He nodded to me, a short, businesslike dip of the head, and was gone, leaving me to swirl my hands in cold water, attempt to clean my face, and then turn the signs to 'Open', all with my head in a fog of thoughts.

Gran was just getting off the bus when I arrived home. I saw her give me a sidelong glance as she unlocked the front door. 'What's the matter with you today?'

'Nothing.' I sounded defensive and I knew it. And she knew I knew, so I just got a raised eyebrow, a cocked handbag and a sniff.

'Place is a mess.'

'Yes, Gran.'

'And someone's been in the spoons again, look.'

'Tea?' I thought I'd managed to remove all traces of the crying jag, but I knew my eyes were still a little bit red. Even though I'd been busy, single-handedly doling out cake and scones and fresh juice to a van load of retired ladies visiting Yorkshire for the first time, I'd still found myself the odd quiet moment to let a few more tears fall for the scared, abused young boy that Josh had been. Watching him through the window of the cafe, talking to his birds as he tidied the shed, and thinking how lonely his life must feel.

'What's upset you then?' Gran was there, in the kitchen doorway, watching me fill the pot. 'You're looking peaky, and it's not like you to be peaky. You've got a face that just doesn't do peaky.'

I sighed a little, hitchy sigh. 'Just ... Josh was telling me about his life. Before he came to Monkpark, I mean. And it wasn't very nice.' To the spout. No further.

Gran sniffed again. 'Making you count your blessings, is it? Knew there was something about that young man, he's got a look about him. What is it they call it these days? PMT?'

I set the pot on its trivet and carefully added the tea. 'What do you mean, Gran, "something about him"? You hardly know Josh, apart from showing us the priest hole you've not had anything to do with him.'

Gran sighed this time. It was a sigh that had history in it. 'I remember my dad, your great-granddad, coming back from the war,' she said, and her voice was distantly dreamy but not in the way it went when she was losing herself to the past, more remembering. 'In forty-five. And believe you me, the man that came back from the war wasn't the same man as went, if you get my meaning. I was only little, but I knew. Knew from the way my mum was with him, the way she had to be so careful what to say all the time. The arguments at night when I was in bed, when he'd storm off out to the pub ... Mum said he'd never touched a drop before he went away. He had the same look as young Josh in his eye, like he'd seen something he could never unsee, no matter how hard he tried or how much drink he took. You've put too much tea in the pot now, you'll be able to bend a spoon in that tea, you will.'

I looked down at my hands. It was a wonder there were any teabags left in the packet, I'd been concentrating so hard on her story. Listening, storing up the words. I'd never really heard Gran talk about her family before, not like this, not making them real people. Oh, she'd said, 'Mum used to do this' or 'Dad always did the garden on a Saturday', but nothing that had told me what they'd been like.

'I think you mean PTSD,' I said, faintly. 'Not PMT. That's something else.'

'Well, whatever.' She shuffled back through to rearrange the spoons again, and when I carried the teapot through she was digging in the back of the old cupboard in the living room, the one where she kept the good china and her grandmother's table linen.

'What are you looking for, Gran?'

I bent down beside her. She had an urgent look on her face, half-worried and half-curious, pulling old albums of photos out and giving them a cursory glance before dropping them and going back in after more. I saw pages flip, old pictures that had fascinated me when I was younger, glimpses back through time into a world when my mother had been a little girl, hair in pigtails and feet in Clarks sandals. A hole in time that I used to love, when we'd still been a family, but didn't want to look through any more.

'Here.' She finally pulled free a single picture in a white, scallop-edged frame. 'Here they are, look.' It was a wedding picture. Not herself and Granddad, that picture was up beside her bedroom mirror, a typical sixties wedding, she and Granddad had married late for these parts. This one looked pre-war; the bride had a sort of 'nurse's headdress' on and the ugliest shoes I'd ever seen, the groom was wearing what I always thought of as SS glasses and a double-breasted suit that looked a bit like a straitjacket. 'My mum and dad,' Gran said. 'Molly and Jim they were called. This is nineteen thirty-six.'

It felt a bit odd, looking at this picture, at two people I was so closely related to and yet so distant from.

'They look nice,' I said.

They were both smiling broadly at the camera, she with eyes modestly downcast towards her bouquet of lilies, him through his bottle-bottom glasses.

'Happy.'

Gran did the straight-mouthed smile that she tended to use on me when I wilfully misunderstood.

'They were happy,' she said. 'Then. After the war it was different, of course. Dad moved back here to work on the estate, but he couldn't deal with loud noises, they had to put him in the wine room at the back, helping in the storehouse.'

She shook her head slightly, her tight, grey pin curls rigid as ever. 'Knew your Josh had a look of that about him.'

'He's not "my" Josh. He's a friend, that's all.'

I handed back the picture.

'Dad was better, by the end.' Gran looked at the picture again. 'It took a lot of patience, and I think Mum was at the end of her line some days but ...' One side of that straight smile curved up a little. '... he was a good Dad.'

This was the most Gran had ever said about her growing up. Oh, she'd told me about the things she wasn't allowed to do, but mostly in the spirit of letting me know how lucky I was to be living in the twenty-first century and therefore able to ... I don't know, go to a party that ended after midnight without having to marry someone as a result, or something.

'What's he doing for Christmas?' Gran asked, suddenly. Her tone was so matter-of-fact that it felt as though she was asking whether he'd be performing the Highland Fling in some kind of Christmas entertainment. 'Maybe you could invite him for Christmas dinner.'

Monkpark Hall was closed on Christmas Day, thankfully. We'd used to have the gardens open so that local people could come and walk off their overindulgence, but the cost of having staff on duty had outweighed any advantages, so now we all got Christmas Day, Boxing Day and a couple of days after as paid days off. Plus all the artichokes we could eat.

'He doesn't like being indoors much,' I said, remembering Josh's desperation in our small, dark living room. 'And he might already have plans.'

Gran wrinkled her nose at the tea. 'If you say so,' she said, and the doubt and disbelief positively dripped from her tone. 'Suppose he could have been invited up the palace for a slap up turkey dinner with Their Majesties.'

It stung. 'Look, I'll ask him, all right?'

Gran sniffed. 'Tell him I'll leave the window open. We can even have the back door open, if it's not frosty.'

The thought of the three of us huddled around a table, wrapped in woollies and trying not to shiver whilst eating rapidly cooling gravy, made me smile. 'That's very understanding of you, Gran.'

'I remember my dad,' she said, enigmatically, and then carried her cup through to indulge herself in another one-sided shouting match with the man who did the questions on *Pointless*.

Chapter Twenty-Six

Josh

I kinda kept away from Amy for a bit. Saw her through the windows, in the cafe, doing stuff, but I didn't go in, just scrounged the odd sandwich from James, drank the cold water from the tap in the men's toilets. She knew about me now and I thought ... maybe she'd look at me and wonder, maybe imagine what it had been like for me growing up. Nothing she could imagine would be close to the truth. And I didn't want her to think about it. Felt as if I'd darkened her life a bit, bringing the filth in from the outside. Like this little bit of Yorkshire, with its big old house and big fields and trees nearly as old as the horizon, had been all clean and shiny till I came in and now it was rusty and rotten.

Stayed away from Sam too. He'd stopped making bloody stupid remarks since I landed one on him, kept his distance now. Hated myself for that, we'd been ... not friends but passing mates and there's not too many of those that I can afford to lose them but ... nah. He'd bad-mouthed Amy. Showed that he had no real respect for her. Looked at her like any other girl, when she's so, so much more than that.

So I hid out with the birds. There was plenty to do with flying them and I was working on getting Bane to come back reliably, not bugger off whenever I sent her up, so there was that. Sometimes I took the bike out off to the coast and sat and watched the waves. Nothing between me and Europe. Or I went up on the moors and looked up to where the sky just went on forever, and I tried to forget what it had been like being shut in that cupboard. How it had felt to realise that I was nothing but property to be sold on to the highest bidder. To be torn between wanting my mum to protect me and wanting to protect her. Tried to move myself on to another place, one where I wasn't touched by all that, one where I could think about a normal life.

Amy seemed to know. She'd grin at me in the mornings as she opened up the cafe, maybe shout a 'morning!' across the yard, but she didn't push for me to come inside. Like she knew that I felt embarrassed that now she knew about me and I had to deal with all that before I could talk to her again. But then, after a couple of weeks had gone past, there she was one day talking to Skrillex up on his perch near the barn when I came in from flying Fae. Skrill liked Amy, far as you can tell with an owl. I'd shown her how to whistle to get him to come to her, and she was practicing getting him to walk to her hand. He was still trying to savage her fingers, but he was doing it affectionately now.

'Hey.' It was all I could think to say, feeling hot and tight inside my own face.

'Hi, Josh.' She looked at me and there wasn't a sign of awkwardness on her face. Like she was just talking to James or Sam, bit of a grin on her mouth and her eyes all bright and a bit wicked. 'Came over to ask you something.'

I looked down at Fae, taking off her tracker and getting her tied back onto the perch, and then I looked down past her, in through the window of the cafe. 'Busy today?' Wanted to say much more, wanted to say *everything*, to tell her how much she was coming to mean to me, but how would that conversation even start, now she knew about me?

'Oh, well, just a bit.' She looked over at the cafe too, but not like me, not like trying not to meet my eye, more like she was checking up. Julia was serving a bloke, he looked a bit familiar, leaning against the counter in a Fair Isle sweater with a shirt collar underneath, like one of those blokes you see in catalogues. 'We had a coach party in earlier. And that's Simon, Julia's latest admirer. Well, I'm not sure he admires her exactly, but he certainly stares a lot. But he's got an F-type Jag, so he's

169

probably seen everything there is to see already.' Then she smiled again. 'Sorry, that sounded really bitchy, didn't it? He's actually quite nice.'

'For a bloke in a Swedish serial killer jumper.'

'I'm *reasonably* sure he isn't one of those, he's from York and he works in a bank. Came a few weeks ago to bring his mum out for the day, and he and Julia hit it off.'

Through the window I could see Julia doing that 'look how gorgeous I am when I laugh' laugh, leaning her head back and throwing her hair all over the place. Then, finally, I managed to look at Amy. 'Sorry about ... all that stuff before,' I said.

She frowned and it made her eyes go all gleamy. 'What stuff? You mean telling me about what happened to you? That wasn't "stuff", Josh, that was your past, and you never, *never* need to feel sorry about it.'

'I meant ... I didn't mean ...' Didn't really know what I meant. She got me all confused when she gave me that fierce kind of look. It wasn't like she was angry with me, more like she was angry with the world we were in that could let that sort of thing happen, but it was me that told her about it so she must be a bit angry at me too. Fae pecked at my hand and I had to concentrate on what I was doing.

'No, I know.'

Amy sort of jiggled about on the spot. She was wearing her cafe uniform so she looked a bit like one of those dolls they sell over in the shop, made from old-fashioned pegs painted up. She even had a little red dot on each cheek. 'I came over to ask you ... well, it was Gran's idea really and I said you might already be doing something but she carries on a bit, so I said ...?' Her voice went up at the end like there was a question in there somewhere.

'Doing something what?'

I could smell her skin now. She smelled of the cafe, of baking and warm butter and then under that was something out of a bottle that smelled like grass and lemons; all together it was the smell of Amy. I'd know her in the dark by that smell.

'Oh, sorry, yes. Gran ... and I ... wondered if you'd like to come to us for lunch on Christmas Day.'

I got this feeling then. It was like a bit of an old memory of something that hadn't happened yet, sitting round a table with Amy, eating and drinking and laughing. Could I do it? Little slice of normality like that, like tempting me with things that I was never going to have for myself? Like watching millionaires on their yachts farting round the Caribbean, sort of programmes that James watched and then told us about when we were hanging round the yard, lives we couldn't get our heads round they were so far away from anything we knew.

I'd left it too long to answer.

'So, I'll tell Gran that you're busy, shall I?' Her voice was all bright, but the kind of artificial bright that people use when they are trying not to show how much they're hurting, and I felt bad that she couldn't show me how she really felt. And I thought about Christmas. When it had just been Mum and me and she'd tried to make it special even though we didn't have a lot. And then the dick had wormed his way in and Christmas was days of trying not to upset him and always, *always* failing, and a belt and then the cupboard. And after that – Christmas was just another day. Then I had that feeling again, that half-memory, half-imagination, of watching Amy across a table, eating and laughing, and I thought, *Hey, don't I deserve just a little bit of that?*

'No. I mean, yeah, I'd really like that,' I said.

'You'd like me to tell Gran you're busy?' She made a sort of pouty face at me.

'I'd like to come.'

She hadn't expected that. Which made me wonder what she *had* expected and what it was that she really thought of me.

'Gran says we can leave the window open for you.'

'Can I not use the front door like everyone else?' God, I was *joking*. Nearly couldn't believe it myself, it felt kinda weird but then normal and a bit great, especially when she smiled that smile that got wider and wider.

'Keep that level of humour up and you'll be lucky to be eating in the garden.' Still smiling. And her face had got softer somehow. 'Okay, good, it'll be nice. It's usually just Gran and me and she falls asleep in her chair after lunch and I end up watching kids' films on telly all afternoon.'

There was a little screw in my chest when she said that. A moment thinking about how lonely it must be for her, and then I wondered why I'd never seen it before. Knew, obviously, why not, because I'm so wrapped up in myself and the birds that I don't often do sympathy, don't have time for it. But now it was there, going through my heart like an auger; a little picture in my head of Amy rattling around the house on her own while her Gran slept, trying to convince herself that she was having a good time, having a great Christmas, when really it was just another day, with a bigger dinner. And if she thought having me there could make things even a little bit better, I'd be there.

'Yeah,' I said. 'It'll be nice.'

Better than the alternative. Better than sitting in the van all day, on my own, except for an hour or so putting the birds up and feeding them and cleaning them out. Having a dinner of some pheasant that Bane had brought down, listening to the silence that was everyone else being with their families.

'Okay then.' Amy gave me another of those smiles. 'I'll tell Gran. We've ordered a turkey from the supermarket, so we only need to double up on the sprouts. By the way, if you've never been in a small room before with an elderly person who really likes brassicas ...' She wiggled her eyebrows at me. 'We may well be glad of the quiet when she goes to sleep.'

She gave me a last smile and headed off back to the cafe, leaving me wondering why I'd said yes. I mean, I knew *why*, it was because I liked Amy. Liked her Gran too, in a funny kind of way, she was a lady who knew she didn't have to watch what she said any more. Like she kind of hid a wickedness behind being a bit mazed, maybe laid on the madness a bit thicker than it was so she could get away with stuff. But mostly, yeah, I liked Amy. Enough that it made me angry I couldn't be with her. But friends was good, friends was all I could handle, and it was enough. Just enough.

Chapter Twenty-Seven

Amy

I yawned and looked at my watch. Two forty-five in the morning, now that wasn't natural. Any given day should only have one two forty-five in it and that should be mostly spent cashing up and wiping down the counter, not sitting in the dark in the Old Kitchen, resting my head against the wall and trying not to fall asleep.

'Anything?' The voice came through the radio that sat on the table.

'Nah. Nothing here.' The young man in the room with me, the one twiddling dials and fiddling with some bit of equipment that kept lighting the place up in shades of green that were so luminous they must have something radioactive going on, shook a meter. 'Not so much as a drop in temperature. Place is a bust, Nev.'

'Give it a bit longer,' Nev said, from his remote location. 'We're getting something promising from the Library.'

I wanted to go home. I wanted to be tucked up in my warmish bed, not sitting here babysitting what sounded like the York Psychic Research and Amateur Broadcasting Unit. But I'd promised Edmund not to leave them alone in the house, apparently a previous group, who we'd allowed to do their investigations unchaperoned, had broken some expensive china and used the huge fireplace in the Hall as an indoor toilet. So here I was, shivering inside so many clothes that I couldn't bend my arms, and failing to stay awake.

'How promising?'

I sighed and shuffled my bottom to try to get comfortable on the old settle. The young man ignored me. He'd been ignoring me ever since we'd been shut in here together.

'Dips in temperature, cold spots, stuff like that.' The static-broken voice sounded quite excited. 'Really random.'

Probably the draught coming from the priest hole, I thought, but I wasn't going to enlighten anyone on that subject. I was keeping the priest hole secret, just in case I ever needed something to bring out and truly stun Edmund with. Or maybe just to hide in and rock gently.

'Can't we come back another time?' The young man stared around at the walls, and me, and sighed deeply. 'It's bloody cold, there's nothing happening here, and the company's not up to much.'

I carried on pretending to be asleep. Okay, I wasn't exactly being scintillating, but then he hadn't bothered to address more than a couple of words to me all night, what was I supposed to be doing, a ventriloquism act?

There was a snort through the radio. 'At four grand a time? You're kidding, right?' Then, softening. 'Look, we'll give it another hour, okay? Nothing happens, we'll pack up.'

There was grudging agreement from our end, but when the radio call was over I could feel the resentment, even from this dark corner with my eyes closed. I carried on the pretend sleeping, and I may even have managed half an hour or so for real, because when I next looked up, they were packing equipment and rolling wires.

As instructed by the presumably tucked up in a warm flat and sleeping peacefully Edmund, I checked that the ghost group had tidied up behind themselves – not even so much as a stray sandwich wrapper was allowed to be left behind – and I saw them off the premises.

'Nev' promised enthusiastically that they would be back, while I smiled politely and wondered about the four grand they'd paid to be here. It seemed an awful lot to pay to sit around in the dark and be totally bored – I'd only charge half that for someone to sit in my living room and the results would be the same.

I yawned and stretched out my back. There was something very homely about Monkpark Hall, alone here in the dark. Obviously the place was familiar, from the smell of the woven grass matting, which made the corridors smell like a haystack, the slight hum of the security lighting that illuminated small patches of each room and the odd slight draught that brushed my cheek. I was as accustomed to being in here as I was to being in the cottage really, with the hours I'd spent hanging round waiting for Mum, and then Gran, to finish work.

I wandered down from the Old Kitchen, running my hand along the panelling, feeling the change of grain where some of the old panels had had to be replaced fifteen years ago. The worn patch in the matting was still there in the doorway, where underneath the stone flagstones dipped, scoured away by generations of feet passing through. My feet felt it but my mind hardly registered, although it did tell me where I was. I could have walked this house blindfolded and still known, from the smell of the air, from the feel of the walls and the way the floor lay, where I was.

History sat heavily in the air, with the dust, as I wandered through into the Library. How many people had polished in here over the years? How many maids had rushed through, using the Library as a short cut to the yard, probably against all the rules? I stood in the middle of the dark room and breathed the smell of old books, floor polish and the faint odour of potpourri from the little bowls scattered around, which made the place smell vaguely of cat wee. The merest suggestion of a draught ruffled the hair on the back of my neck and made the skin down my arms prickle, as though a ghost stood just behind me; not enough to make me turn around, but enough to keep me moving forward, tracking the origin.

I'd been right. The draught seemed to originate from one of the almost invisible cracks that marked the position of the priest hole. I held my hands out in front of me and waved them about, trying to locate the exact position; I must have looked like some sort of Harry Potter of the Hardback, wafting my arms up and down, as though I was trying to conjure the books into life, but eventually finding the point at which the cooler air was making its way in. A tiny hole, which looked as though a mouse had chewed through some of the panelling, was letting the slightest trickle of air through. Almost without thinking I reached up and pulled the moulding. There was a definite 'click', very loud in this silent dark, and the door swung inwards with a reinvigorated waft of cold air and the sudden smell of dusty cupboards.

I stood and stared into the recess for a moment and it felt almost as though the house was holding its breath – no sound, no movement, and even that draught had stopped as soon as the door opened. The Library had been quiet before, of course it had, but the quiet seemed almost to have become a thick silence, as though even the slightest noise was being sucked inwards, into that small square of blackness. It was unnerving and I started speaking aloud to myself just to reassure my own ears that they hadn't gone deaf.

'Well, at least we know that it wasn't ghosts making the Library chilly.'

My words sounded stifled by the dark, almost as though there was something standing there, just in front of me, wrapping them in night. I stretched an arm forward into the priest hole, feeling the change in temperature.

'Bloody ghost hunters. You'd think at least one of them would know the difference between a banshee and a lack of draught proofing.'

I stepped forward, squeezing myself through the doorway and stopping just inside. From this side I could see that there was a proper sort of frame to the door. What from the other side seemed to be just flush panelling, was actually a moulded entrance.

'That's odd,' I said, slightly self-consciously, but the 'talking out loud' thing was stopping me from feeling as though there were a dozen dusty skeletons doing grabby-hands just out of reach. A voice, even if it was my own, made me feel less lonely. 'Why would a priest hole have a proper door?'

Another step inside and I could see the very faintest outline of a staircase reaching up through the dark, between the walls, and I suddenly realised what I was looking at. 'It's not a priest hole! It's the old servants' staircase,' I said.

The layout of the house was there, inside my head like a CSI special effect, the house I'd played in, run through, and sulked in my whole life. I knew this place almost as well as I knew the inside of the cottage, and now the whole thing made sense. The Library had been part of the conversion work done in the early nineteen hundreds, made from part of the old Hall. This had been the way that the servants had come up and down to their jobs from their rooms in the attic without inconveniencing the Posh People by, oh, I don't know, soiling their eyeballs by being seen or something. It wasn't a priest hole and never had been, it was just the door that had become disused when the bustle and activity of the Hall had given way to the bookish quiet of the Library.

I strained my eyes upwards. Yep, right up at the very top of the stairs was a tiny splinter of light, which was providing the illumination by which I could see. So vague as to almost not be there, but making the outline of the top landing visible. Probably the security lighting up in the office suite, shining through whatever gaps there were at the other end of the staircase. I grinned to myself and moved a little further forward into the dark. The stairs must come out somewhere, either in Wendy's office or in Edmund's flat.

At least Gran would be reassured the Hawtons had never had to hide a priest.

My nose twitched with the dust and I stifled a sneeze on the back of my hand. That was real life for you, less romantic hiding places, more allergy and draught. I backed out of the doorway and closed up the concealed door, making sure there wasn't so much as a crack visible. It felt a little bit like my heart.

Chapter Twenty-Eight

Josh

'Hey, Josh,' Amy sidled into the barn, just missing me twatting her with a forkful of shavings. 'Are you busy tonight?'

'Hang on, I'll just check my diary.' I didn't even slow down, shoving another load of old bedding on top of the wheelbarrow. 'Bloody daft question, to be honest.'

'Well, I don't know, do I?' She was leaning against the wall now. She'd got a bit of a look about her like Malkin gets when he's building up for legging it when I send him up on a display. Can't describe it, it's more of a feeling I get. Like he's become a container full of mischief and sometimes it just bubbles over and he takes off for the hills. Yeah, she had a bit of that about her, maybe it was the way she'd got her arms propped behind her. Normally she does this kind of 'arms folded' thing, like she's trying to hold the world a little bit away from her, but today she was using her hands to keep her back from touching the wall. Made her look more ... I dunno. Open, somehow. 'You could be going out.'

'Amy.' Felt good using her name. 'Where the hell would I go?' Thought that was a pretty good line so I picked up the barrow and wheeled it outside to the dump. The wind whipped little bits of shaving up and some of the drier ones flicked into my face; I spat some out of my mouth but a few went in my eyes and I had to stop and blink for a while. When I'd got all bar a bit that was making my eye sting, I turned around and she was standing in the doorway now, watching me.

'Are you trying to wink at me?'

'Got bird crap in my eye.'

'Story of my life.' She sighed and then grinned at me. It made me grin back and lifted the blast of the icy wind up, so it felt like it wasn't touching me any more. 'I've got something I want to show you, but we can only do it when the house is closed.'

'Can you not just describe it to me?' I lifted up the empty barrow and shoved it back towards her. It rumbled over the frozen ground, and I could see the noise disturbing Fae and Bane over her shoulder. Fae baited up off her perch for a moment, lost her footing and sort of flapped down and, as if she hadn't stopped to think about what might happen, Amy went to lift her back up.

'Don't touch ...' But I was too late. She'd done it, made the mistake that I've made so many times myself, that I've seen loads of others make. That instinct to help, something that seems so easy to put right. She had put out a hand to touch Fae and the bird had done what they always do, ripped into Amy's fingers with beak and claws, then righted herself onto the perch and sat back, unconcerned, flipping her feathers back into place as though nothing more had happened than a breeze passing through.

'Well, that was a stupid thing to do, wasn't it?' But Amy wasn't talking to Fae, she was talking to herself. 'Sorry, Josh, I wasn't thinking.' She'd screwed her hand up tight and was holding it against her side.

'Let me see.'

'No, it's fine, just a scratch. It was my own fault, I do know better, honestly, than to touch the birds, she'd just ...' She made a face. 'Stupid.'

It hurts when they get you. Not so much for the first couple of seconds, those claws are so sharp it's like a knife; first you think you've got away with it, then it starts to sting and then it hurts like a bitch with a razor blade.

'Show me. Where did she get you?'

Slowly, and almost like she didn't want to admit it hurt, she held out her hand and opened the palm. Fae had clawed down the thin skin across her wrist and it looked like her beak had gone into the heel of Amy's hand, taken a chunk of flesh out at the base of her thumb. There was quite a lot of blood, so I couldn't see exactly how bad it was.

'Okay, we need to clean this.'

'I'll go back to the cafe. We've got a First Aid kit in there.' She sounded so practical. 'It's no worse than I've done to myself when I've been chopping veg.'

I shook my head. 'Uh huh. I want to get it properly clean. Don't want you coming after me with a case of blood poisoning and trying to sue my arse from here to Barnsley.'

I almost didn't realise. Almost. Was more concentrating on the blood splashing down and the way her skin had peeled back where Fae's talons had dug in. But in that deep part of me where I kept everything normal, where I knew I fancied Amy, the part that made me stiffen in my jeans when I thought about the way she smelled or her hair, down deep in there I knew what I was doing, and reached out. Took her ruined hand.

That feeling. I'd forgotten. Warm skin, although her fingers were chilling now, the way her bones felt under her skin, like a bird that's lost its feathers. Half fragile and half so strong that I almost dropped it. And she'd not been expecting it, was still keeping the load of her wrist in her arm. But then, slowly, she let it drop, let me take the weight of her hand as I turned it, slowly and as gently as I could, more like she was a bird that had caught itself in wire. Touching her. And okay, the blood was pouring from her palm and dripping down her wrist, covering up the other scratches, it was hardly the hand holding romantic scene that I'd sometimes let myself think about, in the night, wrapped up in that van against the cold. But I was touching her. Proper, purposeful touching, not a brush of hands or a pull to get me upright but a gentle skin to skin contact. Like I'd not touched anyone since I'd hugged Mum, asked her to leave the bastard, come with me. Felt her shaking, fragile as a wing, but I'd already known then that

181

he'd crushed the life out of her. She couldn't live without him. She could live without me.

'It's not as bad as it looks,' Amy said, and her voice had gone a bit trembly.

'That's good, 'cos it looks bloody shocking.' I kept my eyes on that hand as hard as I could. 'Come on, there's a kit in the gardeners' hut, we'll use that to wash it off.'

We stayed standing. We'd have to move, the hut was at the top of the formal garden, but it was a bit like neither one of us wanted to be the first one to step away. Her blood was over my shirt now. Started warm, but that sharp December air was making it set and dry.

'Ow.' Amy moved her hand in my grip, as if she was trying to check it still worked. 'Starting to sting a bit now.'

And that was my cue to stop standing around like some kind of gripping pervert and lead her out of the barn. She cupped her own arm while I locked the door up, and then followed me up the cinder path that lay between the formal yew hedging and the sheep hurdles, that the gardeners used to move around without being seen, I dunno what the posh people thought they did, teleport or something.

The hut was empty and I went all hot with gratitude. Amy hurt was all sort of soft. It was like all her practicality went away when there was blood, and she sat down where I put her in the little folding canvas chair that James sits in to eat his sandwiches. I ran some hot water and found some cotton wool in the first aid kit box that hung on the wall.

'This is going to sting a bit.'

'Oh, no, don't, it's so completely painless right now,' Amy said, and I was glad of the sarcasm because I'd got a bit worried by the way she'd gone all obedient on me. Thought shock might have done something to her personality.

I washed and dressed the scratches and bites. Dunno what the lads got up to in that hut, but there was practically an A&E department in that box, if she'd been in labour I could probably have dealt with that too and taken her appendix out on the side.

'I'm sorry, Josh,' she said as I stuck the last of the tape down around her arm to keep the dressing from slipping. 'I wasn't thinking. I usually know better than to try to handle the birds.'

I was reciting the Latin names of all my birds in my head, over and over, to keep from thinking about how silky her skin was just there, along her forearm. How pale it looked against the blood splashed up it. *Falco biarmicus* ...

''S okay. We all do it,' I said. *Tyto alba* ... Was I really touching her? Was this really me? I never touched people. Not now. Like my nerves were tainted and poisoned and it could spread. *Falco tinnunculus* ... I didn't want to stop doing it and I didn't know why. Well, I did, but I ... didn't. I mean, I knew what I wished and I knew what I wanted and just as much I knew none of it would ever happen. *Buteo buteo.*

'I hope I didn't upset Fae, looming in like that and grabbing hold of her.'

She was watching my face. Could see her out of the corner of my eye as I smoothed more tape down. Didn't want to stop dressing the wound, didn't want to stop touching her, but was going to have to soon or she'd have so much surgical dressing up her arm that she'd lose the use of her elbow.

'Nah. She'll get over it.' *The way her skin kind of puckers as I slide the tape over it. The colours, pink that fades to blue and then back to pink. The tiny, pale hairs that rise and fall ...* Those hairs made me want to lay my cheek along her arm and kiss it.

'If you're sure ...' She moved a bit, settling herself against the canvas that smelled like James; sacking and damp. Kept her arm stretched out, laid on the folding table alongside the chair, kept it still under my fingers.

'Yeah.' Couldn't open a new reel of tape. Be too obvious. That wound was already better dressed than the Queen. I went back and checked all the tape I'd already done. Best to make sure.

When we weren't talking it was a sort of perfection in that hut. Okay, smelled of piss and earth and James's mum's home-made pickle, but it felt ... right. It felt like she wanted to be there and I wanted to be there and it must be like what it feels like to be out on a date with someone you really like, only that probably doesn't have the smell of piss and pickles. Her, Amy, sitting there, quiet and warm and me touching her without having that hate coming up in the back of my brain. Like this hut was some kind of magic.

'Hello, the "Hi Ho" brigade are on their way back,' Amy said, when I couldn't check the tape any more without it looking weird. 'Must be lunch break.'

There were voices out on the path, laughter, someone coughing. 'Only two more days and Christmas break, lads,' Sam was saying. 'A week of turkey and shagging.'

'Shagging the turkey, in your case.' More laughter.

I stood up. Moved back from Amy but she kept her arm stretched on the table. 'Better go. Got to ... you know. Things.' Didn't want the lads to catch us in there together. Didn't want to give Sam another chance to have a go. The hut was a well-known banging-site after hours and I didn't want anyone thinking that she and I were ... Not because I didn't want to, and that was confusing me something chronic too, but it was like my body had ideas that my brain wasn't in on, 'cos I knew if it asked my brain's opinion I'd be on the bike and heading for Plymouth about now.

'Yes. You're right.' Now Amy stood up too. 'I've left Julia on her own for too long. We've got a coach party in for a Christmas Tea at half three and there's a lot to do.'

'Yeah.' Her blood was still on my shirt. Jeez. I felt a bit deranged. 'Oh, what was that thing you wanted to show me?'

'Thing?' She went blank. Her face was a bit pale too. 'Oh,

yes.' A look at her arm. 'When Gran gets a look at this she's going to put me under house arrest.' A sigh. 'It'll keep, Josh.'

'Only ... I was thinking ... over Christmas? The house is shut? Can you show me then, or is it something that's going to crawl away and die in the next couple of hours?' Like Evershit. Not much chance, but there's always hope.

Amy did a big, sudden smile. 'Great idea! No one will be around. Edmund is, apparently, going to some friends in York for Christmas. We could do it then, after Gran has, inevitably, overdosed on greens and farted herself into a comatose sleep.'

'You aren't really selling this whole "Christmas at your place" to me,' I said, and I must have looked really serious, because she flickered around the edges like she was panicking.

'It's not that bad, honestly, we have a good time and Gran's really good company. After a couple of glasses of sherry, anyway.'

I raised my eyebrows at her. 'Yeah, and I'm so inundated with alternative offers that I'm about to turn you down.'

A second, and then she laughed. 'You bugger, Josh.'

And then the hut was full of the gardeners coming in for their break, and Amy explaining what she'd done to her arm, and I managed to slip away down the yew walk, back to the birds.

Chapter Twenty-Nine

Amy

I was woken in the middle of the night by a sound I hadn't heard in years. A noise like a tentative hailstorm rattling against my window, making me sit up and rub my eyes. 'What?'

The noise came again, this time accompanied by an equally familiar sound. 'Pssssssst!'

I slid open the sash and looked out. 'What the hell are you doing, Jules? We passed the "sneaking out to drink cider in the woods" mark about a decade ago, did you not get the memo?'

My bedroom overlooked our thin, neglected garden, beyond which the fields stretched, currently ironed into blandness by a thick frost. On the chipped concrete patch right under my window, Julia was standing wrapped in a thick coat and preparing to throw another handful of stones at my window. 'I need to talk to you, Ames.'

'That's why daytime was invented.'

'It's important. *Really* important. Honest.' With her hair loose rather than drawn back into the severe ponytail she maintained because she thought it would stop wrinkles forming, and in a pair of Hello Kitty pyjamas under her coat, she looked younger and more vulnerable than she had in years. 'Please, Ames.'

We'd been a bit off with one another since my outburst about her propositioning Josh, and I knew it must have taken a lot for her to be here, wanting to talk. 'All right, I'm coming down.'

I dragged on my dressing gown and found my slippers and went down to let her into the kitchen, where I put the kettle on and she slumped at the table. Even slumped Jules looked cute.

I checked out my image in the kettle. In my too-small dressing gown and my sturdy flannel nightdress I looked as though I'd been put to bed as a ten-year-old and grown up in my sleep. I felt a bit like that too, sometimes, I reflected, making tea.

'Right. What's up?' I pushed a mug of tea towards Jules, who had her head down on her spread arms. 'Or rather, what's so important that it has to be done round my table in the middle of the night?'

She turned her head to one side so she could look at me. There were rings under her eyes as though she hadn't slept for a while. Without her make-up she looked very fragile and I felt a little burst of fondness for her go off somewhere deep inside.

'It's Simon,' she said and her blue eyes were suddenly vague under the weight of tears. 'He says he's in love with me.'

The fondness hardened. Became something more complicated, something tempered by history into sharp points.

'And?' I hid my face in my mug. She'd forgotten. Forgotten what she'd done to me. Did that make it all right, or worse?

'And I don't know what to do.' Julia turned her head so her face was hidden in her arms. 'I mean, he's got a good job, he's got a lovely flat, nice car and everything.' Now she looked up at me. 'But what if I could do better with someone else?'

I swallowed my tea far too hot and felt the tears of pain sweep over my vision for a moment. Blinked hard.

'What do you think about him? Do you ... love him?' My voice sounded normal. *She's forgotten. Like it never happened, like it never mattered, because it never mattered to her, only to you. And now she needs your advice. Either give it or get out.*

'I don't know!' she wailed and I found myself looking ceilingward in case her increased volume woke Gran. 'Honestly, I don't know,' back to a whisper again. 'I might, but ... whenever I think I do I just start wondering what I'd do if Bradley Cooper came in the teashop and asked me out and if I was going with Simon I wouldn't be able to go out with Bradley Cooper!' And now her tears overflowed her eyes and twisted her mouth.

'Hmm.' The bitterness had gone now. I wasn't sure if it was the ridiculousness of the way she made her case, or her genuine unhappiness that had driven it back underground, but then, that was me, deal with the immediate problem and push all the repercussions away so they can resurface in the middle of the night. 'Jules. How often, on average, has Bradley Cooper, or, indeed, a Bradley Cooper look-alike, come into the teashop in the last six years?'

She half-sat up. 'Well, not yet he hasn't, but they might make a film and use Monkpark as a setting and he'd come in for a cup of coffee and fall madly in love with me.' She wiped her face with her fingers.

'They have catering people for that. The coffee, I mean, not the falling in love with you.'

'Okay, so he might just be walking round the grounds and I'm there serving tea on the lawn and he'll see me and—'

'—fall in love with you, yes. Julia. Does the saying "A bird in the hand is worth two in the bush" mean anything to you?' One of Gran's favourites, that one. I'd never actually had cause to use it in cold blood before.

She sat still for a moment. I'm sure, internally, her lips were moving as she processed what I'd said. 'You mean, I might never do any better than Simon?' she said, slowly.

'It's a possibility.' And, I didn't add, given that you aren't getting any younger or blonder, and we live in the middle of nowhere with a daily throughput of people whose ages are, on average, heading for three digits, maybe you should run for the hills, grasping your good-looking, financially solvent man who says he loves you in one hand, and a tightly drawn pre-nup in the other. 'And given our ongoing lack of anything Bradley Cooper shaped.'

'But what if ...?'

'And what if you win the lottery? Or Monkpark burns down? Or Mister Cooper comes into the teashop and decides that *I* am more his type?'

Julia pulled a 'wry' face. 'You're right. Oh, not those things, obviously, but ... no. Simon is lovely. I mean, really nice, he's kind and he says he'll buy me a car and then I won't have to keep borrowing Ry's all the time, and when I said I'd like to do something with flowers he said he knew a florist who would help me and—'

'You want to do something with flowers? Since when?'

She wiped at her face with both palms, blurring her cheeks for a moment. 'Well, I don't really, but I can't work in a teashop forever. I'm not like you, Ames, I want to run my own business one day in my own premises and everything.'

I drank my tea and muttered into my mug, 'Good luck with tax returns and VAT forms then,' but I didn't say it aloud. Jules clearly felt better if she could be snippy.

'Thanks, Ames.' She stood up and raked her hair back away from her tearstained cheeks. 'Honestly. Thanks for talking sense into me.'

'I haven't got that many years left to me, Jules,' I said with a deep sigh, 'but I'm glad you feel better.'

'Oh I do!' Hello Kitty bounced around a bit under her fleecy coat. 'You've always been the sensible one, haven't you, always done the right thing and all that.'

She let herself out of the back door, leaving me to stare bitterly into my congealing cup of tea. The sensible one. Yep, that was me. Never make a fuss, never stir things up ...

In consequence of my disturbed night, I was a bit later than usual getting to Monkpark next morning. As I swung my bike to a halt, in what I fondly imagined to look stylish in a James Bond way, but probably looked more like a Nineteen Fifties midwife hurrying to a breech delivery, Wendy stuck her head out of the yard door. 'Oh, great, Amy, you're here.'

'I'm always here.' I unzipped my windproof fleece. 'What's up, Wendy?'

'It's a bit ... I'm really sorry to have to ask and everything ...

Look, Sash has had a bit of an accident at nursery and they've asked me to arrange to have her picked up, but my mum has broken her arm so she can't drive, which isn't usually a problem but she's over with my Aunt Janet today so she can't get to the nursery and—'

'You go. I'll cover for you, 'course I will. I'll just let Julia know and ...'

Wendy made a face and her bobbed hair flipped around in the wind. 'It's a bit awkward really though, Amy. Edmund said that I'm not to ask you to cover for me again.'

I stopped, midway to propping the bike against the wall. 'What? Doesn't he know I've done your job before? What about that time you went to Cyprus for a fortnight?'

'He does know, yes.' Wendy did a kind of rotation, obviously desperate to go to her daughter but also torn by her responsibilities to Monkpark. 'But he did say that I wasn't to ask you in future, he said we'd get a temp in. Only ...' She looked over her shoulder. '... he's not in today, he's gone to Middlesbrough to talk to someone about some group thing or another, and I *really* need to pick up Sasha, and it's only for today, so ...?'

I patted her on the shoulder. 'He will never find out from my lips, Wend. You go to her, I'll square things with Jules and then I'll be in your office in ten. Anything I need to know about?'

She shook her head. 'Nothing pending. It'll just be answering the phone and there's a couple of emails need dealing with. I left a note.' And she was gone, drawn by maternal love. I idly wondered if my mother had ever felt that duality, that two-directional pull between wanting to be with me and needing to be someone else, and concluded that she probably had, but that she'd come down on the side of earning, of having a life away from Monkpark.

So I told Julia, mindful of the fact that Wendy obviously didn't want Edmund to know what we were up to, that I was helping out in the house for the morning, because we were short of room guides, and to call me if she needed me, then headed off to Wendy's office, up in the old attics, full of intentions to get the emailing out of the way and then spend a therapeutic few hours doing a nice, slow internet shop in Tesco.

Wendy had left her machine on for me. The phone didn't ring at all, so I got the few emails out of the way, shopped with a lot less rigour than I usually did when I had to get it all done in my lunch hour on the old computer, and then made a coffee. From Wendy's high window I could see occasional glimpses of Malkin, circling the estate on a rising thermal and, once, Fae passed, hovering briefly overhead, outlined by the tinsel Wendy had pinned around the frame in honour of the season, looking for that second like a particularly savage attempt at a Christmas card.

Julia didn't call, so I presumed the cafe was quiet. At around eleven, and bored, I flipped through a pile of papers stacked on the side of the desk; all estate business, Wendy locked away anything Edmund would deem as 'personal'. There were sheaves of data from the Heritage Trust, brochures and colour printouts of Annual Reports and Board of Trustees Reports and I found myself idly turning the pages of the most recent. It looked as though the Heritage Trust was doing all right for itself, the Chairman's report was positive, and there was a lovely picture of her with a small terrier, visiting a property in the Lake District. I licked my finger and turned the page. There, under a pencil sketch of one of the Trust's larger houses in Essex (residence of a famous poet or something), was a list of Highlights of the Year, included in which, to my amazement, was Monkpark Hall.

I read the brief summary, which basically outlined the increased visitor numbers to the Hall in the previous season, the amount that the house had earned for the Trust, and the projected figures for the current year, all of which put Monkpark in the top ten earners for the Trust for the whole

191

of the North of England. There was even a paragraph acknowledging the new events that Edmund had initiated and how 'forward thinking' his approach was. No mention of most of it being my ideas, of course. I frowned at the page, in case I was somehow reading it wrong, but it continued to tell me that Monkpark, far from being in financial difficulties, was well on its way to becoming the flagship property for North Yorkshire.

I looked across the corridor to the locked door of Edmund's flat. He wouldn't be back for the rest of the day, Wendy had said, so I couldn't ask him what was going on, and we were only a couple of days from closing for Christmas, so I wasn't likely to get the chance before then. I looked back at the reports. I must be missing something. Edmund wouldn't run the risk of upsetting the Trust with the ghost hunting thing if there wasn't a good reason, would he? Maybe money had gone missing when John left? But John had gone to work for another property owned by the Trust, surely they wouldn't have given him another job if he'd been siphoning money from them? And besides, all these new events we were putting on were attracting more visitors, so why wasn't that enough?

I shook my head. My degree had taught me that there could be loads of reasons why seemingly successful businesses ended up making a loss: tax avoidance, mismanagement, money invested in building work or new attractions. None of it meant that anything Edmund had told me was wrong.

Above my head Malkin mewed, I could hear him through the skylights, and I wondered if he'd got away from Josh to go hunting along the roadsides. It distracted me from thoughts about the financial situation of Monkpark Hall, and I spent the rest of my time filling in for Wendy experiencing the dual joys usually denied to me of Facebook and Twitter.

Chapter Thirty

Josh

The house closed on Christmas Eve. James said before, before Evershit took over, there always used to be a party, mince pies and mulled wine in the Library and everything. But now we just sort of shut up shop at half four, signs went up and all, and that was that. The lads had a bit of anti-climax going on, been spoiling for a party for months, so they all climbed in the back of Andy's van and went off to Pickering to get pissed and chat up the lasses. James asked me along but ... nah. Not my scene. 'Sides, didn't want to give Sam another excuse to have a go, and ten pints of lager would be more than enough excuse as far as he was concerned, so I locked the birds away and took the bike up onto the high moor to watch the sky.

Funny how I don't mind the dark so much outside. It's inside that's the problem, when it's all dark and small and pinched, and all I can think about is that little room without the windows. Should've got over that now. Keep telling myself that. It's gone. Past. Will never happen again while I've got breath. But still ... when I'm inside and it's dark, when the place is small enough that the air feels like it's been there for years ...

There'd been a snowfall, enough to get everyone excited, and for two of the gardening lads to get sent home for chucking snowballs at each other and just missing some visitors, but the roads were clear. And the moon hit the snow like an orange on glass, the air so cold that it was all just mist unless I blew down; sheep just blobs moving in the dark, keeping me company, kind of. And I thought about Amy.

Pretty much all I ever thought about now, unless it was the birds. Amy. All bright and lovely, smelling of indoor things and cooking, like she was person-shaped comfort in an apron. And

I thought about touching her, proper touching, when I'd done her arm up, and what it had made me want to do, and that I couldn't … like there were two 'me's in my head. One 'me' that wanted her, properly, like a bloke and everything, that tiptoed around the dreams of her lying next to me in a bed all rosy and soft but prickly round the edges so you didn't mess with her. Like Bane, all gentle and feathery and nibbling at my fingers kind of like a kiss but taking a chunk and winging it if you went wrong. Knowing, though, knowing all along that she'd be back, stomping and grim but giving you another chance because it's you and her, always will be.

And the other 'me'? That guy held the first me to ransom, with his memories of the self-loathing and the disgust. The fear that, if I touched her, properly *touched her*, that it would all come screaming back in like Bane in a dive, all talons and beak and pain. And wondering if it was worth it or if I shouldn't just cut my losses and ride away somewhere, take it for granted that I was never going to be a part of anything normal.

Sometimes though, like tonight, first 'me' won out. Sounds stupid now, but I rode the bike back, imagining her behind me, pretending like I could feel her hands tight on the jacket, feel her leaning in to the corners, just pressing herself against me a little bit. Imagination. Pretty much all it could ever be; didn't even know what she thought of me now I'd told her. Did she pity me, was that why she kept getting me over to the cafe to feed me? 'Cos she thought I was something less than a real man because of what happened to me? Because I'd run out on my mum when I could have fought harder to get her to come with me? Because I'd not realised, with all the 'pretty-boy' comments, what my stepdad had in store for me?

My back went all cold under the jacket as I lost imaginary Amy. Like she'd fallen, slid off the back of the bike when we went round that last corner, evaporated into breath-mist and gone and I gunned the engine and roared it home kicking gravel and ice and not caring if I made it or not.

Chapter Thirty-One

Amy

I looked forward to Josh's arrival all Christmas morning. Everything else was exactly as Christmas always went in our house; I woke to a stocking that Gran had secretly packed with little treats, and was relieved to find only the things I might expect, chocolates, a diary, stationery, and not what I'd feared, dog biscuits, jam or a brochure from a photocopier supplier. We went to church, along with all the rest of the Monkpark residents, had mince pies in the vestry and went home to get the rest of the dinner on, by the light of our resolutely artificial tree, since Gran didn't hold with fetching perfectly healthy timber into the house.

At half past twelve Josh arrived and I opened the door to him to find that it had snowed a little bit since we'd got in, and he was standing on the step wearing a suit and a dusting of white that made him look like the decoration off a Christmas cake.

'Happy Christmas!'

He looked me up and down. 'You're a penguin,' he said.

'Gran always gets me a sweater for Christmas.' For once I didn't feel embarrassed about the fact. In fact, the broadness of Josh's grin and the way he was obviously trying to stop himself from bursting out laughing made me very grateful to Gran. His whole face looked lighter, and not just from the snow's reflection. 'Come on in, dinner's nearly on the table.'

I saw his eyes flicker to my arm, well concealed under the fluffy black and white knit, that made me look less like the intended penguin and more like a wine waiter who's undergoing a severe case of moult.

'How's it doing?' he asked.

'If I bang it against anything it hurts like death, but otherwise it's fine. I have a renewed sympathy for voles though, if that's how Fae treats them.'

'She's efficient.' He came through and sat at the table. He had to as we'd pulled it away from the wall to accommodate the three of us and now it took over most of the room.

Gran was sitting in her chair under the window, which was, as usual and as promised, open. The through draught was, as ever, making the fire smoke and her wiry form, seen through the fug, looked a bit like something out of a horror film.

'Merry Christmas if you believe in such things,' she said. 'Window's open and we don't lock the door. You can walk out any time you like.'

Josh looked as though he was about to say something, but then he just nodded. Gran's matter-of-fact attitude seemed to settle him.

'They told Dad to close his eyes and count to ten,' she went on. 'Not sure what good it did him, mind, but we got him back in the end.'

Josh frowned at me and I just shrugged. Explaining Gran was a bit like trying to explain quantum physics. 'I'll start dishing up, shall I? More sherry, Gran?'

We sat around the table and ate. I saw Josh cast a few glances towards the open window, but he didn't seem to have the edginess he'd had inside the cottage before. Sometimes I noticed his eyes widen as though panic was about to strike, but he seemed to be able to bring himself back now from that unspoken brink. As though something had changed.

Josh got on well with Gran, especially once that second glass of sherry caught on, and we talked about Monkpark, about the house and the grounds and the way Christmas had been celebrated in the old days. Gran managed to make 1950 sound like the fifteenth century, but she remembered so much about how things used to be done and the way the house used to be that it was quite entertaining. However, things caught up with her shortly after lunch and she retired to her chair 'to think', whereupon Josh and I went to hide in the kitchen.

Once alone, he seemed to suffer from a recurrence of the nervousness. He helped me stack plates but kept letting cutlery slip between his fingers until the kitchen rug was covered in splashes of old gravy.

'Are you okay? I can open the back door if you want, although I warn you that Gran has a whole host of epithets to apply to people who leave their back doors open. I think it's a symptom of sluttish behaviour,' I said, feeling the irony creeping into my voice. 'Although chance would be a fine thing.'

'I'm ... is that Julia?' It felt to me as though he seized on the sight of Jules, arm in arm with Simon the bank manager, walking through the snow across the field that backed the village. 'And is that ... has she got a dog? Never saw Julia as a dog person. Maybe a Rottweiler or something ...'

'Oh, that's Simon's Labrador. Simon's spending Christmas with her family. Well, the bits of Christmas that are legal, her brothers have got quite a robust approach to "nobody wanted it so we took it". But I don't think she's told him that yet.'

Josh kept his eyes on the couple. I had to admit that Julia looked happy, they were practically a Christmas card illustration, two young people – or people with a skilled hand with the make-up brush, in Julia's case – kicking through an ankle-deep application of snow, preceded by an overexcited black dog with half a tree in its mouth. The bitterness stung the back of my mouth for a second and I began to stack plates much harder than necessary.

'Hey.' Josh stopped me before I broke one of Gran's prized tureens. 'What did those sprouts ever do to you?' Then a glance over his shoulder into the living room where Gran's snores and farts were alternating up and down the scale like a jazz exercise. 'Apart from the obvious.'

'Sorry. Nothing. Just ...'

He must have followed my gaze. 'You can swear if you like. Promise not to tell your Gran.' And he smiled, a bit more relaxed now, as though only one of us was allowed to be wound up at the same time. 'I'll even let you say "bugger".'

'How can I resist?' I tried to sound similarly light-toned, but I knew that my voice still had a bit of that 'sourness' to it, that bit that I always tried to keep under control because I knew it made me sound like a bitch.

Josh kept his eyes on the field. 'So what if she is practically family? Plenty out there hate their families.' And now those eyes darkened. 'I should know.'

'It's not that. Not really. Just ...' My eyes followed Jules, wearing a new coat that was probably a present from Simon and her expensive Dubarry boots that had been a present from a former boyfriend. She was tossing her hair in the breeze like a pony overfed on oats and looked satisfied with her lot. 'I was engaged once, you know.'

Josh made a face. 'Okay.' A spoon clattered into the gravy boat.

'His name was Guy, and we were at university together.' My memory threw up a tall, lanky shape in a grey coat, sandy blond hair hanging over one eye and a ready smile. 'I brought him home to meet Gran and ...' I stopped, but the direction of my gaze and my narrowed eyes must have told the rest of the story, because Josh suddenly stopped picking up the knives.

'Well, that was shit.'

'She didn't mean it, and, let's face it, if he'd really been a keeper he wouldn't have gone with her, would he? I mean, if you look at it that way she did me a favour really.'

'Why does she do it?' He turned on the hot tap and steam billowed between us. 'She's not got to prove anything, she's skinny and blonde and blokes like that kind of thing, why did she need yours?'

I shrugged. Most of the pain and anger had gone now. Over the six years it had seeped away, almost unnoticed, leaving

Julia once more washed up on the shore of Monkpark, where we all knew one another's business and got along because the alternative was feuds and infighting and people being evicted for being nuisance neighbours. I hadn't forgotten though. I thought she had, but I couldn't be sure, although she probably wouldn't even remember Guy's name now. 'She could have him, so she did.'

He stood very quietly for a moment. In front of us, in the sink, dishes slid under the soapy water like tiny floral china *Titanics*. 'That why you were so angry?'

I gave a hollow laugh. 'I'm never angry. It's a waste of energy and it just annoys Gran.'

'When Julia came to me that night. Was it because you knew I liked you? Did you think she knew and put me on the list?'

'I—'

'You were so sad, Amy. You sat with me in the cafe, and you were so sad you cried. Was it me you were crying for, or was it you?' His voice was very soft.

There was a splinter of cold in my stomach. 'I never cry for me. Why would I?'

'Because you've been shat on, Amy. And you can't see it.' He shoved back the sleeves of his suit jacket, pushing them back past his wrists.

'No, I haven't.'

'What Julia did to you? That wasn't shitting on you from a great height?'

'It's what you come to expect when you're me, Josh.'

My words seemed to startle him, he gave a sort of jerk back that made the cutlery sing against the pots in the sink.

'I've got a face like a well-disposed horse, I'm short and I'm chunky and I'm pretty much just podge all the way round. When you aren't slim and pretty, d'you know what happens? Blokes think they're doing you a favour going out with you. They expect you to shag them because you're grateful, they think they can treat you as badly as they want because you'll always take them back because there's so little choice. And women think that you're no competition, they can have your boyfriend with the click of their fingers because they are thin and pretty and men want to be seen with them. And do you know something else? *They can.*'

'Wow.' Josh's hair was curling softly in the steam. 'You really don't think much of blokes, do you?'

'Would *you*?' Aware that I'd sounded a bit shrill, I glanced quickly over my shoulder in case Gran had woken up. Reassured by the soft grunting sound, I turned back to him. 'I never knew my dad, every man I've ever been out with has had an eye out for someone better from the day he bought me the first drink. I'm not stupid, Josh, I know what I look like and I—' I stopped, suddenly and used the first available tea towel to conceal my expression.

'What about me?'

'What?' I dropped the tea towel to see him with his back to the sink now. With the snow light coming in from the window his face and expression were hard to make out.

'Do you think that's what I'm like?' He was very, very still. 'Seriously, Amy?'

The cottage was suddenly silent. All I could hear was the slow, slightly off beat ticking from Gran's inherited clock on the mantelpiece, the occasional eructation from her chair, and a faint settling of china as it came to rest at the bottom of the sink.

'No,' I said, in a tiny voice. 'No, I don't.'

'Why not?'

Chink went the gravy boat against the tureen in the depths of the bowl. Something in his tone told me that this was a very serious question.

'I ... don't know.'

'Not, because, for example, you think I'm too fucked up to make a pass at anyone at all? That I'm safe because I'm not really like other blokes?'

And suddenly I realised what was at the bottom of all this. 'You're not like that because you're my friend, Josh,' I said, trying to keep my tone steady and level. 'Because you didn't just pick me up in some bar or online or something, and pretend to care just so you could have easy sex with someone who wouldn't demand anything of you. Because you are a lovely, decent man who thinks of me as a person, not just as a bag of tits and what have you. You aren't looking at me wondering how soon you can sleep with me or how long it will take to get rid of me afterwards, you talk to me and care what I think about stuff and ...' I stopped and took a breath. 'So, no, Josh. It's not just because of what happened to you. It's because of who you are underneath.'

His head moved away from the blinding effect of the window as he moved across the kitchen and I could see his expression again. There were little tight creasings at the corner of each eye, as though he'd had his face screwed up in pain.

'Thank you,' he said, and it was almost a whisper.

We began washing up the dinner things, a careful but warm kind of silence between us as though an understanding had been arrived at. Josh had uncoiled a little bit further, the shoulder line of his jacket had lost the tension and he'd stopped looking at the window as though to check it was still open. When we'd dried and put away the last dishes and there was still no sign of any activity from Gran's chair that didn't involve digestive disturbance, I said, 'Shall I show you that thing now?'

'This is nothing to do with what we were just talking about, right?'

The loss of tension seemed to have rubbed off on me a bit too. 'I can promise nothing untowardly sexual is going to happen, all right?'

Josh dried his hands. 'Dunno if that's disappointing or what.'

He'd brought the bike, so we rode down the cleared roads

to Monkpark. The few inches of snow that had accumulated over the fields and gardens evened out the humps and bumps of the landscape and made everything look level and neat. It tidied the usual ragged edges of the yew walk under a neat surface and made the house look like an iced biscuit. Josh pulled the bike round by the barn.

'We'll have to go in the way Gran showed us,' I said, quietly, heading down towards the dank stairs to the cellar.

'Why are you whispering? There's nobody here.' Josh looked down at his suit. 'And how bad is this going to be, only this thing costs a fortune to clean.'

'You'll be fine.' I led him down the flagged corridor, through the butler's pantry and into the body of the house. It felt odd, almost reverberatingly empty. The snow light lent all the rooms an otherworldly sort of atmosphere, as though we'd not so much gone through the servants' door as through a wardrobe. I half expected the mirrors to talk to us as we passed.

'Here. Look.' I pulled the moulding and swung open the door to the old servants' staircase. 'Not just a cubbyhole, a way around the house!'

Josh had hung back, peering through from the hall. 'So, where does it go?'

'Up to the attics, I think.'

'Nice.' He took half a step through the door. 'I'm sorry, I still can't … It's too dark.'

'No, it's fine, I didn't expect you to come in. I just wanted to show someone what I found.' I looked up, following the route of the staircase to where it twisted back on itself. 'Was it because you were shut in?'

My question seemed to take him by surprise. 'I couldn't …' A pause and a deep breath. 'Usually I was bleeding too. So it was dark and I couldn't breathe and I could feel this blood dripping but I didn't know where from. And I thought I might die. All bent up in that little cupboard.' Another breath, almost a gasp. 'I need to see.'

I wanted to touch him then. To give some kind of reassurance that everything that was evil was over, that he was free. But he had that guarded expression again as he backed out into the filtered light of the hall, that expression that said everything might be over but the memories were still peering over his shoulder and snarling their way into his dreams at night.

'Monkpark feels weird like this,' Josh said, once he'd reached the middle of the room and the dark was shut away behind its door again. 'A bit like it doesn't want to be empty.'

'I know.' I could feel that atmosphere too, almost as though the house was just holding its breath, waiting for something to happen. The same kind of feeling as a room has just before a party. 'I've got some ideas for some more events, like the thing we did at Halloween, if I can get Edmund to stand still long enough to listen. Nothing that will upset the Trust but things that ought to bring in more cash. Then we could stop doing those ridiculous ghost hunting evenings.'

'Yeah?' Josh seemed to want to turn the conversation away from anything to do with his past. 'Like what?'

'Well, I thought ... Easter things in the gardens, with chicks and rabbits for the children to look at and Easter egg hunts, and maybe a Midsummer picnic – we could get the local drama group to come and do plays in the gardens, or maybe dress up in costume and pretend to be previous owners of the Hall and tell visitors what it was like when it was lived in, and do the house up for Christmas ...'

Josh was grinning now. 'You should be running this place, not Shitface.'

I pretended not to have heard the prejudicial name. 'I love dreaming these things up.'

He wandered over to one of the long windows that looked out onto the garden. For a second he was framed against the snow and, in his suit, looked as though he belonged in this house in another age.

'It's a great place,' he said. 'Glad I pitched up here.'

'I'm glad you came too.' I stood beside him and we watched another snow shower blaze through on a wind that rattled the glass in its frame and knocked the snow from the hedges, only to replace it with a new layer. I could feel his jacket sleeve against my arm through the moulting penguin jumper but I knew better than to move closer to him. Wished that I dared, but didn't want to spark any nasty memories, not when he'd reached a place of quiet.

'I like you, Amy,' he said, eyes still on the falling snow. 'Even more now I know you don't ... that you like me as I am.'

I looked sideways at him. His hair was swept away from his face, leaving his cheekbones clear and the snow gave his skin a blue tint, so he looked as though he'd been carved from the side of a glacier. Grains of stubble grazed along his chin and around his mouth, and then grew almost casually upwards like contour lines. He looked carelessly handsome, a portrait of someone who doesn't care but looks great anyway. I couldn't think of anything to say.

'And I'm starting to ... I can kind of touch you now without it being weird, like when I did your arm?'

Under my jumper I felt my hand twitch in its bandages, as though it wanted him to touch it again. 'Mmmm?' I said, not sure where this was going.

'But I don't know ... I don't think I can ever ... I feel like I want to but ... I'm afraid if I try it will all just come back, what happened with that bloke my stepdad brought in, when he tried to ... touch me, and I don't want to feel like that ever again.' A tiny gust of wind managed to force its way through the casement and tweaked his hair in an almost impossibly picturesque way.

'Hey.' I turned to look at him properly. He turned too, so I could see his face. 'I'm a bit down on sex myself, what with it always being followed by some bastard upping and leaving or, worse, starting to laugh. So ...' I gave a sort of shrug, which

204

was mostly absorbed by the penguin. 'Let's just see what happens, okay? Maybe time will take care of things, maybe it won't, but we'll still be friends whatever, yes?'

A very cautious hand wavered in front of us for a moment, and then he seemed to take a decision and laid it over my wrist. His skin was firm and warm and, once his hand had arrived, his fingers seemed to find a life of their own and curled down onto my hand until they slid over mine. 'Think ... yeah, think I can manage that.'

'Very good of you, I'm sure,' I said, rather tartly, and I sounded so much like Gran that I made myself laugh. 'I suppose we ought to go back. Gran will be waking up soon, and I've got a terrible feeling that there's one of her sherry trifles in the fridge which will be making its presence known later.'

'Yeah,' he said, but didn't move his hand, and we stayed there, side by side watching the snow fall over the gardens until it got dark.

Chapter Thirty-Two

Josh

I sat in the van. Thought about Amy and what she'd said about men. Still didn't know if I really believed her about liking me for who I was – didn't like to tell her about the girls before who'd said things like that. Pretended to like me and then moved on me, all lip gloss and perfume, telling me what they wanted me to do to them in bed. Okay, yeah, they didn't know why, no idea why I wouldn't just shag them. Couldn't tell them. Couldn't tell anyone until her. Until Amy.

And suddenly the van felt cold. Up to then it'd always felt like fresh air, needed it like that to breathe and never really noticed that it was cold. Had the gas burner on sometimes when it got a bit much, but this cold was different. Wasn't just the kind of cold Yorkshire gets in December when the snow comes in and the wind can burn you alive, it felt like the kind of cold you get when something is dead.

Maybe because the cottage was warm, with the fire and all of us in one little room, and her Gran generating megawatts of her own. There was a kind of comfort to it for the first time. Not like I was trapped, I could see the window was open and feel the air coming in and all, didn't feel like I couldn't breathe, it made me feel more like ... A hug. Yeah, like I was being hugged by the air.

I thought about what she'd said about men and I wanted to fight every one of them that had hurt her, like I punched out Sam. Fuckers. Didn't they know, couldn't they see what they were doing, or didn't they care? And that one that got engaged to her and then went off with Julia? I wanted to track him down and then send Malkin in, all talons and beak, and rip his throat out ... no. The birds were above all that. Not their fight, not mine either, but Amy's, and the way she'd looked when she'd told me, like she thought there was no point fighting. Like she'd kind of accepted second best all down the line.

I went to bed, but couldn't sleep. Didn't know why. There was light and there was air and that was all I needed, but my brain wouldn't stop giving me pictures of things I didn't think were ever going to be mine, so I gave up. Got up and put my bird gear on, thought I could go and sleep in the barn. Oh, I took my sleeping bag, wasn't going to put Amy through finding me dead and cold on the floor or anything, wrapped up everything I needed and headed out under the moon. I could think out there, in the snow. Like being outside stopped all those memories of when I'd been shut in, like when I started to get back on that roundabout I could tip my head up and count the stars or put faces in the clouds and it would all go away. Walking and being outside.

Snow showers were still coming over the hills every now and then. They'd blow in, I could see them coming across the fields and then they'd hit and it'd be five minutes of blindness and the taste of ice and then they'd be gone again, leaving another half inch on the ground and everything quiet again. Above me the rooks kicked off as I made my way down through the wood, keeping me company, so I decided to go over the fields rather than down the road. Even with the snow it was better going that way, the rooks gave way to the owls once I got down past the copse, and there were deer grazing along the hedge line, raising their heads just to stare my way as I went down, heading to the river. A couple of hares boxed in the moonlight, it was like nature had put on a film just for me and what with the whole Amy thing, I was feeling pretty good.

The river crossing was a narrow bridge made of railway sleepers, put in so the farmer could drive the tractor over and not have to risk fording. I got there in another blizzard, skidding and sliding down the valley in the silence of another snowstorm. Hit the bridge blind, but the sleepers had iced over and I went arse over tit into the river, breaking surface chilled to the bone and with a tawny owl whooping overhead like it was laughing at me. Dropped my sleeping bag and had to duck back down to get it, had my glove and feed bag and all in it, so I was scraping around on the bottom for a few minutes, not deep, only waist high water but sieving through grit and sand while the snow blew. Felt like I was being sawn about, like the wind had blades, cutting like a turbine. Found my bag, dragged it up the bank and ran down over the field to where I got in through the hedging at the end of the garden, so cold that it was hardly cold at all.

There was no light at the top of the house, Evershit must still be away jollying about with his posh git friends in York for Christmas. Tit. I thought of him living up there, all central heating and hot running showers, fancying himself and reckoning all the women to fancy him, why else would he be fannying around in those skinny cut trousers and brogues like some ad executive trying his hand at life in the country?

I stopped up under the hedge out of the wind for a bit. No good sleeping in the barn, it'd be too cold with my gear all soaked and all. Same for going back to the van, even with the gas burner the sleeping bag wouldn't dry out. Gardeners' cottage was all locked up tight with everyone being on holiday, so there was nothing else for it but to break back into Monkpark down the way Amy took me earlier, in through the old cellar and up through the butler's pantry, into the house proper where at least there was heating on. The butler's room was where all the fancy dress stuff lived that the kids played with when they did school visits, so I found a couple of outfits that near enough fitted, and put those on instead of my wet gear, and felt better.

It was weird in the house at night. That 'waiting' feeling that Amy and I felt during the day was still there, but now it felt like the house was holding its breath. Like the house was like me, couldn't breathe properly at night, was just surviving until it got light again. But the heating was on, just background, just to stop the pipes freezing and everything getting all damaged by damp, but enough that I wasn't going to die, and there was the security lighting and everything, so I found myself a little corner in the back of the Old Kitchen, hunched myself down into a chair, and went to sleep, with the house all secure around me, almost like I was home.

Chapter Thirty-Three

Amy

It was early enough that Gran was still clattering around in the kitchen, rearranging her spoons and complaining that the leftovers from Christmas dinner had been put in the fridge the wrong way. I was up in my room. Not in bed, no, Gran didn't hold with anyone staying in bed past seven o'clock unless they were ill or giving birth, so I was sitting on the little chair, elbows resting on my dressing table and staring at the wall.

The patterns in the paper were so well traced by my eyes that they were like diary entries. I'd sat here, year after year, eyes unfocussed but travelling the swirls and curlicues while my mind roamed beyond the Monkpark Estate, first wondering what life had in store for me and then, once I'd found out that life really didn't care much whether I never married one of Take That or spent the rest of it up to my shoulders in flour, dreaming of alternative lives. Lives in which my mother had taken me to live with her in London, and I'd grown up a metropolitan girl, treating the Tube with comfortable familiarity and visiting museums at weekends. Or a life where I'd married Guy and we lived in a small house in Doncaster; I drove the children to school and gardened at weekends and we sat comfortably together on the sofa in the evenings.

None of my younger self's imaginings had come up with the theory that I'd still be here, still doing the same thing, year after year, the alternatives becoming smaller and smaller with each year that went by. Now they were pretty much variations on a theme – a future where Gran needed a level of care that meant I had to give up my job, so we'd have to leave Monkpark. In that future I became less and less of a person, until future extrapolations could only see a shapeless lump, shopping and cooking and cleaning amid a riot of thwarted ambitions, for an old lady made bitter by fear.

And then, hooked on a fern frond, my thoughts turned to Josh. That beautiful, scared man with whom I shared a friendship that felt as though it teetered on the edge of being something else. I began finding the outline of his profile in the leafy excrescences, the dark shading of his eyes, the high planes of his cheekbones, the straight definition of his chin ...

'This tureen is filthy!' There was a dismissive clatter of crockery from downstairs. My bedroom was over the kitchen, and Gran knew full well that I could hear her. 'They didn't make much of a fist of washing up, did they? Could have done better with a hungry cat.'

That small, rebellious part of me that I'd smothered since my teenage years wanted to respond. Wanted to shout that we'd done our best, it wasn't our fault that her standards were ridiculous, that whatever I did would never be good enough. That we could have scoured the dinner plates until the patterns came off and she would still have found grease or traces of gravy. But I knew it was pointless. The teenage experiences had been enough. Trying to stand up for myself had always resulted in stony silences that had gone on, sometimes, for weeks, until I'd been trained into taking the path of least resistance.

'There's someone at the door now,' her voice, peevish with the unanticipated, floated through the floorboards. 'Who would that be at this time?'

'Just a suggestion, try opening the door,' I muttered, but was already halfway down the narrow staircase. 'It's okay, Gran, I'll get it.' Then, back to the mutter, 'Might be the escape committee with the tunnelling equipment.'

It was Josh. Standing on the step, bike engine running, and wearing ... well, I wasn't quite sure what he was wearing. An army greatcoat, with sleeves far too short, barely covered some velvet knee breeches and what looked like the top half of a peasant's smock.

'Good grief. You look as if you've been dragged backwards through a portrait gallery.'

He shook his head quickly. His hair, I noticed, had rat-tailed around his face, and there was a smear of mud that ornamented one cheek. 'Fell in the river. These are from the dressing up box.' He shrugged his shoulders to indicate the weirdly cross-century clothing. 'I was wet.'

I let out a breath. 'Okay. So ...?' I waved my hands, indicating his appearance. 'Did you just come to let me see what happens when a man is left unattended in the vicinity of seven centuries of fashion, or ...?'

He wriggled his shoulders inside the coat. 'Do you know where Evershott is? I've got a problem.'

'Looking like that you've got more than one. What happened, besides falling into the river?'

He wriggled again in a sort of embarrassed shrug. 'I lost my keys. Bloody stupid, slipped on the bridge and ...' He dropped his head and the rat-tails clunked into place across his face like a door slamming. '... bag fell in. Didn't realise the keys were gone until I tried to get in the barn this morning.'

I stepped forwards towards him. 'You can't get into the birds?'

Now he raised his head and there was a stark look in his eyes. 'No. And they need feeding and sorting and ... I'm a twat. Don't deserve to have them.'

'It was an accident, Josh.' I was thinking furiously fast. All right, Edmund had a set of keys, but I had no idea where he was, apart from York, and it's too big a city to start trawling through at nine a.m. on a Boxing Day morning. 'We can sort it out, though.'

'Can you get him to come back and give me the keys?' Josh was shifting from foot to foot in a sort of shuffling dance, as though anxiety had to turn to energy to be dealt with. 'Only, can't leave them much longer.'

His lower legs were bare, his feet clad in big boots, jutting out from the undersized breeches and beneath the greatcoat in a stretch of shin and rolled down sock. It made him look like a badly prepared flasher and, because I knew this was as far from Josh's intentions as it was possible to get, it made me smile.

'I don't know how to get in touch with Edmund. But Wendy might have a number for him.' Out of habit I groped my mobile out of my pocket and checked it, even though I knew that we only had a signal up at the end of the Monkpark gardens. Down here it was just a decorative bit of plastic. I glanced back behind me into the hall, where our house phone hung on the chilly wall. 'Can I use the phone, Gran?'

Josh followed me into the hall as, not waiting for an answer, I used my mobile for practically the only thing it was any good for in the village, storage, and looked up Wendy's home number. Worrying about the birds seemed to trump his fear of the indoors, because he didn't even look back as the front door slammed itself shut.

'What are you up to, madam?' I'd forgotten Gran's aversion to anyone attempting to contact the outside world.

'Trying to get hold of Wendy.' I dialled. 'It's an emergency.'

Gran looked Josh up and down. 'If it's a fashion one, it might be too late.'

'Birds,' Josh said and dropped his head again.

'Ah.' She patted his shoulder. 'Well, our Amy is good at solving problems, even if she is a stranger to the washing up brush.'

Wendy answered the phone, only to tell me that she had no idea where Edmund was, only that he wouldn't be back for a couple of days. The news made me twist my mouth and Josh shied about, rotating in the hallway as though his panic about being shut in was back.

'Can we break the door down?'

'You'd upset the birds.' Gran surprised me by speaking up for Josh. 'Think properly.'

Josh gave her a grateful look. 'Yeah, they'd panic. Maybe ... y'know, heart attack ... don't like sudden, loud noises.'

'They'd be all right without food for a bit, though, wouldn't they? I mean, until Edmund came back?'

Gran still had her hand on Josh's shoulder as though she was pegging him to the floor. He was twitching around but not shaking off the hand.

'I didn't feed Fae much yesterday, I'm flying her today. She's a little bird, Amy, she can't do without food for long.'

Gran tightened her grip on the outside of the greatcoat and he raised his head to meet her eyes.

'They're all I've got,' he said, quietly.

'Evidently not, or you wouldn't be here now, would you?' she said, tartly. 'So, think. Edmund has the other key, you say?'

I cupped my forehead in my hands. 'Yes, but he's away in York for a few days. Even Wendy doesn't know how to get in touch and ...' A vision of a staircase, winding its way up through the dark. 'Oh.'

I must have sounded as though I'd found an answer, because Josh straightened. 'What?'

'The servants' staircase. It must come out somewhere in the attics, and it can't be in Wendy's office, unless it comes out through the back of her filing cabinet, which would be like the weirdest Narnia, *All the President's Men* mashup ever ... so ...' I rubbed at my head. 'Come on, let's find out.'

He was already at the door, Gran's hand still outstretched as though he'd ducked out from underneath it.

'You be careful with that,' Gran said as we headed out to the bike, still ticking over gently at the kerb like a huge cat purring peacefully.

'It's perfectly safe, Gran, and we're only going a couple of miles down to the house.'

'I wasn't talking about the machine,' she replied, darkly. 'That boy is shot to pieces.'

I looked over my shoulder at where Josh was pulling his

helmet on, squeezing all his features into a little window that made his eyes look intense. 'I know,' I said, softly. 'But I like him.'

She twisted her head like a cat that's heard a fridge door open in another room. 'Well,' she said. 'Well. I remember what happened with that madam over the road there and your fiancé.'

I had the feeling that this was Gran's way of telling me not to get hurt, but she'd perfected the art of Yorkshire shorthand, editing most of the emotion out of anything she said, so it was hard to tell.

'Look, we've got to go. If anything happens to the birds ...'

Gran made a sort of 'tch' noise, that could either have been sympathy or extreme annoyance, and closed the front door on me, so I dashed over to the bike and we rode down to Monkpark in a spray of gravel and a rumble of cattle grid.

'It's less of a secret and more of a revolving door these days,' I said as I flipped the switch and the gaping hole of the servants' old staircase entrance swung open. The darkness seemed to suck at the quiet of the room making it even more hushed, despite the presence of Josh clomping his boots in a nervous fandango against the boards. 'Okay. I'll go up and see where it comes out. You ...'

He gave me a look that was constructed of equal parts guilt and unhappiness.

'... just stay here. If those stairs aren't safe you might have to go for help.'

He nodded, then looked at his feet. 'Should be me, y'know,' he muttered. 'They're my birds, and I lost the key.'

'I'm lighter, the stairs are less likely to give way if they're a bit dodgy.' Then I looked down at myself, intruding my penguin-covered chest into the room, and at his slender, 'mix and match centuries' shape. 'Probably.'

'But I ...'

'Going,' I said, firmly, and headed off into the fusty depths.

The staircase was plain and serviceable, no swanky carvings or polished oak for the oppressed masses at Monkpark. Just unadorned steps that reached up through the three floors and brought me to an equally plain door, bolted with a slightly rusty old catch that looked as though it might have had a former life holding shut a garden gate. I wriggled it open and cautiously pulled the door until there was a gap large enough for me, and my knitted penguin, to enter.

Obviously the staircase had once opened onto a landing, but now that had been incorporated into a small kitchen, and the door opened into a space which was full of pots and pans and wall-mounted spice racks, like a kind of walk-in larder. I pushed my way through the stacked casserole dishes and baking sheets, stepped over a bag of potatoes and unlatched the outer door to reveal the mysteries of the rest of what was obviously Edmund's flat.

'Wow,' I murmured as the full glories of How the Other Half Lives was gradually exposed. Edmund's kitchen area was fairly basic, but he'd got some top of the range equipment in there, a set of knives that Jamie Oliver would have killed for, a bowl that looked so utterly useless that it had to be a designer piece and some glassware so beautiful that I found myself running my fingertips over it, trying to get close to its elegance through touch. An enormous American coffee machine shone its red 'on' light into the windowless space and illuminated everything with a satanic glow.

Telling myself that I was looking for the keys, course I was, honestly, I went through into the living area, to be met by the most luxurious throws and covers that I'd ever seen outside one of those aspirational lifestyle magazines that Gran didn't hold with but still went through every time one was delivered, with an expression somewhere between martyr and sour milk. Wool so soft that it actually didn't register on my skin, artwork on the walls that I'd seen featured in a Sunday supplement, rugs and lamps and one of those huge candles in a lantern holder, where lighting it would have made you look like an old-style ship wrecker.

I spun on the spot, muttering 'wow' again. There was some seriously expensive kit in here too: a top of the range laptop purred gently on top of a sheaf of stationery and a hi-fi with speakers that looked more like some kind of high tech torture device. On my third rotation I spotted a bowl, carved from tree rootstock, inside which I could see a handful of keys, each bearing a paper label as all the estate keys did. I rummaged and came up with the bird barn key, and only the knowledge that Josh was waiting, increasingly desperately, stopped me from checking out the rest of the flat. I could only imagine what sort of bedroom Edmund would have, if his living space was this lavish.

Then I paused, keys swinging from between my fingers and a memory of that Heritage Trust report knocking gently on the door that lay between Edmund's flat and Wendy's office. Feeling horribly guilty, and also a little bit proud of myself, I went over to the laptop, which sat on the speakers. The screen was black, but a blue light indicated that it was switched on and running, illuminating the beautiful sepia sheets it rested on top of, like a modern police car appearing in a black and white film. Almost as though I expected sirens, I crept over and touched the mousepad with the tip of one finger then jumped back as the machine whined into life and the screen lit up.

His desktop background was one of the brochure pictures of Monkpark, spread under summer heat with the gardens alive with flowers, but the picture was barely visible under all the documents and files, peeping out in snatches of colour like a jigsaw half done. Still at fingertip level, and keeping the hand with the keys cocked at what was, I knew, a comedy angle, I swirled the mouse around the desktop and opened a random document.

It was a spreadsheet. I felt my long atrophied financial nerves twitch at the sight of the columns of figures and, almost before I knew it, I found myself sitting in front of the computer and scanning through. Then I closed that file, checked over the desktop, and opened another, related file.

Edmund was practically printing money. There were letters, headed by the Monkpark logo and probably printed out on the Trust stationery beneath the computer, and emails from his official Heritage address, all to various 'ghost hunting' companies, both local and national. He'd got a standard letter, which he was using to tout for custom and then more personalised replies and he was keeping track of the earnings, both actual and potential on the spreadsheet. Four thousand pounds for an average night in Monkpark, two thousand for midnight till three, and we'd had – I checked over the final column on that spreadsheet – five all nighters, seventeen groups and individuals for part of a night, and one, the Northern Ghost and Supernatural Investigation Group, who had stayed (presumably either in the attics or the unused wine store) for three days.

I looked at the bottom line. Profit. Edmund had, so far, cleared nearly a hundred thousand pounds. *A hundred thousand pounds ...* no wonder he'd got that coffee machine and all that lovely, tasteful art, and *I'd been helping him*. Monkpark in financial trouble my arse. If he'd been putting the money into wages, or offsetting Trust costs for the running of the house, that would have been one thing but – a quick browse through other documents and Edmund's search history showed – he was using the money for, among other things, keeping a racehorse in training, a portfolio of stocks and shares, and an account at John Lewis with a balance that made my eyes water.

I flopped away from the keyboard, suddenly boneless with guilt. All those groups that I'd let into the house, kept an eye on, and there were others I'd never even known about. All of them paying money to keep Edmund in the style to which, I looked around the beautifully furnished room, he had evidently become most accustomed. Something sharp dug into my palm and I realised I'd still got the bird barn keys, that Josh was still waiting for me downstairs. That I *had* to do something, or Edmund would keep on using Monkpark as his own personal earning potential, while the rest of us lived in our tied cottages, owing our living to the estate.

I bit my lip. What could I do? I daren't steal the laptop, if he thought his earner was in danger then he'd probably shut it all down and deny everything, there'd be no … proof.

Out of Edmund's front door, wedging it open with a handmade brogue, across the landing and into Wendy's office, cold and silent without the rattle of the keyboard and the hiss and hum of computers and photocopiers. Into the third drawer down of the desk where all the consumables for the computer were kept, a new mouse, the cables to connect things to other things and … the USB flash drives that Wendy used when she needed to save work to finish off at home or to back up files. There were four in there, one still in its packaging and, muttering a silent apology to her, I pulled this one free of its bubble casing, tearing at it in frantic desperation and leaving a shredded bit of cardboard and tatters of plastic in her bin.

I ran back across the landing to Edmund's flat, kicked the shoe away from the door, and copied across everything I could think of to the memory stick, which, not having any pockets, I shoved under the sweater, tucking it under the shoulder strap of my bra. Then, still carrying the keys to the bird barn at a stupid 'these keys are not incriminated in any way' angle, I squeezed my way through the back of the kitchen cupboard and out onto the dark, enclosed staircase beyond.

After the designer-scented air of the flat, this smelled of dust and possible dead mice. 'Did you get it?' Josh's voice was a cross between a hiss and a whisper.

'Yes. Why are you whispering?'

'I don't know. I think the house might be listening.'

I grinned to myself and started down the staircase. Which

surprised me by shuddering like a wet dog and revealing a sudden, gaping hole halfway down, which swallowed my legs and left me pinned by the waist, digging my elbows into the wood to stop myself from plummeting down into the darkness. My bird-chewed arm was agony. I must have caught it against something, because it throbbed with each heartbeat, the pain fogging my head for a moment.

Josh's voice was suddenly louder, echoing up the stairs. 'What? Amy, what's happened? Are you all right?'

I wriggled. Everything I'd seen upstairs suddenly whirled away into insignificance compared to my current plight, caught between two sharp-edged planks of wood where a step had given way underneath me. My feet were suspended and, for the first time ever, I was thankful for my sturdy build, which seemed to be the only thing that was stopping me from dropping through the hole. In fact, not to put too fine a point on it, I was wedged, but the cracking sounds coming from the wood around me, and the wobbly feeling of the planking on either side, led me to believe this may be a temporary state of affairs. The pain in my arm stopped me from being able to prise myself free the same way I went in. I'd have had to lean on both elbows to raise myself up and – nope, my forearm screamed at me and my vision went all red.

'I think so. But I daren't move, I can't see how bad the damage is or how far I might fall.'

A pause, during which I could hear his worried breathing.

'I'm not sure what to do.'

'I can't,' Josh said, quickly. 'I can't come in there, Amy, I'm sorry.' And he sounded so torn and unhappy that I could almost feel the split inside him, half wanting to overcome his fears to help me and yet nailed to the past by horror.

'It's okay,' I said, as soothingly as I could given that I could be facing a sudden drop to a broken neck. 'There's nothing you could do anyway. Any more weight might send these stairs into splinters. My arm hurts when I try to lever myself free, so I can't go up but I think I might be able to wriggle out and go down ... I just need to be able to *see* ... can you push the door right open, try to get some more light in?'

A feeble beam of light appeared, whirled around the cavernous space and didn't help at all. 'That's my torch. Got a bit fried in the river, but it's something.'

'I need it up here so I can disentangle myself without falling down the hole.' There was one of those creaking noises that is always described as 'ominous' and I stopped breathing until it settled back into the dusty silence again. 'And I think I might need it quickly.'

There was the vague flickering outline of Josh's head, illuminated by the Library lights and accentuated by the pinpoint glow of the torch. He got as far as head and shoulders, then I heard the raspy sound of his breathing, the sudden snatching in of air as his fear descended over him again.

'Can't.'

The little part of me that wanted to yell at Gran, wanted to tell Julia what I really thought of her, muttered in my head, but I shut it up. He would if he could. I knew that absolutely. The stair creaked again and the bit under my supporting elbow bent in a little.

'Can you throw it up?'

'Can't see you enough to aim.' His panic seemed to have subsided a bit, maybe subsumed under the practicalities of having something to sort out, which was good because I was beginning to brood a nice case of dread of my own. Although I couldn't see, I estimated I was about halfway up the staircase, leaving me a good floor and a half to drop. Even if I landed chest first, I couldn't see myself bouncing out of this one and my heart was beginning to thump so hard that my penguin was twitching. 'Throw me the keys.'

'*What?*' My brain tried to process this. Was he going to leave me here?

'I've got an idea, but I need the key for the barn.'

The keys were in my hand, embossed on my palm by panic. I managed a feeble swoop of the arm without causing more than a shudder of staircase, and heard the flap and rattle as they hit the wall near the door.

'Got them.' His whisper was back. 'Don't move.'

And he was gone. I hung there, in the dark. Above me I could see the faintest smear of light coming through from the door to the flat, inching through from the bright, airy living room. Below me ... well, I didn't want to think too hard about 'below', it was probably lots of bits of loose wood, splinters and a fifteen foot drop. My mind briefly dwelt on shattered ankles before a renewed creaking and distinct wobble made me concentrate my thoughts on hanging on for grim death. If anything happened to me ... what would happen to Gran? Where would she live? Who would listen to her monologues about spoon theft and disturbed curtains?

I tried a small wiggle to see if I could get any part of my torso free but the knitted sweater was thoroughly snagged on the broken wood. I could feel sharp edges digging into me even through the wool, my arm hurt if I tried to put too much pressure on it, and I daren't even try to untangle myself when I couldn't see what I was doing or how much more unstable the stairs were getting.

'Hurry up, Josh,' I breathed into the dark. '*Please.*'

There was a noise. Cutting into the dust-laden quiet came a clicking, shuffling sort of noise, like someone trying out their new fingernails on a desk. Behind that sound I could hear Josh's whispered, 'Go on then.'

And I knew what he'd done. The mental image was so clear that I could almost see through the dark.

'Call him,' Josh said, his voice confident as it always became when he had the birds. 'He'll come to you.'

And he did. Practically the only creature that could see in that ghostly non-light came shuffling towards me, hopping across broken wood and kicking his way through splintered rails.

'Skrillex ...' I whistled, the way Josh had taught me, although Skrill was so dim that it was unlikely to make a difference.

'The torch is tied to his leg,' Josh said from the doorway. 'It was all I could think of.'

I wanted to laugh but was afraid that any disturbance of my chest would send me downwards, so I lapsed into a slightly disbelieving grin.

Skrillex loped his way up the broken stairs, lopsided with the Maglite taped loosely to his leg and hampering the already hampered bird. When he reached me he stopped, baffled as to why I didn't immediately hand him some food, and tried to attack my fingers.

'Got it!'

Josh whistled and, with an almost audible sigh, the owl turned around and began hopping and waddling his weightless way back down the stairs. If I'd been closer I bet I could have heard him muttering, 'There had better be some food *this* time.'

The torch showed more clearly how stuck I was, but enabled me to disentangle myself, and illuminated those bits of stair that had kept structural integrity. Using my uninjured elbow to lever myself onto the firm steps, and kicking my legs onto others, I managed to worm my way free. I tucked the memory stick further inside my bra for added safety, from where it jutted like misplaced underwiring, and slid on my stomach to spread the weight. I arrived at ground level, spreadeagled and with my penguin jumper unravelled all the way back to my point of impact, like Ariadne's thread if the Minotaur had had a second floor apartment and an ambiguous attitude to novelty knitwear.

Josh, with a sleepy looking Skrillex on his wrist, helped me out of the doorway. He seemed to feel ashamed of himself, he clearly found it hard to meet my eye, although the fact that my chest was revealed in all its chain-store serviceable bra glory might have had something to do with it.

When we'd closed up the door and stood in the middle of the Library, Skrillex making a beak-clacking noise of annoyance, Josh sighed deeply and broke the silence.

'Should've come and helped you,' he said. 'I crapped up.'

'It's okay,' I said, the adrenaline of relief making my tongue stick to my lips. 'I'm out now, and Skrill was brilliant. Weren't you?' I addressed to the owl, who rotated his head to blink at me and shifted his claws up and down the glove. 'It was your idea to send him in with the torch, so you didn't crap up at all, Josh,' I said, more gently.

Josh's face was grey, his skin tight over his bones.

'Not very heroic though, was I?' He lowered his lips to the feathered head, just brushing them against the deceptively fluffy outer layer. 'Even as your *friend*, Amy ... I should have tried ...'

'Josh ...' I began, but it was no good. With a shrug of his shoulders and an adjustment of Skrillex, he turned and walked out of the room, every line of his body telling me that he felt a failure.

Chapter Thirty-Four

Josh

Didn't think I'd ever been this low before.

Yeah, there were times when it was tough, when I saw girls I'd liked, arms wrapped round some tosser, all snogging on the benches and stupid, giggly morning gossips with their friends. Times when I wondered what it would be like.

But back then I still thought there was some chance I'd get a go. Maybe one day I'd wake up and, hey, I'd forget what had happened when I was younger. The cupboard with the blood dripping and then that bloke, looking at me like I was a car he was going to buy. Then I'd find someone, someone kind who wasn't all about the way I look, and we'd be friends. We'd start being more than friends. We'd kiss and ...

It kind of broke down there, the fantasy. And I knew that I'd got it arse-first, most guys would be fantasising the other way round, shag a girl and then maybe see how it went, but I never got as far as the shagging, because I wanted to make love. A girl who was so into me that I'd forget that sex wasn't just something that was taken from you, but something you gave. But I couldn't even help Amy in the dark. How could I ever love her when I was still so hung up that she could have died on that staircase and I wouldn't have been able to walk in and save her?

So I went through the motions. Flew the birds, did a bit of mending and sorting, ordered a new glove 'cos Skrill had eaten through the fingers on my old one. Watched the house open up to the public again. Saw Amy cooking in the cafe, but only through the windows, I never went in even when she saw me looking and kind of waved.

Loser. Such a loser. Every time I saw her I felt it again. And I knew she didn't care about what I was, but I did and I couldn't look at her knowing that she'd been helpless there in the dark and all I could do was send the bloody owl in to rescue her. Even Skrill, even a bird that has never been able to fly, was more use than I was. So I decided.

I hired a carrier for the birds that'd go on the bike. Checked the bird mags for places that were hiring, found somewhere out East Anglia way that wanted birds flown and would give me a place to live. Norfolk, all sky and water, no distracting girls with their penguin jumpers and beautiful eyes to make me feel guilty about what I was. Took the job, packed up the van and flew the birds one last time over Yorkshire.

I was back at the barn boxing up the kit when she found me.

'Hi, Josh!' she called, for all the world like nothing was wrong. 'Brought you some coffee cake that's left over. For some reason everyone's on a healthy eating kick and those granola bars are going like nobody's business. I am absolutely *not* going to mention how much butter goes into them.'

I couldn't look at her. 'Thanks.'

'What are you doing?'

I shoved some more of the spare leatherwork into the bag. 'Packing.'

She made a little noise, like she didn't want to attract my attention, and a few moments went by. The birds were perched, but all rousing their feathers like they expected action. 'Why? And why not say something?'

I shrugged. Nothing to say, still.

'I've been wondering, you know,' she kept talking as if I wasn't getting set to leave, 'about this stuff I found in Edmund's flat.'

'Stuff?' I stopped for a moment, just to rest my fingers.

'While I was up there … he's got all this fabulous gear, it's like something out of *Country Living* in his flat. I looked some of it up, the music stuff is worth over three grand,

and there's a coffee machine that cost more than my year's salary.'

She bit into the piece of cake she'd brought for me and my mouth watered. Looked so good.

'And his laptop was just sort of ... *there* and I was wondering and yesterday James came into the cafe and we were chatting, and he said that you and he helped move Edmund's stuff in when he arrived?'

A question. She wanted an answer, her sideways look and that raised eyebrow were full of it. 'Yeah.' Still tipping her head in my direction, wanting more. 'He had stuff but nothing that amazing.'

'Coffee machine? Huge thing, so big we could use it in the cafe?'

My mouth wanted to smile at her. Even though I was leaving, even though I'd let her down, she made me want to smile. 'Nah. I'd remember. The hernia would remind me.'

'So where did he get the money from to buy that kind of kit?' She licked icing off her fingers and my jeans puckered. Hated my body, sometimes. 'And I thought, maybe he could have inherited it. He does drive a posh car, after all.'

''S not that special.' Didn't want to but something about Amy was pulling me into the conversation. Like I couldn't *not* talk. 'Maybe he earned enough. He's single, don't think he's got a load of kids he's paying for ...'

Evershit wasn't the 'dad' kind. Not that I'm much cop at recognising father material, I know that someone who cares that much about the clothes they wear isn't going to be up for mucky fingers and sicky babies.

'Well, I was once in the office when Wendy was doing John's wages and she left the machine on and I ... well, just professional curiosity and everything.' And she gave me the cheekiest smile. 'And I don't think Edmund got a huge raise to come here, so ... nope, not in the industrial coffee machine purchasing bracket at all.'

I could smell that vanilla and sugar smell from her now. It overpowered the smell of the birds – that dry, powdery kind of smell that is just feather and droppings and leather, and kind of rose to fill the whole barn like she'd been cooking in there. Made my mouth water again.

'Is he creaming off money from the ghost hunting thing?' Interested now, in spite of myself.

'Well, this is where it gets interesting.' She licked down the last of the coffee icing and crunched on a walnut. 'While I was in there I just sort of ... *borrowed* some of the documents he had on his computer, because it seemed a bit odd, him saying that Monkpark was in trouble when the official line is that we are, like, mega success of the year.'

A sudden image of Evershit, all cocky tailoring and that half-sneery look on his smooth face. 'The estate isn't in trouble at all?' I'd stopped packing. Only realised when I took a step towards her. 'Seriously? All that getting up like some seventeenth century prick and I thought it was for the good of the Hall? When really—'

'Oh, the events have all been put through the books, all official. Even if they were my idea and he's taken the credit for them, they were kind of legit. No, it's just the ghost hunting business that was all Edmund earning himself a nice little lump sum.' She brushed off her fingers and wouldn't look at me now. 'You were going.'

'I ... how did you know?'

She did a sort of jump, like she was stiffening from inside. 'Oh, I dunno. Maybe the fact that Wendy did your references, or could it be that you are bloody *packing up* right in front of me? Josh ...'

Couldn't look at her face now. Started sorting out Fae and Bane for the trip.

'I let you down, Amy. When it came to it, I let you down, and I don't want to have to think about that every time I see you.'

'But I—'

'Look. It was bad enough all those years ago, leaving my mum behind. Walking out knowing I couldn't help her, and this was like it all over again. Something really bad could have happened on that staircase, and I wouldn't have been able to help. I'd have let you die in there rather than walk into the dark, and nobody needs a friend like that.'

I untied Bane from her perch, but she wouldn't move onto the glove.

'You went up there for me and I couldn't even ...' The words went down into my chest, hiding from the light.

'You sent Skrillex in with the torch, Josh. Okay, you couldn't come in but you did the next best thing and if you hadn't, I'd probably still be hanging there, or lying in a pile of matchwood on the floor with a broken leg!'

She moved in now, further in, and the birds were all looking at her as if she was going to set them free. Bane roused her feathers again.

'Being a friend isn't asking you to overcome every fear you've ever had, you know.' She quietened her voice like she knew the birds were listening. 'Some really serious shit happened to you, Josh, stuff that won't just go away because you or I want it to. You left your mum because you *had* to, to survive and you are living with that guilt. Even though you know there was nothing you could do, she was an adult, she made her own decisions. Like Gran says, it took her dad years to get over the war, even when he had a wife and a daughter and a lovely settled life to come back to, he couldn't just forget it all. It changed him, and it took more than just wanting to change back and a few months to make it happen.'

She was touching me now, very carefully, making sure her fingers and her hand were out of Bane's reach. Guess she'd learned from Fae.

Half of me wanted to pull away. Didn't want that touch,

229

that sympathy, that *understanding*. Because if she understood even a part of what had happened to me, that meant she was pulled in further than I'd ever want her to be, to a world of horror and the dark. But the other half of me ... the other half leaned in to that touch like it craved it. Her touching me made me feel human.

'What if it won't ever go?'

'Time, Josh. Time and determination. And, if great-granddad was anything to go by, an enormous amount of whisky, but let's just skip that stage, shall we?' Her fingers were there, on my arm, above the glove. Warm through my shirt. 'Don't go.'

Bane shivered her feathers again but still didn't step onto the glove. When I looked round the birds were all averting their eyes, Skrill looked as if he'd gone to sleep, and even Malkin was focussing very hard on a beetle crawling across his perch.

'I'm no kind of friend,' I said. Almost whispered it.

'Hey, at least you haven't slept with my fiancé.' She was whispering too, but there was something that was almost a giggle in her voice. 'So, you know, brownie points for that and all.'

And suddenly it was bright, the sun sliding in through the part-open door and I could smell the air on her, fresh and open, and see her face a bit mischievous with that half-giggle still trapped on her lips and I leaned in there and I took it off her with my own mouth. Just touching her, like I sometimes kissed the top of Skrill's feathery head when he sat on my hand all sleepy and vulnerable and I thought what could have happened to him if I hadn't picked him up and that there could be a world without him in it.

Amy stood very still. 'Did you just kiss me?'

'I'm not sure. I think so.' My body thought so too. A kiss. My first, real kiss. Intentional and wanted and I could taste the coffee on my own mouth. And I wasn't freaking.

'Well. Oh God, I sound just like Gran.' I could feel her hand on my arm, it had got a lot warmer, and her other hand came up and sort of fanned at her face. 'That's, umm ...'

'That's progress,' I said.

'Oh, definitely. Yes. Progress.' She was still fanning and her cheeks were red from her forehead down.

'Do you think I should stay?'

I knew I'd made the decision already. Would it have been different if Bane had stepped onto my glove? If the birds had boxed up instead of hunkering themselves down onto their perches and pretending to ignore me? Was all of life like this, balanced on a two-way pivot? If Skrillex had never been hit by that car, if he'd never learned to like Amy ...

'Of course I think you should stay, you fruitcake.' No sting in her words, just the dying of the blush on her face and a little tightening of her fingers on my shirt. 'When have I ever said I wanted you to go?'

My body had had a chance to process what had happened now and my heart was going so fast that it was making me sweat. 'I dunno.' Didn't want to break contact or lose that warm hand, but I needed the space so I stepped back and covered myself by brushing my hair with my fingers.

'All right, all right.' She sounded a bit shaky too. 'How about staying until we've managed to bring Edmund down? I mean, I seriously can't believe that he's been using us all, and our fear of being out of our houses and jobs, just to make himself money. If he was nursing a sick mother or something then maybe I'd understand, well, no I wouldn't because it's still bent as anything but ... honestly, Josh, he's got that flat looking like he's expecting *Tatler* round to do a photo shoot, and here's me staying up all night to stop dubious blokes from pissing in the cupboards!' A deep breath. 'So. Are you in?'

I thought of Norfolk. Of the flat landscapes and the bleak skies over the sea, and being able to watch the birds fly for miles. And then, of being so far away from Amy.

'Okay. I'm in.'

Everything about her relaxed then and I realised how she'd been holding herself tense, afraid that this was it, I was walking away. And I felt a tiny bit of guilt that I'd made her feel that way, but it was massively outweighed by the pride I felt in kissing her and making her blush.

'Yeah. I'm in,' I said again.

Chapter Thirty-Five

Amy

Edmund had been using me. That also shouldn't have come as much of a surprise. Josh was the only man I'd known who hadn't looked in my eyes and seen something leaping up and down behind them waving a banner saying 'low self-esteem! Will drop knickers for dubious excuses!' Even though I hadn't dropped so much as a handkerchief, and Edmund would have run a mile if I had, the principle was the same. I had thought Guy ... I'd thought he was different too, as different as he'd pretended to be, but, in the end, he'd come down on the side of being Just Another Bloke.

And, I thought, as I waited for Gran's bus to pull in, seeing her already standing up as though if she weren't ready for immediate disembarkation the bus would drive past, what had I expected, seriously. Edmund had used me, and I'd let him. For the sake of a plan that a bunch of teenagers and a talking dog would have seen through, I'd gone along with him. All right, I'd thought I was doing the right thing by Monkpark, but ...

'Place is a mess.'

'Yes, Gran. I'll tidy up later.'

'I mean, look at those curtains, just look!'

I flipped the kettle switch down. Somehow, with the knowledge that Josh had kissed me, her comments had become easier to bear. That one little action that came so easily to other people yet was a massive hurdle for him, had been overcome. Okay, he may never kiss me again, may never manage to be in that headspace that let his thoughts free for long enough again, but he'd done it. He'd become the man he wanted to be, just for that second.

'What are you smiling about, madam?'

233

'Nothing, Gran.'

'Hmm. Someone's been at these spoons again. Look at the state of them.'

Sweet, lovely Josh. Who didn't look at me and see a fat, plain girl so bound up with Monkpark that I might as well have had 'Property of the Hall' tattooed on my forehead. He didn't see a lack of ambition, the hatred of confrontation that kept my tongue bitten into soreness all wrapped up in an Edwardian uniform that did its best to squeeze me into an acceptable shape. He saw … what did he see? A friend. Someone he could talk to. Someone he could *kiss* …

'And you can take that expression off your face and pour the tea.'

Behind us, in the passage, the telephone rang, its bell as loud and peremptory as the bells to summon the servants that hung in the Old Kitchen.

'Who'd be ringing us?' Gran looked put out and baffled. 'Nobody rings us. Except your mother, and she only rings on a Saturday or birthdays.'

We stood and stared at the telephone as though it might be about to explode. 'Just a thought, but answering it might sort out the whole "Who's ringing us" question,' I said. 'I'll get it, shall I?' Silly question, I'd never yet known Gran to leap up and forestall anything I might be about to do, unless it looked as though there might have been fun involved. 'Might be important. Or a sales call.'

'Miss Knowles?' The voice was efficient. 'This is Malcolm Webber from the Heritage Trust.' A no-nonsense voice. 'There is to be a meeting tomorrow morning at Monkpark Hall and the Trust is most anxious that all members of staff should attend.'

He sounded senior. He sounded as if he meant business.

My stomach wobbled. I'd made the phone call anonymously, phoning from Wendy's office when she'd left for the day and Edmund had been in the Library, sorting out a flooring issue.

I'd thought they might ignore it, but evidently not. 'Um,' I said. 'What is the meeting about?'

'I'm not at liberty to discuss that, Miss Knowles, but the Trust looks forward to seeing you tomorrow. I've been unable to contact a Mister Scott, perhaps you could pass on the message? It really is most important that all staff are there.'

When I put the phone down I must have looked a bit dazed because Gran noticed. 'Kettle's boiled and you look like someone's slipped a teacake down your pinnie,' she said. 'Better get the tea made.'

'Gran, will you be all right here for a bit? I need to bike down to the van and talk to Josh.'

Gran grunted. ''Course I'll be all right. I keep telling you, Amy, there is nothing wrong with me. You think I'm daft just because I'm old—'

'And because you always think someone has been in the house when we've both been out all day!' The words were unintended.

'Someone has. Those curtains do not disarrange themselves, young lady, and someone has been rotating my spoons. Don't you try and tell me differently.'

'But—'

'I know the evidence of my own eyes. Now, you said you were going out. Just pour the tea and put *Pointless* on before you go.'

I was on the bike and halfway up the hill before she could reconsider, or stop to think and decide that only 'girls who were no better than they should be' went out visiting unattached young men at this time of the evening. Sometimes Gran came over as if she'd been raised in the eighteenth century.

The roads were all cleared, the snow had been washed back to frilly edges along the verge and silent humps under the hawthorns, so cycling up and over the hill and freewheeling down the other side didn't take too long and I arrived at the van just as Josh was emptying a bucket outside the door.

'The Heritage Trust called. They're coming tomorrow to have some kind of big meeting and they want everyone there.'

Josh shook the bucket. 'Okay. I shall try to fit it in to my busy schedule.'

I stayed on the track, still straddling the bike and looked at Josh. There was a more relaxed look on his face now, as though he'd made a decision that had been gnawing at him for a while.

'What are you doing?'

He looked back behind him. 'Cleaning out the van.'

'Because ...?' The thought that he might have decided to move on again, even after our discussion – and the kiss – crossed my mind.

'Thought I might get somewhere a bit more ... well, somewhere with a floor, for starters. This was great when I came, but I want somewhere I can ...' He gave a shrug and looked down at the grass where there was steam rising from the tipped water. 'Y'know.' Now he raised his eyes and looked directly at me. There was a kind of burning hope in that brown gaze, a patient sort of optimism. His life was changing. Slowly, but still changing.

'Josh ...'

'Yeah. Never going to be easy, not for either of us. But, maybe, I thought, if we want it enough ...' He stepped back into the doorway of the van. 'Coming in?'

'Being in there isn't "coming in". It's like "sheltering" or something. This van is basically outdoors with a roof.' But I leaned the bike against the hedge and followed him up the steps. 'So. The Trust are coming tomorrow.'

Josh looked at me, raised his eyebrows and wiped a rag along the cracked melamine of the work surface. 'Cleaning' was probably not the right word for what this caravan needed, but flame-throwers are hard to come by.

'Anything to do with you, Amy?'

'Might be.' I couldn't meet his eye. 'I helped him, though,

Josh. Technically I'm as guilty as he is. I might lose my job over this, Gran will lose her house. All I know is that I can't let him keep getting away with it, so I had to do something.'

He threw the rag into the bucket and I felt the floor dip and buckle as he came over to where I stood in the doorway, not quite sure whether I should come further in. 'You thought everything could go. You went along with him to keep our jobs and houses, did you think of that?'

I shifted about. 'Well, yes, sort of. It's not much of a legal defence though.'

Now he was standing so close that the boarding of the van floor was creaking under our combined weight. I could feel a kind of heat from his skin and the urge to brush a hand through his disorderly hair was immense. I settled for putting a hand on his arm. He didn't shake it off or move away, in fact, he stepped a little bit closer, until his body touched mine.

'Then we'll go down together,' he said.

And this time the kiss was stronger, more urgent. As though his previous kiss had broken some kind of barrier and now he knew how things went. His mouth was on mine with no tentativeness, his arms went around behind me and held me in close and I felt a surge of desire that burst up through the layers of me that they'd been submerged beneath. The layers of lack of self-worth, the duty, the knowing that I was always going to be second best, they all shattered as I kissed Josh back, burning from the core of me with wanting. Fighting with myself not to panic him, not to push him, just to take that kiss as it was offered, and losing myself in the feel of his stubble tickling my skin into an almost unbearable arousal.

'Wow.' He stepped back and lowered his hands to his sides. He looked so surprised that I started to laugh.

'I guess all those millions of years of biology knew what they were doing.' There was a warmth to my skin that told me I was blushing, and my eyes felt as though they'd been stretched open. Against my body my clothes felt different, as though my shirt hung in a new way and my jeans were tighter and thicker than they had been. 'But this can be all there is, Josh. We never have to take it any further, I will still be your friend.'

He was still looking stunned, now raising his hands to rake through his hair. 'No. I want … I think I can do this, Amy. I want you and me to be like all those other people out there that we see. Like Julia and her bloke. Holding hands.' Now he stretched a hand out and took mine, naturally, as if he'd always done it. 'Kissing.' A light brush across my mouth that made my body leap again. 'Making love.'

'Don't rush it,' I whispered. 'We've got time, we've always got time.'

'Oh, I don't mean *now*. We'd get hypothermia, and besides, I've never … I need to put in a bit of time on Google, put it that way. I want to get it right with you, Amy. I want *us* to get it right.'

'You think we can be an "us"? I mean, I've got Gran and you've got … well, complications.'

He ran a light finger over my cheek, almost in wonder. 'Never thought I'd get to know what this feels like,' he said, very quietly. 'And that is worth all the complications.'

I breathed in the warmth and the scent of him. He smelled of cold air, the outdoors and my face smiled almost without my knowledge. 'Just checking,' I said, and leaned in to drop a quiet kiss on his lips. 'Just making sure.'

There was a comfortable familiarity in the feel of his body next to mine, even through the many layers of my wool duffel coat. As though this had been in the past, and would be again in the future, and it would be him. Always Josh. Untidy and wayward, but with the face that could have graced a magazine cover.

'Josh …'

He seemed to sense the change of subject in my body language, because he shifted beside me. 'Yeah?'

'If anything happens, if they take me away or something, will you look after Gran? Just until I can find somewhere for us. I don't think they can put me in prison or anything drastic.' I swallowed hard. 'But it might take a while for me to find another job and somewhere to live. You'll still be here, so. You know. Keep an eye on her.'

Josh turned his head and looked down at me. 'That won't happen, Amy,' he said, fiercely. 'You were misled. More than that, the bastard lied to you and threatened you with losing the cafe, that has to count for something!'

I swallowed again. 'Yes, but if. Just if. I have to know that Gran will be all right.'

He shifted again, and I could feel his unease. 'How can you trust me? I left my mum behind with a bloke who punched her, Amy. I ran out on her. I should have stayed and—'

'And what? You were a *child*, Josh! How were you meant to force her? She didn't want to go with you, well, it was her decision.' I stepped in closer, turned, so that I could see his face. 'You have never failed anyone. Ever. And I know you won't fail Gran, if it comes to it, all right?'

He rubbed his knuckles over his forehead as if he was trying to rub my meaning into his brain. 'You really trust me?'

'Yes. I really trust you. You are the nicest person I know.' And then, my practical side reasserted itself for a moment. 'But then, I've lived here all my life, and I am aware that Monkpark isn't exactly the last resting place for moral rectitude.'

His fingers knotted through mine and he stared down at our conjoined grip. 'It's nice to be trusted, even when I don't really trust myself, you know. Yes, if the worst happens I'll take care of your gran. But it's not going to. And here's where you can trust me again, because you're not a criminal. You're just a lovely girl who sees the best in people, for which I am bloody glad.' He stroked my knuckles with his thumb. 'Now, you'd better get back to your gran and those spoons.'

'Subtle way of getting rid of me,' but I laughed and slowly

unwound our hands, then looked around the van. 'Any ideas where you're going to go?'

Josh leaned against the worktop, which creaked and one end went a few inches up in the air. 'Not really. But I want something a bit more ...'

'Indoorsy? Warm? Not quite as much like a bit of corrugated iron over some mud?'

He smiled. There was a new set to his face now, one that almost wiped away the wary creasing around his mouth. 'Permanent. Can't make much of a life from here. I was never going to stay here, y'see, just passing through, until ... well.' The smile turned a bit shy. 'Now I want to start a proper life.'

'In a house? Are you sure?'

A strong, level gaze which had a layer of darkness taken out of it and replaced with hope. 'Reckon so. Think I can cope with a roof and a door now.' And now he met my eyes. 'Reckon I can cope with a lot of things now.'

'You're a very brave man.' I said it very quietly, hoping he'd know what I meant.

'You listened, Amy.' His reply was equally as quiet. 'You didn't just look like a lot of people do, you wanted to know what was under the surface and, okay, that was all shit and darkness and guilt, but you never flinched.' He was still looking into my eyes and the hand not trying to prevent the work surface from tipping him up stroked my duffel-coated arm. 'That's what's helped me to cope. Knowing that you know me and you don't think I'm something too damaged to mend.'

There was one of those moments then, where the whole world seems to have forgotten that you are in it. As if the caravan had somehow slipped into a crack between universes, no longer belonging anywhere, and outside the rooks called as they swung home to their nests in the gathering darkness. Josh gave me the briefest of cheek touches, and then I was away, heading back to Gran with a head full of beckoning newness.

Chapter Thirty-Six

Josh

I'd put Bane up, watching her ride the wind. Could almost feel that freedom on the cross-breeze, like someone had taken this great lead sheet off me; a sheet that had kept me warm and a weight I'd kind of relied on, but now I could feel the air for the first time. Made my heart sort of lift in my chest, and when I thought of Amy and the kind of future that we, maybe, could have ... well, then it swooped and dived like Bane, like Fae, homing in on something it really, really wanted.

Amy was in the cafe. I could just see her through the window if I squinted, and I could smell the baking coming at me on the cold air. Warm. Promising. Like Amy.

'Hey, Josh.' James came up, careful not to upset the bird. 'Boss wants us all in the Old Kitchen in ten minutes.'

'What for?' Even though I knew, I didn't want to let on. Even though it was James, and he's the kind of bloke who wouldn't care. Evershit could have been an international art thief and James wouldn't be bothered, as long as the onion sets got put in on time and Artichoke Sam didn't get himself arrested.

'No idea, mate.' He leaned in a bit. 'Bloody great Volvo just arrived though, so probably some posh twat he wants us to hang out the bunting for.' He shrugged. Didn't care. 'Okay?'

I whistled Bane in to the lure and she dived down, coming over James' head like she knew it'd make him jump. Don't tell me the birds don't have a sense of humour. 'Yeah.'

Over my shoulder I could see inside the cafe, Wendy had come down from her place up in the offices to tell Amy and Julia the same thing, it looked like. James and me were being totally 'bloke', staring at Bane sitting on the glove, while the women were breaking out the buns and having a chat session. I got a little shiver then at the differences between us – could Amy and I really get something going? Seriously? Could I really let myself believe in her? And then she looked up, her eyes met mine through the window and across the yard and she gave me a little bit of a wink that she hid behind a cupcake so the others couldn't see and I knew then. *Knew*. 'Course we could make it. She knew me right through, like I knew her. Knowing was what it was all about.

Bane stepped onto the perch and I fastened her on. 'Come on then, mate, don't let's keep the boss man waiting.' James waited till I was clear then gave me a punch on the arm. It was like he could feel I was different too, he'd always kept a distance before. ''Sides, they might have some more of that free booze going.'

Wanted to tell him not to get his hopes up, this was not a 'meet and greet' but something bigger. Wanted to tell him that Evershit had put us all on the line just so he could fill his wallet, but I didn't dare.

'Yeah.'

I followed him down to the Library doors. Everyone was trickling in from various parts of the house and garden, all chatting excited-like, the lads wiping their hands down their jeans when they saw that there were women there, all trying to tidy themselves up without looking like they were doing anything special, knocking the mud off their boots on the wall outside. Room guides came fluttering in from 'their' rooms, some carrying the big files they used to answer questions. I saw Wendy nip out and put the 'Closed' sign at the entrance to the yard – must be bad if they were closing the house …

We all kind of funnelled down the corridor to the Old Kitchen and I found myself next to Amy. Maybe she'd waited for me. She was all pink from the ovens and she had her white coat on, all smeared in icing like she'd wiped her hands down it. I looked down at my hands then, if everyone was at it maybe there was some point, but they looked clean enough so I didn't bother.

'Here we go, then,' Amy whispered to me. Her breath felt hot on my skin but all my little hairs prickled like I was cold. She showed me her hand with the little black memory stick in it. Dynamite.

'*Josh* ...' She lowered her voice even more and I couldn't tell if she was angry or what.

'Worried?' I whispered back.

She pulled a kind of 'bad smell' face. 'I thought I would be, but now it turns out that I'm not.'

Gave her arm a little squeeze. Didn't need to say anything. She was the bravest person I knew, but telling her might upset her, so I just walked through with her into the big room.

It was weird in the Old Kitchen. Made me realise how this lot had 'Monkpark' tattooed on their souls – there were a load of chairs in there but they all had 'please do not sit on this chair' signs on them, and not one person even leaned on them, or the table. All just sort of milled around by the walls. And there was a bloke there that I didn't know, looking kind of 'workaday posh', good clothes that must have been expensive, proper tweedy jacket and cords with those shoes that look handmade, but all worn and a bit crumpled. But he had these eyes, falcon's eyes, like he wouldn't miss anything, for all he was smiling and saying, 'Good morning,' to everyone as they came in. Like he could afford to be relaxed.

'I think that's Malcolm Webber, from the Trust.' Amy was still beside me, her head bobbing against my shoulder in the crowd and little puffs of icing sugar coming up off her coat.

Everyone started to go quiet then, someone else closed the door that led through into the house, and then, there we all were, shut in. Big room, but shut in. My hands started to sweat, but I calmed down when Amy leaned over and slid open the little window near the stone sink.

'Stay near here,' she whispered. 'Plenty of fresh air.'

I was just about to, maybe, touch her hand, let her know I was grateful, when there was a little buzz of noise. Everyone had seen Evershit come in, being led by a woman who looked like she was built of plastic corners.

'If you could just take a seat, Mister Evershott,' she said, and there was like this intake of breath when he sat on one of the 'do not sit on this chair' seats, though, to be fair, I didn't see where else he could have sat, unless he'd squatted on the table.

Malcolm Webber got started then. Told us all that there'd been 'information received' that there'd been 'misuse of the house' and that they'd interviewed Evershit and now they wanted anyone to come forward with anything they knew. And all the while Shitface had this kind of smile, like he knew he was getting out of this, that no one would say anything against him because they all wanted to keep their jobs and their houses. Besides, who knew anything, except for him and Amy?

Amy had this look on her face like she'd sort of frozen. And I knew what was happening, she was thinking about her gran, about losing everything. Wanting to speak but afraid of the consequences, and I knew all about that, even if my consequences had been a leather strap across the face. And I suddenly thought 'he's going to get away with it'. That bastard was going to get off with making her sit up all hours to keep an eye on the groups, and taking all the money. So I kind of took a deep breath.

'Ask him about the cars coming down to Monkpark at all hours,' I said. Voice a little bit shaky but I did it. 'Late at night.'

Webber and the sharp woman exchanged a look. Her eyebrows moved a fraction, that was all.

And then Sam said, 'Yeah, he's right. I was out ... just out, few nights back and this bloody van came up the drive, must have been eleven, twelve o'clock. Thought it was just some bugger lost, but he never asked directions, just drove up to the house like he knew where he was going.'

Turned out that a lot of us had seen or heard something. Some people had been stopped and asked if they worked at the Hall, and then given the third degree about ghosts and stuff. Wendy, looking all sheepish and apologetic at Evershit, said that someone from a TV production company had rung her up, saying that they'd heard Monkpark ran ghost hunting sessions and could they come and film one? She'd sent them away with a mouthful, but ... just thought she'd mention it.

We were all looking at Evershit now. But he'd just crossed his legs and started picking at the chair arm with a nail, all kind of bored, just this little smile on his face that I wanted to smack so hard it would make him sit funny. Like, it didn't matter what we said, he knew he was getting out of this all rosy.

'All right, all right.' Webber held up a hand. 'This is meant to be an initial conversation, not a witch hunt. Mister Evershott, perhaps you'd like to give your perspective on things?'

And maybe it was a premonition or something, but I'd swear I felt the hair on the back of my neck start to prick, all itchy and tight. Evershit stood up, chair screeching on the tiled floor, and sort of brushed at his trousers with a fingertip, like he didn't have a care in the world. 'I'd actually just like to say ...' And it was more of a drawl than actual words. '... that you've all got completely the wrong end of the stick. I'm as much a victim of this as everyone else and I am shocked and horrified at what I have allowed to happen here.'

He'd got that smile again. All condescending, like he knew we'd made a stupid mistake but he was going to forgive us because we were all so stupid and heavy-brained that it was a surprise to him that we ever managed to get dressed of a morning.

'So, perhaps you'd like to give us your perspective on events?' Webber had a bit of an edge, like he *wanted* to believe Shitface but couldn't see how.

'With pleasure.' And now that smile was looking round the room. 'You see, it was all Amy Knowles' idea, and she is the one who has been profiting from it.'

Chapter Thirty-Seven

Amy

All I'd been thinking was how much Gran would miss the place if we were forced to move. How she'd not really known anywhere else, and how hard she'd find it to settle in a new house, how it might mean she got even more confused, how I wouldn't be able to look after her if I had to work longer hours to afford a commercial rent. So when Edmund said my name it made me jump and I slowly managed to force my gaze around until I was looking at him.

He met my eye but his expression never changed. He was half-smiling, almost with an expression of pity on his face.

'What?' I said, and then felt that it needed something more but couldn't think of anything. '*What?*'

'A few months ago Amy came to me with a proposition. Oh, I'm not proud of myself, but who here hasn't had his head turned by a ... pretty face?'

There were a few nods, a small laugh of agreement from somewhere. Had nobody else noticed that little pause that changed the whole meaning of his sentence? That little gap before the word 'pretty' that made it all mean the exact opposite?

'And I'm sure that many people here will have been aware that Amy and I were quite ... close, at one time. James, you remember us meeting in the yard? And Tegan, you were there when we went out for dinner together?'

My teeth ground against themselves. So *that* was why he'd taken me to dinner, and why he'd chosen that restaurant, so he'd have witnesses.

'Well, they was all whispering and stuff,' Tegan spoke up from among the crowd.

247

Malcolm Webber was looking at me now, as though he was weighing me up. 'Miss Knowles?'

Edmund didn't give me time to reply. 'I'm sorry, Amy,' he went on, smooth as ice cream. 'And I know you only wanted to fund the care that your grandmother so sorely needs.' He swung his head round to take everyone in. 'You all know that Amy's grandmother is becoming senile, and that Amy is worried about caring for her, don't you?'

A few people exchanged glances, there were some more raised eyebrows.

'She in't bonkers. Evadne Knowles has got more marbles than all of us lot put together.' That was Julia's mum and I felt ridiculously warm towards her for a moment. 'She's a crabby old cow and she made their Karen's life a misery after she got in the family way, but, senile? Nope.' And then she looked down at her feet with her mouth pursed as though she'd said too much, by which time my warm feelings had evaporated a little.

Edmund frowned a bit, but went on. 'Amy had come up with a plan ... that she'd pose as a ghost and Monkpark would attract ghost hunters so that we could charge a fee. Oh, we ... that is, *I* ... knew it was against Trust rules, but Amy can be, ahem ...' He looked down as though ashamed of himself. '... most persuasive.' Another smile, wicked, assuming complicity between himself and his audience. 'And, well, with the state of modern healthcare being what it is, I just wanted to help.'

I opened my mouth to call him a liar, but the past twenty-eight years of being told to be 'nice', that nobody would like me if I spoke out of turn dragged the words back down my throat and nearly choked me. All those years of being 'just fat, plain Amy', backroom girl extraordinaire, unwanted by my mother, dumped by my fiancé, gagged me, bound me and left me standing hopelessly in the middle of the kitchen. And Edmund was *smiling*. I felt every eye in the room on me, a hot weight of collective gazes, assessing me.

'Well, I don't believe it.' It was Wendy, pushing through the crowd to stand in front of Malcolm Webber. Little Wendy, who always seemed grateful for my help in the office, but otherwise not particularly friendly towards me. 'Amy's fabulous. She works really hard in that cafe and she'll help anyone if she can. I can't see her being a fraud.'

And suddenly I unfroze. So what if the Trust sacked me? I'd find something else somewhere, Gran would be fine. Wendy had faith in me. Josh had faith in me. All I needed was for *me* to find some faith in me. 'I've got proof,' I said, quickly, before I chickened out.

'Aye.' James cut in. 'I expect you have, Amy love. They were no more "quite close" than I am with Sam's artichokes. And if anyone can see through a daft plonker like Edmund Evershott, it's our Amy. What have you got?'

Malcolm Webber, looking a little bit left behind with the staff takeover of his investigation, raised his eyebrows at me. '*Do* you have proof of wrongdoing, Miss Knowles?'

Everyone was looking at me. I straightened my spine. Shucked off those years of being nondescript, channelled some of the anger I'd managed to find when Julia had tried to seduce Josh, and went out to fight my corner. 'I have. I copied a load of files off Edmund's computer, spreadsheets, bank statements.' I handed the little black plastic stick over. 'It shows that he's been using Monkpark Hall to make money for himself.'

Edmund jumped to his feet. 'You broke into my flat!'

I smiled a smile that I'd copied from him. A smile which got no higher than my upper lip. 'I broke in nowhere, Edmund,' I said. 'And you should always shut your computer down if you're leaving it, you know.'

Edmund had sat back down again and gone very still. The knowing little smile had died from the corners of his mouth and his fingers curled along the chair arms. 'I have no idea what that is,' he said, his voice icy calm again, 'but I have no doubt that Miss Knowles has concocted some spurious "details" in order to save her own skin.'

After a moment's consultation, the very smart woman who'd come with Malcolm Webber pulled a laptop out of a bag and the memory stick was plugged in. I heard her mutter half under her breath to him, 'He will still have needed help, there are witnesses to him being absent from the house on nights when people were ghost hunting. *Someone* had to let them in.'

'I agree.'

The pair of them looked at us all again, then at the screen, then back to us, settling on me.

'And someone showed them around the house. So there was an accomplice.' Mister Webber looked from her to Edmund, and then to me. 'If Mister Evershott and Miss Knowles could stay, I think the rest of you had better return to your duties.'

There was a collective air of disappointment. Nothing this exciting had happened at Monkpark since the Civil War. 'Hang on now.' James held up a hand. 'You're accusing our Amy of something that none of us think for one minute she did – am I right? Well, we are not leaving this room until you've looked at her evidence and heard her out. We'll not let you hold some kangaroo court, not without us there to back her up.'

There was a mumbled chorus of agreement and, to my total surprise, all the staff stayed where they were. Even Artichoke Sam gave me a nod and a wink and a small hand gesture that I was fairly sure had nothing to do with root vegetables.

Malcolm Webber and the woman exchanged looks. She had tilted the computer screen towards her so that none of us could see what was on it, but she gave the faintest of nods. 'Well, I suppose …' he began. 'And you understand that Miss Knowles …' A slight indication of the head towards me. '… could still be in quite a degree of trouble here?'

Edmund's smile was back when he heard that.

'It was me.'

Everyone looked up at that.

'I beg your pardon?' Malcolm Webber tore his attention away from his current perusal of the laptop to look at Julia, who had spoken from the back of the crowd.

'I said, it was me. I did it. I mean, I helped Edmund. The whole ghost thing was my idea. I mean, I got Amy to pretend to be a ghost, I thought it would be funny. And then when it all got in the papers and Edmund had the idea for ghost hunting, he came to me and said we could make some money, but he needed help.'

What?

She ignored my wiggling eyebrows. 'It was me. All of it. I let them into the house and made sure they paid and everything.'

The woman toggled back and forth between a couple of computer pages. 'You must have been very sure that nobody would say anything about your ... *venture*.'

'Nobody knew.' A defiant glance thrown my way. 'And I did it for the money. I'm saving up to get married and move out.' She was carefully not looking at me now. 'It's nothing to do with Amy. Edmund and I were in it together. For the money,' she added again.

Edmund's mouth had gone all agape, he met my eye and, for one tiny second, we were united in our stunned disbelief. Malcolm Webber looked from the laptop screen to Edmund, then to me, and back again. 'Well, there does appear to have been a large financial motive in any wrongdoing,' he said.

'And then Amy found out,' Jules went on, warming to her theme and playing the part of 'evil genius' for all she was worth. 'She tried to make me stop but it was like the money was a kind of drug, I just wanted more all the time.'

Edmund had now gone completely blank faced and my eyes couldn't have got any wider without my eyeballs falling out. Jules had struck an attitude I recognised from our schooldays, the 'woman trying to do the right thing'.

'But then she made me realise how wrong it all was. She

told me to stop and pay the money back, tell Edmund I couldn't have a part in his schemes any longer!' I recognised that too, Julia had had the lead in our school production of *When a Fool Comes Calling*. She'd got a lot better at acting in the intervening years, I had to say.

Josh muttered into my ear. 'What is she doing?'

'I have no idea,' I whispered back.

Edmund was opening and closing his mouth like Skrillex in a moth-filled room. He looked from me to Jules and back again, not so much as if he was lost for words, more as though all the words were rushing away from him and refusing to be caught. 'Wha—?' was all he could manage.

'I don't think they was plotting when they was out together,' Tegan now spoke up into the confusion. 'He looked like he was trying to get her drunk. Maybe he just wanted a shag.'

Everyone made 'hmm' noises, as if this could have been a possibility, and I felt my back straighten a little bit more. For Malcolm Webber the evidence of the laptop seemed to speak for itself. He looked at it once more, flicked between folders a few more times, and then nodded slowly. 'In view of your very frank and full confession, Miss Neville,' he said, 'we have no option but to terminate your employment with the Heritage Trust.'

Julia flounced. It was the only possible word for the way she drew up her skirts and headed for the door. 'I'm marrying a bank manager. I don't need this poxy job any more.' And, with considerable dignity for someone wearing a bustle and a liberty bodice, she swept from the room. I had to force myself not to applaud.

'And me?' I faced him now, ignoring Edmund's rather sweaty attempts to get some words out. 'I'm sorry I didn't come to the Trust earlier' – well, that bit was true, anyway – 'but I didn't know what to do for the best.' And so was that bit. Especially when you took into account that I'd thought the ghost hunting evenings had been 'for the best'.

'Miss Knowles,' Malcolm Webber began. 'I'm not sure about—'

And then Wendy broke in again. 'All those ideas, you know? For the pretend beach by the river and Shakespeare in the gardens? That was Amy too.' I looked at her and she gave me a little smile and a wave. 'I was listening. Oh, come on, he treats me like I'm deaf and stupid and all that "Amy's not allowed to sit in for you in the office" rubbish? How did he think we'd get a temp if my Sasha was suddenly ill and I had to go? Amy's *always* covered if I've been off, John used to like having her in the office sometimes. Said it gave her a chance to keep up with what was going on behind the scenes – and then I thought that Edmund just didn't *want* her to know what was going on.' She took a deep breath. 'And I had my suspicions too, about the ghost thing, and *I* never said anything either, so if you're going to sack Amy, then you have to sack me too!'

'Thank you,' I said. I couldn't believe how cool I was feeling about all this. Here I was, standing up for myself, and other people were standing up for me too. All right, every molecule in me wanted to sink down through the stone flagged floor, apologising for giving them all this trouble as I went, but I'd spoken out and the world hadn't ended. Gran had been wrong about nobody listening to 'the workers'. It seemed she'd also been wrong about Julia too. And so had I.

Mister Webber looked from me to Wendy to the computer screen. There really was a lot of figures on it, maybe Edmund's exploits went further than we knew. 'Can you confirm that, Miss Knowles?'

'Yes,' I said, but my voice was smaller, and less certain than I would have liked.

'Come on, we all know Edmund Evershott doesn't have an original thought in his head!' James again. 'Those ideas had Amy all over them. She's always liked a bit of Shakespeare, has Amy.' Since I'd never even discussed any form of literature with James, apart from remarking on the salaciousness of the covers of some of the paperbacks he sometimes sat reading in the yard, I *knew* this was a fib, but I loved him for it.

'Yes,' I said again, and now my voice was strong and loud. 'They *were* my ideas, and Edmund never even said "thank you" to me. He's been defrauding the estate, taking my ideas, and I don't even think he's a very good administrator either.' There was a slight echo as my words bounced off the ancient wood furniture, the stone tiled floor. I felt the old house empowering me, the weight of centuries giving me strength. 'And thank you, everyone, for speaking up for me.'

'Well, you're one of us, aren't you?' Sam, keeping his eyes on his boots, took his turn. 'Not like that poncy Evershott, who's never done a day's work in his life, all shiny shoes and gay boy glasses.'

'Thanks for the sentiment, Sam, even if the words were a bit ... inflammatory.' I turned to Malcolm Webber now. Somehow, it didn't matter what he said. I knew the whole of Monkpark – the people, even the house – was behind me. Even if he fired me, here and now, I'd go with that knowledge. That, for once, *I'd been right.* 'So.'

Malcolm Webber, looking rather tired now, pinched the bridge of his nose, glanced once more at the smart lady, who still hadn't been introduced and I was a little bit concerned at whether this was Heritage Trust sexism at work, and blinked hard. 'Yes. Of course,' he said, and even his voice sounded a bit grey. But then, the full force of the Monkpark estate team en masse would do that to an unprepared person. 'Miss Knowles, thank you for obtaining this evidence for us. It would seem conclusive, and in view of the full and frank confession from your co-worker and the evidence from your team ...'

I had a momentary flash of pride. *I had a team!*

'... plus the excellent reviews that your cafe has garnered – well, I must completely exonerate you from any blame in this matter. The Trust are very grateful for everything you've done for Monkpark Hall. Now, Mister Evershott?'

Edmund had a blank kind of expression. Either shock at being discovered or just plain confusion at the way things had turned out, I had no idea which. He turned his head slowly. 'I suppose it's too late to hand in my resignation?'

Malcolm Webber did a nice line in single raised eyebrows. I made a mental note to tell Jules.

'I think, Mister Evershott, for you it is too late for anything else. Because no actual laws have been broken, only Heritage Trust guidelines, and because we hold the good name of Monkpark Hall in such esteem, the police will not be involved on this occasion.' Did I imagine the flash of relief that crossed Edmund's smooth face? Maybe. 'But, be assured, you will never hold a post in any Trust properties nor, if we have anything to do with it, will you be employed in any position more senior than that of asking if someone would like fries with that.' A decisive slap of the laptop. 'Everyone, you may go.'

Josh's hand cupped into mine and we all walked out of the room. When we got out into the fresh air of the yard, there was a smatter of applause.

'Got rid of the posh twat at last.' Artichoke Sam grinned at me. I knew that he and Josh were still a bit uneasy in one another's presence, so I was glad to see a matey shoulder-slap take place. 'Great. What a pranny.'

I left Josh to the admiring crowd and went in through the kitchen door to the cafe where I finally found Julia, one hand against the counter, breathing hard. 'Jules? What the hell was *that* all about?'

Julia loosened her bodice a notch and flapped it. 'Bloody hot. And a simple "thank you" would work.' Then she raised her head and there was something in her eyes, something that pulled at something inside me. 'I owed you, Ames. That was payback.'

I picked up a cloth and began to wipe down the surfaces. Displacement activity, the place was, as usual, clean as a surgical ward. 'You *lied*.'

Julia laughed. 'Not about all of it, Ames. I *am* marrying Simon and you *can* shove your bloody job.'

Behind us, at the main doors, there was a creak and disturbance of the air as Josh came in, slowly and steadily, as though he was walking into the bird barn, careful not to upset anything.

Julia gave him the briefest glance. 'I'm getting out of this place. Simon's got a great little flat in York, somewhere there's shops and internet connection and pubs – all that kind of thing. Real life, y'know?' Now she was looking at me again. 'So I really don't care what's been going on here, but I know you, Ames, and I know you'd never get tied up in anything illegal or even slightly bent, not unless there was a very good reason.'

'Evershit's bent as a pergola,' Josh said, laconically.

We both ignored him. 'And no one has broken the law,' Julia said. 'Not really. Only Trust guidelines, so it's not like I've confessed to murder, is it? And, like I said,' she shrugged, 'don't care if I never see this bloody place again.' She shook her hair back and began stuffing it under her cap. It looked as though she was 'displacing' nearly as hard as me, as I began wiping the hot milk nozzle more thoroughly than it could ever need. 'And, I owe you.'

'Guy,' said Josh, quietly. I was surprised he'd remembered.

Julia nodded. 'Yeah. That was shitty. Shouldn't have ... well. If it means anything, he came on to me, but ... guess it doesn't. Not now.' She threw a quick glance at Josh. 'And you were right about me coming on to Josh. It was a bloody stupid thing to do.'

There was a slow moment, then I threw down the wiping cloth and hugged Jules even tighter than I had on the night she got dumped by Finn Walker when she thought she might be pregnant. 'Thank you.'

Jules sniffed and wiped the back of her hand across her face. 'Like I said, I owed you one.' Then she surprised me by hugging me back, her face pressed against the top of my head. I could feel the salty stickiness of tears against my hair. 'I've got Mum and Ryan and Jason and Aaron, and now there's Simon, and you've only ever had your gran, and I've sometimes been a shit to you, but you've always been there, Ames. You've never called me on any of it, even when I was a complete cow, and sometimes I just wanted to watch you scream and throw things, but now I know …' She pulled back a little bit and looked in my face. '… now I know that's not who you are. You're just *nice*, Ames. And I didn't want to see that get shafted by the Trust people, when all you've ever done is be *nice*.'

I carried on hugging, even if a teeny weeny little bit of me felt quite smug. I'd broken the 'nice' mould today. I'd spoken up for myself, the world hadn't ended. In fact, people had supported me, people who I'd always thought had had me down as just a big blob of 'nice', they'd seen me as worth something. But then, didn't I have Julia fixed in my head as the slightly heartless, slightly tarty girl who only thought about boys and money? And here she was, being so much more.

'Thanks, Jules,' I said again and began a slow release process that saw us both tidying our faces and adjusting our necklines. Behind us, Josh helped himself to a bun and perched on one of the table corners to start eating.

'New start all round, then.' Julia shook her hair into place and looked out through the window. Wendy was moving the 'Closed' sign to allow a Volvo, now containing three people, to inch past up the drive. I saw her give Edmund a cheerful wave as the car went by. I'd been delighted to find that she hadn't liked him any more than we had.

'Good riddance.'

'Yep. We'll need a new administrator – hopefully one who doesn't think about investing in art, and I'll need someone else in the cafe.' I took a deep breath.

'And you and Josh …'

I looked at him and he smiled at me over the top of a Raspberry Crunch. His face looked more open now, and he'd gained at least an inch in height from not being so hunched around his memories. His cut-throat cheekbones were touched with a hint of pink in the warmth of the cafe and the sight of his long fingers twisting the cake around to keep the worst of the stickiness from getting in his hair gave me a pleasurable shiver. One day ... one day, we'd get there.

'Yep.'

'Your gran will go ballistic.'

'Actually, she really likes Josh.' But then I had that horrible 'duality' feeling, the one that had always meant I thought twice, three times before I even looked at a man. 'Although I have no idea how we'll make it work, I don't really fancy us bunking up in the cottage, and I don't want to leave Gran on her own, with the spoons and the curtains and everything.'

Julia made 'heavy' noises with the cake tray. 'Look, are we opening up again, or what?' She sounded a bit peevish. 'Or, since I just pulled your arse out of the fire, can I call it quits, hand in my notice now and start a tragic addiction for "Your Wedding" magazines? You're bridesmaid, Ames, and if you're not really nice to me I'm putting you in primrose yellow trimmed with puce. And those heels. Well, one heel, one flat, so you sort of lurch.'

She leaned back against the counter and grinned. To my slight astonishment, Josh grinned back and gave her a tiny wink, and I felt a small knot of worry, that had co-existed in the bottom of my stomach with all my doubts and fears, begin to untangle. Things just might be all right.

Chapter Thirty-Eight

Josh

I've been proud before, course I have. When I realised Skrill was going to make it. When Bane let herself be unhooded without going crazy. Even when I passed my bike test. But this, this feeling that my heart was so full of love for Amy that it felt like a big balloon of gas in my chest, making me walk with only my tiptoes on the ground, well, that was something else.

I went out to the birds. Everyone was going back to work like it was a normal day. Shitface had been carted off in the back of the Volvo, technically we could all have sat around and drunk tea until closing, but none of us did. It made me think, as I started sorting out the birds, maybe we weren't so far from the time the house was first built as we thought. All going on with our 'duties' while the estate went to buggery around us. Wonder if this was what it was like in the war that Amy's gran keeps muttering about? Everyone trying to pretend that the real world isn't out there?

'What about your lass then, eh?' Okay, we were working, but some of the lads weren't really putting their backs into it like they would have if Evershit had been watching, and Sam had his tools in the wheelbarrow and was leaning on the wall. 'Never would have thought it of her, she's got balls all right!'

I took a deep breath. He was talking to me. Like what had happened had pressed some kind of reset button and I'd never punched him. But I remembered, and so did my fists, if he said anything bad about her now, I'd launch him. 'Yeah.'

'She was like James Bond in there! Cracking his computer and getting his bank stuff.' Sam sort of eyed me. 'She can't do that to *everyone*, can she? I mean, sometimes people don't want to stop and listen, know what I'm saying? If they see something, some kinda payment thing that they might not get, they might think it's summat it's not, you get me?'

I nearly laughed, and I don't laugh much. Everyone knew Sam was the go-to man for 'off the books' artichokes. 'She only does what she has to,' I said and he looked happier.

'That's what I thought. She's cool, our Amy.' And then he slapped my arm. 'Nice one, mate,' and took the barrow off somewhere, the noise the wheel made stopped when he got up to the gardener's shed, so he'd probably gone for more tea with James.

So, I carried on getting the birds out, doing a bit of maintenance, checking the hoods and the leather and stuff. I could see Amy through the cafe window, bustling around doing something with the machines in there. Every now and then she'd just stand. Stop, like she was pulled by what she was thinking and freeze with her hand on the counter and put her head down. I even saw her lips move like she was talking to herself. And sometimes she'd laugh, I could hear it right out here, and it made me feel like laughing right back with her.

Because I knew. Knew how it felt to have stood up, said something. Got out of being who everyone thought you were. *Done something*. Seeing her there, knowing how hard it had been for her to speak up, seeing her face when everyone was on her side, it made me feel something different. Like, I'd known I couldn't save my mum, not really. If she'd come with me when I ran, she'd have made another dick choice soon enough, because she *wouldn't* stand up. Thought her life was all some big mistake she couldn't change, she needed a bloke to make her feel, and if what he made her feel was small and stupid, she thought that was what she deserved.

And I looked up. Looked around. Bane was chewing her foot, Malkin had closed his eyes, Fae was watching something, something so far away I couldn't see it, and Skrill, well, he was watching me. There was a little yellow ray of sun just touching us all, squeezing between the bare old tree and the wall of the garden like it wasn't meant to be here but wanted to be in on this, and I thought *this is my place. I belong here.* I'd got away, but I didn't have to keep running. This was the place I'd been looking for all along, and Amy was the woman I was meant to be with. One day, yeah. Maybe. Maybe I'd go looking for my mum. See if she was ready to leave. See if she understood now that she didn't have to sit there, didn't have to be some piece in a stupid bloke's game of control.

But for now, this was it. Beautiful, brave Amy, with her skin like buttercream and those eyes that were always half-smiling even when she wasn't, and me. And her gran, obviously, and the birds. We were like a family, and this was our home, whatever.

Chapter Thirty-Nine

Amy

I'm sure all the visitors that afternoon thought I was what Gran would call 'a bit mazed'. I kept thinking of Edmund's face when I'd brought out that memory stick, the way his jaw had gone so that his lack of chin had become even more apparent and his eyes looked as though they would fall out, and giggled to myself.

I felt a little bit as though I'd been at the gin. Warm inside, with little moments of disbelief that I really could have been that person who stood up for herself. That wasn't me! I was head-down, hard work Amy, 'nice' Amy with not a bad word to say for anyone, even when they were pulling my life to pieces. But I hadn't stood up for myself alone, had I? Okay, even given that they were desperate to get rid of Edmund, the others hadn't had to join in. Hadn't had to say what they said, especially when it was massaging the truth to an extent that the truth should be completely relaxed and probably smelling of jojoba oil by now.

The phone rang in the back and I had to dash to answer it, my skirts getting tangled around my ankles as I went. *Maybe we could bring in some different costumes? Something a bit easier to wear? What about those flappers in the Twenties? They would be eye-catching as waitresses.* I caught sight of Josh as I went, quietly getting on with sorting out the birds, and a different kind of warmth spread over me, and coming from a different place than the pride in myself. He'd stood up for me too; when even I had thought I was going to bottle out and keep quiet, Josh had put himself in the firing line by speaking up. And, a small and less well-developed part of my personality whispered, he's got a hot body and he actually wants to be with you.

It was Wendy on the phone. 'Malcolm Webber is coming back in a couple of days, Amy, and he wants to talk to you.'

Right, this was where it all went wrong. 'Oh. Yes, of course. Well, I'll be here, won't I? Unless the Trust wants me out before then.' The little warm bubble had burst, turned into ice cubes. It couldn't be that easy, could it, of course not. I had, after all, spied, broken into Edmund's flat, stolen information from his computer. They could probably get me for misuse of estate property too, if they tried.

Wendy's voice got a little squeak in it. 'He wants to talk to you about being administrator! He's spoken to John, apparently, who told him that he always had you in mind for the post, that's why he used to let you sit in on my job to find out about the background stuff. You could be running Monkpark, Amy!'

Running Monkpark? 'Don't be daft, Wendy,' and there was Gran's voice again, even the intonation was hers. 'I don't know anything about running a Heritage Trust estate. They need to find someone who—'

But Wendy just talked right over the top of me. 'It will be great to have you in charge, you're so much easier to talk to than Edmund and we've all got ideas, all of us. Even some of the lads in the garden have got things they'd like to try, but the place has got so stuck. We're still doing stuff we were doing in the Fifties. I've seen the paperwork. Amy, you *have* to take over.'

Gran would be convinced I'd got ideas above my station. But I had a degree in business, surely that had to count for something? 'Well, I'll see what they have to say first, Wendy, before we all start getting excited.'

Wendy squealed a bit more down the phone, but I gathered my taking over the Hall would be a popular move. When I put the phone down and went back through to the cafe to serve a couple of ladies who, very rightly, fancied a cup of tea and a sit down, I found my mind wandering with my eyes. Outside, into the weak sunshine that was throwing the shadows of the old trees across the yard. Where young Imogen was chatting animatedly to a visitor, pointing out the line of the river that ran past the house and down along the bottom of the valley. *Imogen would make a good guide for walks round the estate.* My mind's eye continued, seeing the whole of Monkpark sitting in its green bowl among the hills, the house and its history like a great weight on an emerald sheet, with Josh's birds criss-crossing the skies above.

'I think I might already have got a *bit* excited,' I said, quietly to the coffee spout.

Epilogue

Josh

It was a great wedding. Amy looked so ... *so* cute in a kind of blue thing with a big tie round it, even if she said it made her look like a whale having a heart attack. Julia looked okay too, and Amy's gran managed to keep her voice down when she watched Julia walk up the aisle and said, 'Why buy the cow when you're getting the milk for free?' but she sort of smiled when she said it, and she thinks Simon is a good thing for Julia. Same as Julia's mum, really, and her brothers, who've apparently already turned her old bedroom into a TV and football room.

The sun shone too. Simon said they'd picked June for a wedding date because it was statistically more likely to be nice weather, but he's not as much of a prat as that made him sound. After the ceremony, I flew the birds so Julia could have her picture done with Bane on her wrist, all 'look what a country girl I am' and she had wanted Skrill to deliver the ring until I told her it would take him half an hour to get down the aisle and everyone would have got fed up waiting and been halfway through the cake and posh pastries before he got past the first pews.

Everything ... everything was better now. Oh, not all forgotten, never going to forget that cupboard, the dark, but, got a nice place to live, got Amy. Got my birds to taste the sky for me. So, yeah, life is good.

They made Amy the new administrator, even though she complained, said she wasn't experienced enough, but they reckoned she was, what with knowing the place inside out and having done admin sitting in for Wendy and all, and she's doing this business course, which looks like it's all numbers and 'feasibility studies' and shit like that, and she moans about it but she sits there every evening tapping away on this huge computer with a smile on her face like she's just won some job lottery. And we live in Edmund's old flat, only with a lot less crap in it. Amy's gran has stayed in her cottage, so we pop in there a couple of times a day, even though she's just as snarky as she ever was and keeps telling us not to bother. She's okay, Amy's gran. She sometimes takes me into a corner and asks me whether the PMT is getting any better, and then she kind of smells my breath and nods and mutters something about 'No whisky yet, then'. So, yeah, weird as all get out, but she means well. I think.

And the spoon obsession? When Amy told me about that, about how she thought her gran was going senile because she thought someone had been in every day, messing the place up and fiddling with the spoons, I laughed until I was near on sick. And then I took Amy to the window – the window that's always open, rain or shine, and I pointed to the tree and I just waited. Took her a moment or two, but when she saw the magpies sitting up there and eyeballing us, she got it. They've not actually caught one in the place yet, but those corvids? They're clever. And they're obsessed with shiny things. So I told her gran, it's either close the window or get your silverware messed with. And she looked at me, looked at the magpie which had its head on one side, all assessing us, and she left the window open.

She likes birds.

So, life? Pretty good. We've even … well, it took time, bit kind of awkward at first and I had to keep all the lights on, but after the first couple of times … yeah. Turns out practice does make perfect, after all.

There's a couple of young lasses running the cafe now. I go through every now and then, old times' sake and all, but they're a bit mean with the cheese and their cakes are no way as good as Amy's, but they get all giggly when I turn up and it gives me a bit of a kick, tell the truth. All those years when I didn't dare, when I was so afraid of being looked at, turns out I really quite like it, especially when Amy's there to pull faces and do all this 'comedy muttering' stuff.

I'd never hurt her. She knows me. Understands that sometimes I have to go outside, stand under the unending sky, put Fae or Bane up and watch them spiral off into the air, just breathe and feel all the space around me. Understands that sometimes the dark is too much and I have to sleep with the light on, and her body all wrapped round me like she's keeping the bad things out.

And that's what love is. Always wondered. Thought it had to do with possessing and not wanting to let go and all, but turns out it's just being there, through the dark and the nightmares for me, through the fear of being left, for her. We are there. Together.

* The End *

If you loved Jane's story, please leave a review on Amazon or the retail site where you purchased this novel. Reviews on retail sites really do help the author. Thank you!

A Thank You note from Jane next ...

267

Thank You

Hello!

Sorry, didn't mean to sound surprised there, it's just that I don't often see many people here, lurking round the back of books like this. I mean, I'm here because I'm the author, I have no idea what your excuse is. Anyway. Thank you for reading this book, I hope you enjoyed it. If you'd like to read something else by me, then I'm sure there's a list of 'other books by this author' around somewhere close by. If you aren't feeling strong enough for an entire book, then there's my blog and website at www.janelovering.co.uk, which is full of my ramblings and news about books and some quite nice pictures of puppies and kittens. I'm on Facebook as Jane Lovering, Author, and twitter as @janelovering, if your need for puppy and kitten pictures is limitless.

As ever, if you feel up to it, please leave a review on Amazon, we authors live or die by reviews. That's a bit of an exaggeration, but other people like to see whether other people have enjoyed a book that they, the first lot of other people, might also like. You might also like to check out the full range of Choc Lit books – we've got all sorts of things, paranormal and historical and time-slip as well.

And, if you read the acknowledgements to *Little Teashop of Horrors*, you'll have found out that it's based on Nunnington Hall in North Yorkshire, so if you'd like to visit, have a look at the website, because they are often closed on Mondays. Besides, the website has some very nice pictures on, almost none of them are puppies or kittens, though. https://www.nationaltrust.org.uk/nunnington-hall

Jane

x

About the Author

Jane was born in Devon and now lives in Yorkshire. She has five children, three cats and two dogs! Jane is a member of the Romantic Novelists' Association and has a first-class honours degree in creative writing.

Jane writes comedies which are often described as 'quirky'. Her debut *Please Don't Stop* the Music won the 2012 Romantic Novel of the Year and the Best Romantic Comedy Novel award from the Romantic Novelists' Association. Her Christmas novella, *Christmas at the Little Village School*, won the Rose Award from the Romantic Novelists' Association in 2018.

Jane's other Choc Lit novels are: *Please Don't Stop the Music, Star Struck, Hubble Bubble, Vampire State of Mind, Falling Apart, How I Wonder What You Are, I Don't Want to Talk About It* and *Can't Buy Me Love*. She has also published three eBook Christmas novellas: *The Art of Christmas, The Boys of Christmas* and *Christmas at the Little Village School*.

For more information on Jane visit:
www.janelovering.co.uk
www.twitter.com/janelovering

More Choc Lit

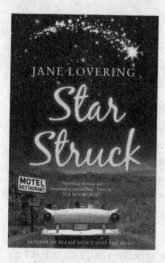

Star Struck

Our memories define us – don't they?

And Skye Threppel lost most of hers in a car crash that stole the lives of her best friend and fiancé. It's left scars, inside and out, which have destroyed her career and her confidence.

Skye hopes a trip to the wide dusty landscapes of Nevada – and a TV convention offering the chance to meet the actor she idolises – will help her heal. But she bumps into mysterious sci-fi writer Jack Whitaker first. He's a handsome contradiction – cool and intense, with a wild past.

Jack has enough problems already. He isn't looking for a woman with self-esteem issues and a crush on one of his leading actors. Yet he's drawn to Skye.

An instant rapport soon becomes intense attraction, but Jack fears they can't have a future if Skye ever finds out about his past …

Will their memories tear them apart, or can they build new ones together?

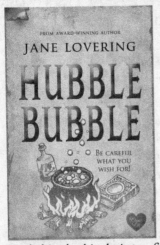

Hubble Bubble

Be careful what you wish for ...

Holly Grey only took up witchery to keep her friend out of trouble – and now she's knee-deep in hassle, in the form of apocalyptic weather, armed men, midwifery ... and a sarcastic Welsh journalist.

Kai has been drawn to darkest Yorkshire by his desire to find out who he really is. What he hadn't bargained on was getting caught up in amateur magic and dealing with a bunch of women who are trying *really hard* to make their dreams come true.

Together they realise that getting what you wish for is sometimes just a matter of knowing what it is you want ...

How I Wonder What You Are

"Maybe he wasn't here because of the lights – maybe they were here because of him ..."

It's been over eighteen months since Molly Gilchrist has had a man (as her best friend, Caro, is so fond of reminding her) so when she as good as stumbles upon one on the moors one bitterly cold morning, it seems like the Universe is having a laugh at her expense.

But Phinn Baxter (that's *Doctor* Phinneas Baxter) is no common drunkard, as Molly is soon to discover; with a PhD in astrophysics and a tortured past that is a match for Molly's own disastrous love life.

Finding mysterious men on the moors isn't the weirdest thing Molly has to contend with, however. There's also those strange lights she keeps seeing in the sky. The ones she's only started seeing since meeting Phinn ...

FROM AWARD WINNING AUTHOR
JANE LOVERING

I Don't Want to Talk About It

What if the one person you wanted to talk to wouldn't listen?

Winter Gregory and her twin sister Daisy live oceans apart but they still have the 'twin thing' going on. Daisy is Winter's port in the storm, the first person she calls when things go wrong …

And things *are* wrong. Winter has travelled to a remote Yorkshire village to write her new book, and to escape her ex-boyfriend Dan Bekener. Dan never liked her reliance on Daisy and made her choose – but Winter's twin will *always* be her first choice.

She soon finds herself immersed in village life after meeting the troubled Hill family; horse-loving eight-year-old Scarlet and damaged, yet temptingly gorgeous, Alex. The distraction is welcome and, when Winter needs to talk, Daisy is always there.

But Dan can't stay away and remains intent on driving the sisters apart – because Dan knows something about Daisy …

Available in paperback from all good bookshops and online stores. Visit www.choc-lit.com for details.

Can't Buy Me Love

Is it all too good to be true?

When Willow runs into her old university crush, Luke, she's a new woman with a new look – not to mention a little bit more cash after a rather substantial inheritance. Could she be lucky enough to score a fortune and her dream man at the same time?

Then Willow meets Cal; a computer geek with a slightly odd sense of humour. They get on like a house on fire – although she soon realises that there is far more to her unassuming new friend than meets the eye …

But money doesn't always bring happiness, and Willow finds herself struggling to know who to trust. Are the new people in her life there because they care – or is there another reason?

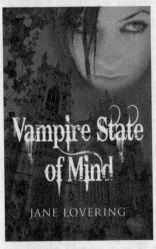

Vampire State of Mind

Book 1 in the Otherworlders

Jessica Grant knows vampires only too well. She runs the York Council tracker programme making sure that Otherworlders are all where they should be, keeps the filing in order and drinks far too much coffee.

To Jess, vampires are annoying and arrogant and far too sexy for their own good, particularly her ex-colleague, Sil, who's now in charge of Otherworld York. When a demon turns up and threatens not just Jess but the whole world order, she and Sil are forced to work together.

But then Jess turns out to be the key to saving the world, which puts a very different slant on their relationship.

The stakes are high. They are also very, very pointy and Jess isn't afraid to use them – even on the vampire she's rather afraid she's falling in love with ...

Available in paperback from all good bookshops and online stores. Visit www.choc-lit.com for details.

Falling Apart

Book 2 in the Otherworlders

In the mean streets of York, the stakes just got higher – and even pointier.

Jessica Grant liaises with Otherworlders for York Council so she knows that falling in love with a vampire takes a leap of faith. But her lover Sil, the City Vampire in charge of Otherworld York, he wouldn't run out on her, would he? He wouldn't let his demon get the better of him. Or would he?

Sil knows there's a reason for his bad haircut, worse clothes and the trail of bleeding humans in his wake. If only he could remember exactly what he did before someone finds him and shoots him on sight.

With her loyalties already questioned for defending zombies, the Otherworlders no one cares about, Jess must choose which side she's on, either help her lover or turn him in. Human or Other? Whatever she decides, there's a high price to pay – and someone to lose.

Available in paperback from all good bookshops and online stores. Visit www.choc-lit.com for details.

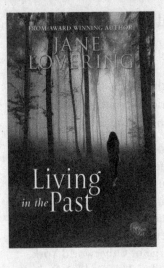

Living in the Past

Do you ever wish you could turn back time?

Grace Nicholls has a few reasons for wanting to turn back the clock … although an archaeological dig at a Bronze Age settlement on the Yorkshire moors is not what she had in mind. But encouraged by her best friend Tabitha, that's exactly where she finds herself.

Professor Duncan McDonald is the site director and his earnest pursuit of digging up the past makes him appear distant and unreachable. But when a woman on the site goes missing, it seems that his own past might be coming back to haunt him once again.

As they dig deeper, Duncan and Grace get more than they bargained for – and come to realise that the past is much closer than either of them ever imagined …

Available as an eBook on all platforms.
Visit www.choc-lit.com for details.

The Art of Christmas

Novella

What if the memories of Christmas past were getting in the way of Christmas future?

It's been nearly two years since Harriet lost Jonno, but she's finally decided that it's time to celebrate Christmas again.

Then she finds a stash of graphic novels belonging to her comic book-loving husband in the attic, and suddenly her world is turned upside down once more.

With the help of eccentric comic book dealer Kell Foxton, she discovers that the comics collected by Jonno are not only extremely valuable, but also hold the key to his secret life – a life that throws Harriet's entire marriage and every memory she has of her husband into question.

As Harriet grows closer to Kell, she begins to feel like she could learn to love Christmas again – but first, she needs to know the truth.

Available as an eBook on all platforms.
Visit www.choc-lit.com for details.

The Boys of Christmas

Novella

Who are the boys of Christmas?

Mattie Arden has just escaped from a toxic relationship so when, a few days before Christmas, she receives a letter informing her that she has inherited a house from her great aunt Millie, it's a welcome distraction.

Except it comes with a strange proviso: if Mattie wants the house, she must fulfil Millie's last wish and scatter her ashes over 'the boys of Christmas'.

In the company of her best friend Toby, Mattie sets out for the seaside village of Christmas Steepleton in the hope of finding out the meaning of her aunt's bizarre request.

Whilst there, a snowstorm leaves them stranded for Christmas, and still no nearer to finding 'the boys'. But as the weather gives Mattie time to reflect, she realises the answer to the mystery might have been under her nose all along – and that's not the only thing …